THE GOLDFISH BOY

Lisa Thompson

SCHOLASTIC INC.

For Mum and Lynne

This book was originally published in hardcover by Scholastic Press in 2017.

The publisher does not have any control over and does not assume any responsibility for author or third-party websites or their content.

ISBN 978-1-338-05393-7

10 9 8 7 6 5 4 3 2 1   18 19 20 21 22

Printed in the U.S.A.   40
This edition first printing 2018

Book design by Christopher Stengel

CHAPTER ONE

THE ARRIVAL

Mr. Charles had sunburn right on the top of his head.

I saw it while he was inspecting his roses. He studied each flower, giving the larger ones a little shake to see if any petals fell off as he edged along the pathway. The big, bald patch on his head was now a bright red, shiny circle surrounded by white, fluffy hair. He should have been wearing a hat in this heat, but I guess it's hard to notice if the top of your head is burning when you're busy doing things.

I noticed though.

I noticed a lot of things from the window.

It's not like I was doing anything wrong. I was just watching my neighbors to pass the time, that's all; it's not like I was being nosey. And I didn't think the neighbors minded. Occasionally Jake Bishop from number five would shout things up at me—things like *weirdo*, *freak*, or *nutter*. It had been a long time since he'd actually called me *Matthew*—but then, he was an idiot, so I didn't really care what he said.

I lived on a quiet, dead-end street in a town full of people who said how great it was that they didn't live in that big, smelly city of London—and who then spent most of their mornings desperately trying to get there.

There were seven houses in our little cul-de-sac. Six of them looked the same, with square bay windows, front doors with frosted glass panels, and whitewashed walls. But the seventh house, stuck between number three and number five, was very different. Built from blood-red bricks, the Rectory looked like a guest at a Halloween party where no one else had bothered to dress up. Its front door was black, with two triangular windows at the top that were covered from the inside with some old cardboard. Whether it had been put there to stop the drafts or to stop anyone from peering in, who knew?

Dad told me a developer had tried to flatten the Rectory twenty years before when our houses were being built, but it dug its hundred-year-old foundations in and somehow managed to stay, like a rotten, old tooth. The vicar's widow, Old Nina, still lived there, but I rarely saw her. There was a lamp in the front room window that she left on day and night: a glowing orange ball behind the gray curtains. Mum said she kept a low profile because she was frightened that someone from the church was going to make her move out, since with her husband dead, it wasn't really her house anymore. On her front step she had three pots of flowers that she watered every morning at ten o'clock.

I watched her and the other neighbors from the spare room at the front of the house. It wasn't quite as perfect as my bedroom, but I liked it in there. The lemon walls were still shiny-clean and it had that freshly decorated feel, even though it had been five years since it had happened. Mum and Dad called this room the office since we kept the computer in there, but we all really knew it as the nursery. Hanging in a corner there was a baby's crib mobile made of six padded, stripy elephants, which dangled pointlessly over a tower of unopened boxes and shopping bags. Mum had put the mobile up as soon as she'd gotten home from her shopping marathon, even though Dad had said it was unlucky.

"Don't be silly, Brian. We need to make sure it works, don't we?"

She had wound the little key at the top and we'd all watched as the elephants twirled around and around to "Twinkle, Twinkle, Little Star." When the music had stopped I'd clapped—I was only seven then, and you do silly stuff like that when you're that age. Mum said she'd unpack the rest of the shopping another time, but she never did. The bags are still where she left them: diapers, bottles, a sterilizer, a monitor, tiny vests. Everything my baby brother would have needed if I hadn't . . . Well, if he were alive.

The office had a window that looked out onto the street, and I saw my neighbors begin their day:

9:30 a.m.-Mr. Charles is deadheading his roses again. He's using some new clippers with red handles. The top of his head looks sore with sunburn.

Mr. Charles could have been anything from sixty-five to ninety-five years old. He never seemed to get older. I figured he'd found an age he quite liked and just stopped right there.

9:36 a.m.—Gordon and Penny Sullivan appear from number one. Gordon gets into their car as Penny waves to Mr. Charles from across the street.

Mr. Charles waved back and twirled his garden clippers on his finger like a cowboy, then snipped at the air three times, the silver blades glinting in the sunlight. Penny laughed. Her eyes squinted and she put her hand up to shade them, but then her face dropped. She'd spotted something: me. Mr. Charles followed her gaze and they both stared up at me, watching them from my window. I quickly stepped away and vanished from view, my heart thumping. I waited until I heard Gordon's car reverse out of the driveway and then looked out on the street again.

9:42 a.m.—Penny and Gordon leave to do their weekly supermarket shopping.
9:44 a.m.—Melody Bird appears from number three dragging their dachshund, Frankie, behind her.

It was the weekend, which meant it was Melody's turn to walk their dog. Her mum, Claudia, took him out during the week, but I didn't know why they bothered—he never seemed happy about it, and he spent the length of our road trying to turn back. Melody picked at the wool on the sleeve of her black cardigan as she walked along, stopping every three steps for the little dog to catch up with her. She practically lived in that black cardigan, even though it was about a hundred degrees out there. They stopped at a lamppost while Frankie had a sniff before digging his paws in and trying to get home, but Melody dragged him onward, and they disappeared down the alleyway that led to the graveyard at the back of the Rectory.

9:50 a.m.–The door to number seven opens and the "newlyweds" appear.

Mr. Jenkins and his wife, Hannah, lived next door on the side we're not attached to. People called them the "newlyweds" even though they'd been married for nearly four years now. Hannah was always smiling, even when she didn't realize someone was watching her.

"I'm not sure it's good for you to run in this heat, Rory," she said, grinning away.

Mr. Jenkins ignored her as he reached his arm up high and stretched over to one side. He taught PE at my school, and in his opinion, anyone who didn't exercise regularly really had no reason to even exist. I tried my best to keep off his radar.

He lunged along their driveway in a tight white top and blue shorts, his hands on his hips.

"Don't be too long," Hannah said. "We've still got to decide on a car seat, remember?"

Mr. Jenkins grunted at her.

I looked down at the step and flinched when I saw her large, pregnant stomach. She rested her hand on top, patting herself rhythmically, and then she turned and disappeared into the house. I let go of a breath I'd been holding.

Mr. Jenkins set off toward High Street, waving at Mr. Charles, who was too busy with his flowers to notice. He studied each rose as they bobbed in the breeze like tight bundles of pink cotton candy on a fairground stall. Any that weren't up to scratch he snipped off and dropped into a plastic pot. When he was finished he walked back around the side of the house carrying the pot of dead roses.

10:00 a.m.–No sign of Old Nina watering her pots.

It was no surprise I hadn't seen her yet, considering how busy the close had been so far this morning.

The door of number five opened and a boy my age appeared. He walked down his driveway and looked in one direction only. Straight at me. This time I didn't duck away but stood my ground and stared back. Stopping in front of our house, he tipped his head back and made a grotesque, gagging noise before launching a great lump of phlegm onto our path. I gave him a slow handclap through the window, ignoring how sick I felt. He frowned when he saw my hands, and I quickly put them behind me. Giving our wall a good kicking, he turned and headed off down the street.

10:03 a.m.-Jake Bishop-still an idiot.

Once Jake had gone there wasn't much to see. Mr. Jenkins returned from his run, his white T-shirt dark with sweat. Penny and Gordon Sullivan unloaded eleven shopping bags from their trunk. Melody returned from her walk holding Frankie under one arm; the dog looked rather pleased with himself.

And then the cul-de-sac was still.

Until the Rectory door slowly opened.

10:40 a.m.-Old Nina is on her step looking very nervous. She has her little silver watering can in one hand.

The elderly lady was dressed in a black skirt, cream blouse, and peach cardigan. She trickled water into each pot for a count of five before moving on to the next one. As she did this her eyes flickered around the neighborhood. She'd just begun to water the final pot when a car turned onto the street. Leaving the watering can on the step she slipped back inside, slamming her heavy front door behind her.

The car driving slowly down the road was one of those that Dad would say costs "a small mortgage." It certainly didn't belong to any of the neighbors. It was so shiny our houses were reflected in its black doors as it circled the cul-de-sac, coming to a stop outside number eleven. I grabbed my notebook as I watched, waiting for the doors to open.

10:45 a.m.-There is a really posh black car on the close. I've never seen it before and it's parked right next door! Does Mr. Charles have a visitor?

I knew my neighbors' schedules inside and out; they didn't surprise me much. But this was something new. I tried to see inside the car, but it had heavily tinted windows so I couldn't make anything out. It hummed quietly for a while and then the engine was turned off. The driver's door opened.

A woman, wearing sunglasses that were so big they covered most of her face, got out and looked around the cul-de-sac. She brushed her hair from her face and then slammed the door shut. Mr. Charles appeared and walked quickly down his path, wiping his hands on the front of his shirt.

"Darling!" he said, stretching his tanned arms toward her.

"Hello, Dad."

She held him at a distance and turned her cheek for him to kiss, then she went to the car and opened the back door. A small girl of around six or seven climbed out carrying a porcelain doll. I stood closer to the window but could only catch a few words.

". . . must be Casey! And who's this? Is she coming to stay?"

Mr. Charles went to stroke the doll's hair, but the girl twisted around so it was out of reach. It looked like something from an antique shop, not a kid's toy. The woman in the big sunglasses emerged from the backseat of the car with a blond-haired boy who she plonked down on the pavement. Mr. Charles held his hand out to the toddler.

"Pleased to meet you, Teddy. I'm your granddad."

The boy cuddled a pale blue blanket, rubbing a corner against his cheek as he stared at the crinkly hand reaching toward him. The hand dangled there awkwardly between them, and then Mr. Charles gave up and went to help his daughter with the luggage. They talked for a while, but their backs were to me so I couldn't hear what they were saying.

The woman put two black suitcases by the gate and then held each child's face in her hands, saying something before giving them each a quick kiss on the forehead. Squeezing Mr. Charles on the arm, she got back into the car. The engine purred to life and the dark, shiny car drove slowly to the end of the road. The three of them stood there watching until it was out of sight.

"Right! Let's get you two inside, shall we?"

Mr. Charles flapped his arms at the kids and herded them like sheep toward the house, his face a mad grin. The little boy stopped, still rubbing the blanket to his cheek as he reached for one of the roses next to the pathway.

"Ah, ah, ah, no touching!" said his grandfather and he waved his arms again, steering them in through the front door.

A minute later he was back, dragging the two black suitcases behind him. He glanced up at me and I quickly stepped away, but not before noticing his wide smile had vanished.

CHAPTER TWO
MY SECRET BOX

Under my bed I had a secret box.

I would have liked to say it was a mysterious old wooden box that I'd found buried in the garden, smuggled upstairs, and hid behind the folds of my duvet. It would sit there patiently, keeping its treasures locked inside. Once I knew I could trust you, I'd let you kneel beside me as I carefully opened the crumbling lid. Clumps of mud would fall onto my carpet, but for once I wouldn't care. Your mouth would drop open, your eyes getting wider and wider as you gazed at the riches inside.

I wished my secret box was like that.

But it wasn't.

My box was clinical. It was made of white and gray cardboard and was the size and shape of a small shoebox with an oval hole in the top. The manufacturer's name was printed around the sides, and in the bottom corner at each end it read, in bold, black type:

CONTENTS: 100

I'd say there were probably around thirty-two left.

When I say *probably* I mean *exactly*. There were exactly thirty-two left.

Mum knew all about my secret box, but Dad didn't. He'd be upset if he knew. Not so much at me, but more at Mum for "encouraging" me.

"It's not right, Sheila. What're you doing giving him stuff like that for, eh? You're just making him worse."

That was how Dad would react.

He wouldn't understand that at the moment life without that box was impossible for me.

I lived, with my secret box under the bed, at number nine, Chestnut Close. It was a very ordinary duplex house with three bedrooms, two bathrooms, a kitchen/diner, and an oblong backyard (mostly grass) with a shed and a conservatory. Until recently the conservatory had housed a wicker sofa and matching armchairs, but they'd been replaced with a new pool table. I had watched from my bedroom as the delivery men struggled to fit it through the front door a couple of weeks before, and every day since, my dad asked if I was up for a quick game.

Which I never was.

If I looked down from my bedroom window, and if the blinds on the conservatory roof were in an upright position, I could see Dad playing pool, all by himself. The day before, he had glanced up and caught me. I'd ducked behind the curtains, but within about fifty seconds he was banging on my bedroom door:

"Why don't you come down, son? Give your old man a game?"

"Not today, thanks, Dad."

He went away after that. I knew what he was trying to do, but honestly—pool? Where did he come up with that one? And I was determined I would never, ever, ever go into the conservatory again. Our cat, Nigel, had vomited up endless bird and mouse guts onto those cold, white floor tiles; can you imagine what would be crawling around in there? In the summer heat the whole room had to be boiling with disease. And as if to crush any tiny urge I might have had to join Dad in potting a few balls, Nigel had decided to adopt the pool table as his favorite place to nap. Every day he stretched across the green cloth as if he were being sacrificed to the Gods of Pool. The only way to clean that table now would be to smother it in disinfectant, and I wasn't stupid enough to try. That table must have cost Dad hundreds.

My bedroom was the best part of the house. It was safe. It was free from germs. Out there, things were dangerous. What people didn't seem to understand was that dirt meant germs and germs meant illness and illness meant death. It was quite obvious when you thought about it. I needed things to be right, and in my room I had complete control. All I had to do was keep on top of it.

Spending so much time in my room meant that I'd gotten to know the place well. For example:

1) The front right-hand leg of my bedside cabinet was loose and at a slight angle.
2) The paint on the underside of my windowsill was flaking—definitely made worse by my cleaning.

3) High in a corner above my bed there was a piece of wallpaper that, when you considered it from a certain angle, looked like a lion.

It wasn't a fierce "king of the jungle" lion, but a funny-looking, gummy lion. It had a scruffy mane, a long, flat nose, and a drooping eye—ten-year-old textured wallpaper with umpteen coats of emulsion could do that to you, I guess. Sometimes, I would talk to him. I know the whole talking-to-an-object thing is a bit "out there," but I'm sure there's a textbook somewhere saying that what I was going through was completely normal:

On around day ten it is inevitable that the unfortunate person who has chosen to spend the majority of his or her life inside will become so bored that they'll begin to talk to items around them. This is a normal occurrence and should not cause undue concern.

In my case it was day eight. I'd stayed home from school again and was having a bad afternoon, and I could feel the Wallpaper Lion's eyes staring at me from the corner of my room. I knew who it was straight away. I'd been watching him on and off for a while, wanting to say something but not letting myself. I finally got to a bursting point and couldn't hold it in any longer.

"I know what you're thinking! You're thinking: *Aw, poor Matthew, stuck indoors all day, isn't it tragic? Why doesn't he go to school? Why doesn't he go out there and actually do* something? Well, it's NOT going to happen, so DON'T bother worrying about me, okay?"

Once I'd said what I wanted to say I felt calmer. I felt like I'd won an argument with him. Now he was just something I talked to now and then, like Mum talked to the cat. It was nothing weird. What *would* have been weird was if he'd answered me. But that had never happened.

No one knew I talked to him, of course. That was another little secret I had. In fact, the whole cleaning thing was a secret too, until quite recently. My friend Tom was the first one to notice something was up. I'd gone to the bathroom during science class, and when I got back to our desk he was staring at me, his head resting on his fist.

"Matt, what's going on?"

I looked at him.

"What do you mean?"

Tom leaned in to whisper.

"The toilet thing? You've been during every lesson today and at break. Are you okay?"

I'd been washing my hands. That's what I'd been doing. They were never clean enough, so I had to keep going back to try and get the germs off. I opened my mouth to tell him but I didn't know how to say it, so I just shrugged and turned back to my work. I pretty much stopped going to school after that.

Now that I was at home I was much more in control and could clean pretty much whenever I liked. The bathroom caused me the most stress, because every time I went in there it felt infested with germs. A couple of weeks before, I'd gotten really carried away while Mum was at work, and before I knew it the afternoon had passed and Mum was home, standing at the door staring open-mouthed as I wiped the insides of the taps with cotton wool buds dipped in bleach.

"*What on earth are you doing, Matthew?*"

She looked around at the sparkling white tiles. You'd have thought I'd been scrawling graffiti everywhere, the face she was pulling.

"*This isn't right . . . Stop it now, enough is enough.*"

She took a step forward. I moved away and felt the sink press into my back.

"*Matthew, you need to talk to me about this. What's wrong? And look at your poor hands . . .*"

She reached out to me, but I shook my head at her.

"*Stay there, Mum. Don't come any closer.*"

"*But Matty, I just want to have a look at your skin. Is it bleeding? It looks like it's bleeding . . .*"

I tucked my hands under my armpits.

"*Are they burnt, Matthew? Have you burnt your hands? You can't get bleach on your skin, darling.*"

"*It's fine, just leave me alone.*"

I quickly scooted past her and went into my room, kicking the door shut behind me. I lay on my bed, my hands throbbing as I tucked them under my arms. Mum stood outside the door. She knew better than to come in.

"*Darling, is there anything I can do for you? Tell me, please. Please,*

Matthew? Your Dad and I can't go on like this. The school rang again today. I can't keep telling them that . . . that you've got a virus . . ."

She made a little choking sound like she'd suddenly forgotten to breathe. I shut my eyes and called one word back at her.

"Gloves."

Silence.

"I'm sorry?"

"Latex gloves. Disposable ones. That's all I need, Mum. Okay? Now, can you leave me alone? Please!"

"Okay. I'll . . . I'll see what I can do . . ."

And that was it.

That was my secret box that I keep under the bed. Not a dusty old box of treasure but a box of one hundred disposable latex gloves, which now held just thirty-two. A secret agreement between me and my mum: She'd supply me with gloves, and I would stop burning my skin with bleach.

We didn't need to tell Dad—he wouldn't understand.

CHAPTER THREE

THE POND

I put on some gloves (fourteen pairs remaining) and squirted the top of my bookcase using some antibacterial spray I'd stolen from under the sink in the bathroom.

"Look at the state of Mr. Charles's yard. I bet he's really angry," I said to the Wallpaper Lion as I cleaned.

It had only taken a day for the little kids to trash it; the once tidy lawn was littered with a freak rainfall of toys. Buckets, spades, an assortment of different-sized balls, plastic cars, three jump ropes, and a blue tartan picnic blanket covered the thick green grass. I picked up my notebook.

1:15 p.m.—Mr. Charles's grandson, Teddy, is playing in the backyard. There's no sign of his sister, Casey.

Using a stick, Teddy was poking at something in the flower bed. I squinted to try and get a closer look, then flinched when I saw what it was. It was a dead baby bird—the bald kind, with bulging, just-hatched eyes. He picked up a plastic orange spade from the grass and, dropping to his knees, wiggled the spade underneath the bird to scoop it up. I put my cleaning things down to watch.

It took Teddy a bit of effort to stand without dropping the bird, but he managed and quickly toddled off toward the pond. Stopping a good meter from the edge, he tossed the bird up, and it somersaulted over and over and then splashed, disappearing beneath the surface. There were a couple flashes of orange as Mr. Charles's fish darted to the bottom. Teddy stood and watched the water for a bit, perhaps to see if the dead chick was going to float to the top, and then he went back to the flower bed and began to dig with the spade. I took out a book and began to wipe it as I kept an eye on the yard.

Casey appeared carrying a plastic bag and the porcelain doll she'd had with her when she'd arrived. Teddy skipped over to her.

"Casey! Casey! Bird dead!"

Acting like he was invisible, she pulled the tartan picnic blanket toward some shade as Teddy danced around her.

"Bird, Casey! *Dead!*" He shouted the word as if that would make her understand him. I guessed he regretted throwing it into the pond now; he could have shown her first.

"Go away," Casey said, placing the pale-faced doll in the center of the blanket, stretching its legs so that it wouldn't topple over. She tipped the plastic bag upside down, and an assortment of ribbons, brushes, and hair clips rainbowed onto the blanket.

"Casey. It *dead*! It DEAD, Casey!"

Teddy ran to the pond. He pointed at the water as he jiggled around on the spot. Casey watched him for a moment before sorting through the hair accessories, lining up the various brushes and combs and winding the ribbons into curls. Teddy wandered back and sat next to his sister. He picked up a purple brush and attempted to run it through his blond hair, but he got the angle wrong and it scratched down the front of his face.

Casey said something to him and snatched the brush away. The little boy got up and went back to the flower bed. He squatted down, peering under the plants, maybe looking for more dead birds to show her. Fanning her pink skirt around her legs, Casey began to talk to the doll as she brushed its hair.

My heart was pounding. Seeing the dead chick and knowing all the diseases it must have crawling over it had made me feel worse. Even though I was watching from next door, the majority of my brain was overloaded with worry that germs were spreading around my room and sneaking into all the little gaps here and there. One speck of dirt can quickly escalate to a whole infection, nobody realizes that. These things have a domino effect, and if I'm not careful I could be cleaning all day. I turned away from the window and concentrated on taking each book off the shelf and wiping the cover and spine.

I was on my third book when there was a scream from outside. Teddy was flat on his back and Casey was dragging him off the blanket by his ankle. Once he was on the grass, she dropped his foot with a thump and went back to her doll. Teddy lay there for a moment, staring up at the dazzling blue sky before scrambling to his feet and lunging for the porcelain doll. Grabbing a fistful of its hair, he raced toward the pond, pulling it along the ground.

Stunned, Casey sat openmouthed. There was a few seconds' delay as her brain caught up with what was happening, and then she shouted with all her might:

"GIVE HER BACK TO ME, NOW!"

The little boy turned, the doll dangling from his fist with its legs jutting out at awkward angles. No one moved.

"No, Teddy! Mum gave her to me!"

Casey's voice shook as she pleaded with him.

Maybe Teddy wanted revenge for not being included in her game, or maybe he was just a kid who wanted to see if the doll sank as quickly as the dead chick; either way the temptation was too much. With a large swing of his short, chubby arm the toddler threw the doll into the air, where it hung for a moment before plummeting into the dark, green water.

Splash!

Casey froze as the doll lay on the surface like a doomed heroine. Its cream dress ballooned and for a moment it looked as if it was going to float, but then the fabric deflated and it slowly disappeared beneath the surface.

"I've got a bad feeling about this," I said to the Wallpaper Lion.

Casey's body went rigid, her hands splayed at her side. If I'd been watching a cartoon, white steam would have erupted from her ears. Teddy was facing the pond, hypnotized by the water, maybe wondering if the doll had landed on top of the dead bird. Stretching her arms out as if she were about to do a conjuring trick, the little girl ran at her brother. Her hands hit him with such force his little head jolted back, and then he toppled forward, straight into the pond.

It didn't seem real at first. It was as if my window were a TV screen and any minute now the commercials would kick in. Casey stood and watched as her brother splashed desperately in the deep pond.

"Where's Mr. Charles? Why isn't he coming?" I said to the Wallpaper Lion. I thumped my gloved hand against the window.

"Help him!"

Casey jumped and her head slowly turned as she tried to work out where the sound was coming from.

THUMP, THUMP, THUMP!

"Get your granddad! Go and get your granddad! Now!"

THUMP, THUMP, THUMP!

My hand slapped hard on the glass, but Casey just glared up at me, her arms hanging by her sides as her brother's splashes rained around her. I ran out of my room and nearly tripped over Nigel, who was stretched across the landing in a square of sunlight. Standing at the top of the stairs, I fixed my eyes on the front door. I could just run down, pull on my trainers, sprint over, and pull Teddy out of the pond. But I couldn't move. The thought of going outside, let alone putting my hands in that dirty pond water, made me feel sick. Instead I ran into the office, the elephant mobile spinning around as I brushed past.

A hose snaked along the pathway of number eleven, but Mr. Charles wasn't anywhere to be seen.

"Where's he gone? Where is he?!"

I looked around the close, and then I saw him, chatting with Penny and Gordon at number one. The three of them were laughing about something, and Mr. Charles was red in the face. I banged loudly on the glass.

"Mr. Charles! It's Teddy! Quick!"

He stopped laughing and looked around at the other houses, trying to work out where the noise was coming from. Then Penny spotted me and pointed.

"MR. CHARLES!! QUICK! HE'S FALLEN IN THE POND!"

THUMP, THUMP, THUMP.

For a moment Mr. Charles looked dazed, as if he couldn't make sense of what I was saying, but then he seemed to come to his senses and ran toward his house. His spindly arms and legs looked like they were traveling in slow motion. I ran back to my bedroom window. Teddy was still splashing as Casey watched. The old man appeared and Casey grabbed her brother by the arm, yanking him half out of the pond.

"What's happening? Teddy!"

"He fell in, Granddad! I couldn't reach him! I called for you but you didn't come!"

She began to sob as her brother coughed and spluttered on the grass. Mr. Charles rubbed his back.

Penny appeared with Gordon right behind her.

"Oh my goodness," Penny said. "What's happened?"

Mr. Charles jabbed his finger at Casey. "Can't I leave you for a second? What were you doing playing near the pond? I've got fish in there!"

Her crying became louder, but he ignored her and scooped the boy up under his arm.

"Have you got any blankets?" said Penny, waving her arms about. "We'll need to keep him warm. He's probably in shock! Gordon, go back home and get some blankets. Grab at least three!"

Gordon sloped off around the corner without a word.

Mr. Charles looked up at me as he walked toward the house. I was expecting a grateful nod, but his face was blank. Teddy stretched his hands in front of him like Superman.

"Bird, Granddad! Dead bird!"

Considering he'd nearly drowned, he didn't look too bad at all.

After they'd gone inside, Casey instantly stopped crying and grabbed the stick from the garden that Teddy had used to poke the bird. She stuck it into the pond and fished around for a bit until something bobbed to the surface. Kneeling, she pulled the object out and clutched it to her chest. Water poured out of the doll. Its golden hair was now dirty brown and it was missing a shoe. Kissing its face, she tried to smooth its dress and hair and make it look neat again. She took a couple of steps toward the house, then suddenly looked straight up at me. My heart thumped. Not wanting to duck away and make myself look stupid, I held her gaze. Her mouth circled into an O shape and she slowly smacked her lips together three times. Just like a fish. I shivered, then turned away and carried on cleaning.

———————

That night I lay awake in the silence.

Tap, tap, tap.

Somebody was tapping on my bedroom wall from next door.

Tap, tap, tap.

I guessed it was Casey trying to torment me. I didn't move, listening to the silence.

It started again, harder this time.

Tap, tap, tap!

I rolled over and turned my back to the wall.

Things had certainly changed since they'd arrived, and I wasn't sure I liked it.

CHAPTER FOUR
WHAT DO WE DO ABOUT MATTHEW?

Every day Mum delivered my meals to my room on a tray. Lunchtime's selection consisted of one prewrapped ham-and-cheese sandwich, one sealed carton of orange juice, one banana, and three unopened bottles of water to drink throughout the day. Very safe. Very sterile.

Food was always accompanied by Mum trying to have a chat from the doorway. I tried not to say much and to avoid her eyes if I could.

"Mr. Charles's grandchildren look sweet, don't they? It'll be nice having some kids next door for the summer, won't it, Matthew?"

"Yep, I guess so."

I had decided not to say anything about the pond episode or the tapping on my wall.

"His daughter is in New York for a month. She's some hotshot banker, apparently. It's odd. I've never known her to visit him, have you?"

I shook my head. Mum knew how much I watched the neighbors and that if anyone had seen Mr. Charles's daughter visit before it would have been me.

"Isn't that funny? Those kids have probably never even met him. Maybe her usual childcare let her down or something."

"Yeah, maybe."

I kept my eyes on my lunch. I didn't like to be too talkative in case she launched into her favorite subject: "What Do We Do About Matthew?"

"I'm at the salon for a few hours this afternoon. Is that okay, Matthew? Will you be all right on your own?"

Mum had opened the Head to Toe beauty salon five years before. Her original plan had been to let the new manager run the place while she popped in to do the odd treatment and keep up with the gossip. Lately it appeared she had to be there every day, but I knew it was just so she could escape the problem indoors: me. She held the tray out, and I took the items off one at a time using my fingertips and placed them on my bedside table.

"Matthew? Is that all right?"

"Sure." I looked up at her and accidentally met her eyes and then *bam*—she was off . . .

"Good. Oh and I've made an appointment for us to see the doctor in the morning. See if we can get you sorted out. Okay?"

She tucked the tray under her arm like a handbag.

"What?"

"The school keeps calling and now the council is writing letters. We've got to sort you out before September or me and your dad will be in big trouble. You do realize that they lock parents up nowadays if their kids don't go to school, don't you?"

Mum and Dad had been lying to the school; they said I had mono. Of all the illnesses they could have picked, they chose the "kissing disease"—when I had no intention of ever kissing anyone! They must have thought it was a good choice because you can be off school for weeks with that. I think Mum even managed to convince herself that I actually had it, as in the first few days I was off she kept asking me how my throat was feeling and offering me painkillers. Desperation—that's what it was: willing me to have something treatable, something with an end in sight.

"I'm not going."

"Don't be silly, of course you are. It's only Dr. Kerr. You've been seeing him since you were a baby."

As she spoke she tried to look over my shoulder. I pulled the door closed a little bit.

"Why don't you open a window in there? Let some of that stuffy air out?"

Her bare foot landed on my carpet as she stepped across my doorway.

"What are you doing, Mum?"

She flinched but didn't move. I stared down at her painted, pink toenails wriggling on my beige carpet.

"Can you get your foot out of my room, please?"

Her leg twisted at an awkward angle, but she stayed exactly where she was.

"Mum? Please!"

"Why, Matthew? It's just a foot. It's not going to hurt you, is it?"

She giggled nervously, her naked toes snuggling into the pile.

I began to shake.

"I'll tell you what, let's make a deal. I'll move if you promise to come and see Dr. Kerr tomorrow morning. How does that sound?"

She'd have been in the conservatory this morning, her bare feet padding around the cold tiles where Nigel chucks up fur balls and mouse guts. She must be riddled with germs—germs that were now escaping in their millions into my room. I gripped the edge of the door and thought about slamming it against her toes, but if I did that I might end up with blood on my carpet, and that made me feel dizzy. I didn't look up.

"Okay, okay. I'll go. Now can you move? Please?"

Her foot froze.

"Promise?"

"Promise."

I had absolutely no intention of going through with it.

"You really, really promise? On Callum's angel?"

That's my baby brother. He didn't come home from the hospital and he never got to gurgle over his elephant mobile, but he had a grave with a white marble angel. I couldn't break a promise on something like that—especially considering what I'd done.

I closed my eyes, weighing the options. I felt the door being pushed slightly as she tried to edge her way in.

"I promise! I promise on Callum's angel," I said.

She waited a couple of seconds and then her foot retreated into the hallway, her face beaming.

"Wonderful! I'll be home in a few hours. Why don't you sit in the garden today? Try and get a bit of color in those cheeks? I'll put a chair out for you, shall I?"

"Whatever, Mum."

I shut the door and dived under my bed to grab my box of gloves (ten pairs remaining), the bottle of antibacterial spray, and a cloth, and I did my best to try and clean the carpet. I felt my insides squirming, the way they always did whenever Mum or Dad mentioned Callum. The guilt of what I'd done lived inside me like a vicious black beetle, scuttling around in my stomach.

Some days I almost felt like I could just plunge my hand in my tummy and pull that beetle out. I'd throw it on the floor, its little legs frantically kicking at the air, and all my fears would miraculously vanish. I'd finally be free of the guilt. But the beetle didn't go away. It lay there, snoozing, waiting for me to relax, and then it started up all over again: *scuttle, scuttle, scuttle.*

I scrubbed the carpet and sprayed and wiped and then I went to the bathroom to throw the gloves away and wash my hands until it felt right. It took eleven washes. When I got back to my room I inspected my lunch closely. Everything looked unopened, so I quickly ate it up before it became infected. I put the trash outside my door and then went into the office to see if anything was going on outside. I took some notes.

Tuesday, July 22nd. 4:11 p.m. Hot and sunny.
Cars on the street = 4
People on the street = 1

As Melody disappeared into the overgrown tunnel, her arms were folded and her head down, as though bracing herself against an arctic wind.

Mr. Charles appeared on his front path wearing a red checked shirt and beige trousers. He looked like he was getting ready for a rodeo. He jabbed at his concrete path with a stiff brown broom, and clouds of dust flew up around his ankles. There was no sign of Casey or Teddy. He stopped for a moment, wiping sweat from his forehead, and then he opened his iron garden gate and began to brush the pavement outside his house, each sweep directed toward the gutter. My heart started beating faster. My hands were beginning to feel unclean again. I went to the bathroom, but on the seventh wash our doorbell rang. I froze. I wasn't feeling clean enough yet. I rubbed the soap into my cracked skin again and ignored the door. There was another ring on the doorbell, and then someone knocked on the glass. I quickly rinsed my skin in scalding water and ran downstairs, opening the door using my sleeve.

"Ah, Matthew! You're in. Is your mum there?"

I shook my head at Mr. Charles, who was now standing on my front door step. His arms were folded awkwardly on top of the broom handle, and he looked like he was about to burst into song. I could hear the devil cat, Nigel, meowing behind me.

"How about your dad?"

"He's at work," I said and closed the door slightly. I looked behind me to see where the cat was. He was safely in the kitchen, brushing himself against the cupboard where his food was kept, moving this way and that, showing off.

"Okay, okay, no problem," he said, laughing much too quickly. "It was you I wanted to speak to, actually. How do you fancy earning yourself some spare change?"

He rubbed the top of his head where the sunburn was. Maybe it was because I hadn't seen him close up for so long, but his head looked huge, like a tanned walnut. I could hear a steady *thump, thump, thump* coming from his house through the downstairs wall.

"I think they're playing football in your living room, Mr. Charles," I said.

His eye twitched as he listened.

"Oh that's just . . . just a game . . ." He pinched the top of his nose for a moment, shutting his eyes, and then he was back.

"So, how do you fancy doing some babysitting for me? It'll just be the odd afternoon here and there when you're off of school so I can get on with a few jobs, do my shopping and all that. How does that sound?"

I folded my arms.

"I don't know . . ."

"It'll be good money! They're such easy kids—*so* easy!" he said, blinking rapidly.

Thump, thump, thump.

"I'm quite busy, to be honest . . ."

He nodded as if he understood how hectic my life must be, spending most days indoors doing nothing. I really needed to finish washing my hands. The germs were definitely beginning to spread, and Nigel's meowing was getting louder. He had made his way into the hall and was sitting right behind me.

Thump, thump, thump.

I could hear Casey screaming now. Mr. Charles raised his voice in an attempt to drown them out.

"I guess a whole afternoon could be too much . . . How about a couple of hours? One, even? I'll pay double!"

I shook my head.

"You just tell me how much you'd like, eh, Matthew?"

If he could have got his hands around the door, I think he would have tried to shake a yes out of me.

Thump, thump, thump.

"I'm only twelve, Mr. Charles. I don't think I'm old enough."

Nigel was by the bottom of the stairs now, brushing his face against the step. A tiny, dark spot appeared on the cream carpet where he'd dribbled. He saw me looking and came straight toward me, the germs dropping from his fur and running in all directions into the carpet. I quickly took a step back and opened the door wide. The cat blinked at the bright sunshine and then trotted out-side, darting around Mr. Charles's legs and down our driveway. I pulled the door closed again. My hand was sweating through my sleeve.

"I'm sure you can babysit at your age." He laughed. "Why, I was looking after my brother when I was only seven!"

"I don't think so, Mr. Charles," I said as he continued to laugh.

Thump, thump, CRASH!

"GRANNNNDAAAAAAD!!!"

Mr. Charles's laugh stopped instantly, his shoulders slumped forward, and without saying another word he turned slowly back home, dragging the brown broom behind him. I slammed the door and ran up to the bathroom to wash my hands again.

When I got back to the office, the noises from next door had stopped and I could hear a TV blaring. Out on the street every-thing was quiet, the road steaming in the heat. Nigel was in Mr. Charles's front garden, carefully tiptoeing onto the lawn, his nose dabbing at the grass as he sniffed. He didn't hear the old man approaching him from behind carrying a washing-up bowl full of water. Mr. Charles let out a roar and threw the water into the air; it splashed over Nigel in one big wave.

The cat froze in shock, and so did I. I wasn't a fan of the old vomiting fleabag, but I wouldn't *ever* do something like that to him. His fluffy, ginger-and-white fur was now dark brown and stuck to his skin. He looked utterly petrified. Mr. Charles dropped the bowl on the grass and swung his foot at the cat, his body nearly twisting around from the force, but fortunately Nigel had come to his senses and swerved out of the way. He squeezed through the gate, turned right, and scurried up our path. Sitting on our step he meowed feebly, then began to lick at his fur.

I watched Mr. Charles as he picked up the washing-up bowl and took two steps toward the house. He stopped for a moment as if he'd forgotten something. Taking a step back, he tucked the bowl under his arm, looked up at me, and glared.

CHAPTER FIVE

DR. KERR

When I was younger I thought a mirage was something you'd only see if you got lost in the desert. Delirious, you'd drag yourself along the scorching sand, inch by inch, as you desperately search for water. Suddenly you spot something shimmering on the horizon. It's a pastel-colored ice-cream van! You can almost hear the tinkling music. It beckons you closer and closer with its promise of deliciously cold Popsicles waiting in the deep, dark freezer. Your mouth floods with precious saliva as you try to reach it, but when you're just inches away it vanishes! All that's there, in the exact spot where the ice-cream van just stood, is a shriveled-up cactus.

I saw lots of mirages on the road on the way to the doctor. Not ghostly ice-cream vans but dark pools of water puddled along the tarmac. They looked so real I could almost hear the splash as we drove through them. Dad told me once that they were called *highway mirages*, which sounded about right. He knew a lot of stuff, my dad. Brian's Brains was always one of the top three teams in the monthly pub quiz. You could ask him anything and he'd immediately have an answer.

"Dad, who was on the throne during the Black Death?"

"Edward III."

"What is the capital of Latvia?"

"Riga."

"What is the chemical symbol for copper?"

"Cu."

"What is wrong with your eldest and only son?"

"He's crazy."

Not that he would have said that out loud, but I was pretty sure he thought it. I figured they both did.

Mum had the air-conditioning on. It was directed downward so my feet felt like blocks of ice. I would have twisted the dial around but I didn't want to touch it.

"Mr. Charles's grandchildren seem to be settling in okay, don't they? That must be nice for him, to have a bit of company for a change," Mum said as we crawled along High Street.

She was trying that conversation thing again.

"I don't know how he'll manage for a whole month though, do you? He's no spring chicken."

I kept my mouth shut. I certainly wasn't going to talk to her after the way she'd embarrassed me in front of the whole neighborhood.

She'd sat in the car with the engine running while I remained paralyzed on the doormat. Mr. Jenkins had come back from a run as I stood there, spotting me as he turned into his driveway. He stood there for a moment with his hands on his hips, sweat running down his face as he looked me up and down.

To minimize any possible health risks, I was wearing: a long-sleeved shirt, which I'd buttoned up to the neck; jeans; socks;

rubber boots; and two pairs of latex gloves (six pairs remaining). It was about ninety degrees outside. I was pretty hot.

"What *are* you doing, Corbin?" he said, but he didn't wait for an answer, just shook his head in disgust and went inside.

I don't think Mum heard him. She rolled down her window and hollered at me.

"Two words for you, Matthew Corbin. Callum's angel!"

Her voice bounced off the houses like a pinball. Old Nina's curtain twitched and her dark shadow peered through the thick nets, trying to see what all the noise was about. Penny and Gordon Sullivan appeared in the front yard of number one and began to walk over. They always pop up if it looks like something interesting is going on.

"Everything all right, Sheila?" Penny called.

They arrived at our driveway each holding a *Harrington's Household Solutions* catalog, which I'm sure they'd just grabbed to use as a cover. Penny and Gordon went everywhere together. It was as if they were tied at the waist with a piece of invisible string, and if one ventured too far from the other they'd just ping back together again. In fact, I didn't think I'd ever, *ever* seen them apart.

Mum waved at them from the car.

"Yes, all fine here, Penny. Hello, Gordon. Thank you! Just a preteen pushing the boundaries . . . You know how it is . . ."

She forced a laugh and the retired couple laughed along with her, but they soon stopped when they got a good look at me.

"We'll leave you to it then, Sheila," Penny said, raising her eyebrows at me. She muttered something to her husband and the invisible string twanged as she turned back to the house with Gordon following.

"Come *on*, Matthew! We're going to be late!"

"But Mum, you don't realize what this will do to me . . . please."

A loud meow came from behind me in the hallway. Nigel.

"Matthew. You swore on Callum's angel. Nothing is more sacred than that. Now. Get. In. The. Car."

The meowing was getting closer. I looked around and saw Nigel sauntering along, looking for something to brush against. He stopped for a moment, his eyes fixed on me.

"Matthew. NOW!"

I flinched as Mum shouted, jumped off the step, slammed the front door behind me, and got in the car.

So there we were: at a standstill in a traffic jam on High Street.

"Oh look, that's your friend Tom, isn't it? Shall I give him a beep? He'd be so glad to see you out and about!"

Mum waved madly through the windshield at a group of kids in white shirts and blue ties. Fortunately they didn't notice.

"Mum! Stop it!"

I slid down in my seat as Mum sat back and huffed.

Standing a few meters from my window and sipping from a can of Coke was my best friend, Tom. My *old* best friend. He was with a boy from school called Simon, and they were both laughing and swaying as though they'd lost the ability to stand upright.

"Simon Duke?" I said under my breath. "What's he hanging around with him for?"

Simon Duke was a bit of an idiot who made stuff up. For example, he once said that his dad was a top agent with the FBI. Apparently they were only living in England temporarily and at any moment they could get a call telling them to jump on a plane to wherever the next assignment took them.

"If I don't come to school one day, you'll know we've gotten the call and I'm outta here," he announced to our math class last year, slipping into a dreadful American accent as he tapped the side of his nose.

Simon's downfall came about when someone spotted Mr. Duke in a hardware store wearing an orange apron and helping a customer lift a new toilet into a shopping cart. He got a lot of grief after that.

"Simon, we thought your dad worked for the FBI, not in DIY!"

"What happens when he needs to arrest someone? Does he ask them to 'stick 'em up' and shoot them with a glue gun?"

Amazingly, Simon managed to shrug the comments off:

"Dad's got to keep up an appearance of normality, doesn't he?"

And now, even more amazingly, Tom had decided to hang around with him.

We edged along the line of traffic and I watched them in the side mirror.

"You can ask your friends over any time, you know, Matthew," said Mum. "You don't want to lose contact with them."

I ignored her and watched Tom and Simon shrink in the mirror as we moved onward.

The urge to wash my hands was intensifying, and I was so hot that my eyelids were sweating. I closed them and tried to calm my breathing as Mum continued with a running commentary about her clients at work, the neighbors, anything she could think of to fill the silence.

". . . the girl, Casey, is only six and little Teddy is fifteen months, so he'll have diapers to deal with! Can you imagine an old man coping with that? He'll be exhausted."

I listened to her chattering, trying to swallow the sick feeling I had in my stomach, and then finally the car engine slowed as we pulled into the doctor's parking lot. I opened my eyes and blinked at the bright sunlight.

"I'm very proud of you, Matthew. I'm sorry I shouted earlier about you getting in the car, but I just want you to . . . be . . . to have a normal life. That's all. I'm just thinking of you."

I nodded, unable to speak. After a deep breath, I opened the door.

The waiting room was quiet and I sat in the front row of seats, which were all empty. Mum stood at the reception desk waiting to check us in. An aqua-blue fish tank bubbled away in the corner, a toy shark on the other side of the glass, its mouth opening and closing with a three-second delay. I spotted a thumbtack in the crease between the carpet and the baseboard, the sharp end pointing upward. Directly above it, on the wall, was a laminated sign stating that in the month of *June* there had been *24* missed appointments. *June* and the number *24* were written in black felt pen, which the reception staff must rub out and change each month. The bottom left-hand corner of the poster was not pinned down and gaped away from the wall slightly. I very much wanted to pick the pin up and put it back where it belonged. If the pin was back in its place, then everything would be all right. I would be all right. I looked over at Mum, who was heading toward me, but she changed direction when she spotted someone she knew at the back of the room.

"Hello, Claudia! Isn't it hot? I love it though, don't you?"

I kept my eyes on the thumbtack. I was not looking at anyone around me, not listening to a man with a hacking cough or feeling the infested chair beneath my legs. *Just concentrate on the pin. Take deep breaths and count to three. One . . . two . . . thr—*

"What you in here for then?"

I caught my breath. Someone had sat next to me. Close. I could see a blue school cardigan out of the corner of my eye.

"Is it a skin condition? Is that why you've got those gloves on?"

I turned to face Melody Bird, the girl from my class who lived across the street. The one who visited the graveyard a lot. Claudia was her mum, who my mum was now talking to. The hairs on my arm bristled. Melody made me nervous. Apart from her unnatural interest in the cemetery, she lived next door to Penny and Gordon at number one, and her house was number three; and those two numbers next to each other were bad news. "Tenplusthree" was becoming an issue for me, and I was trying to avoid it as much as I could. I'd found out that in some cities around the world, there were skyscrapers that didn't have a "tenplusthree" floor and they just called it 12A or something, or else skipped right from 12 to 14. People wouldn't do something like that unless there was a good reason.

Fortunately Chestnut Close stops at Mr. Charles's house, number eleven. We'd once had a Christmas card delivered that was addressed to *Mr. P. James, tenplusthree Chestnut Close.* That unopened card sat on the windowsill next to our front door long into the summer because Mum couldn't bring herself to throw it away, even though the house, and possibly Mr. P. James, didn't exist. I was thinking about all of this while Melody talked. I didn't really hear what she was saying, but I noticed she was sitting really close.

"Can you move back a bit?" I said.

Her large brown eyes squinted at me as she shuffled back a little in her chair.

"Why? Are you contagious or something?"

"No."

She scratched her nose with a chewed fingernail and I turned away, focusing again on the thumbtack. A bead of sweat trickled slowly down my spine. A fan on the reception desk blew a blast of warm air every four seconds around the waiting room.

"So, can't you tell me what's wrong with you then?"

"No."

She was quiet for a minute, and then I felt the heat from her arm as she edged toward me again.

"Can't or won't?"

I turned and faced her, leaning back slightly as if she had bad breath.

"Won't."

Tucking a long strand of brown hair behind one ear, she held my gaze for a moment and then shrugged.

"Fair enough."

I looked at the thumbtack and pictured myself picking it up and pressing it into the corner of the poster on the wall. Everything where it belonged, then all would be okay. I took some notes in my mind:

Wednesday, July 23rd. 10:45 a.m. Doctor's waiting room.

Number of people in waiting room = 9

Number of reception staff = 4

Number of fish in tank = 12

Number of thumbtacks on poster on wall = 3

Number of thumbtacks on floor = 1

"Verrucas."

I shut my eyes for a second before turning to Melody again.

"Sorry?"

"That's why I'm here. I've got a cluster of them on my big toe. They hurt like crazy. Got to have them all burnt off, I guess. You had a verruca before?"

"Nope."

"They're *really* painful."

She whipped her head around to take a look at our mums.

"Your mum's really pretty, isn't she?"

I couldn't think of an answer to that, so I kept quiet.

"Hey, I hear your neighbor has his grandchildren staying with him. That'll be good, won't it? Having some new faces around?"

I scowled at her.

"It's just a couple of kids."

She crossed and uncrossed her legs and then picked at the hem of her gray skirt.

"Apparently their mum is some kind of top businesswoman. I bet she's rich, don't you?"

I rubbed my forehead. My head was pounding.

"It was *so* hot in class yesterday. I can't wait for summer vacation. I've got science after this, but I'm not going to rush back. They're not going to know, are they?"

She studied her left palm and traced her fingernail along a couple of the lines before turning back to me.

"What doctor are you seeing? It's not Dr. Kerr, is it? I can't stand him. He must be about ninety and he's always got bits of food on his shirt. Urgh."

The fact that I wasn't answering any of her questions didn't seem to put her off. I closed my eyes, hoping she'd take the hint.

"Do you want me to get you some water? You look like you're going to melt. Those gloves must be roasting."

I shook my head and wiped the back of my neck with the cuff of my shirt, trying to soak up a bit of the perspiration. If I could just get that pin back on the poster, then things would be right again and maybe Melody would go away.

"Are you friends with Jake Bishop?"

"No."

"Good. I hate him. He can be so evil sometimes. I can't believe he lives on our street. I mean, out of everyone in the world he is the *last* person I'd want to have as my neighbor. Don't you think?"

I jolted as a loud *BEEP* blasted the waiting room. A gruff, male voice came over the speakers asking for Mr. Andrews to go to Room 2.

"Ha! You nearly fell off your seat. You should have seen your face! You really jumped!"

As she laughed, her arm brushed against my shirt, so I slid onto the seat next to me.

"Where're you going? Look, I'm sorry. It was just funny, that's all."

She was still giggling as she moved closer. I could hear my mum behind us:

". . . I just don't know what to do, Claudia. I've got the

attendance officer on my back now. Why can't we just get him to school? What did we do that was so wrong?"

The general hum of the waiting room had silenced as every ear strained to hear what my mum was going to say next. I cringed. Fortunately summer was right around the corner, so I figured it would all be fine soon. And when September came around, I'd make an effort to get back to normal and go in every day.

The button on my top collar was tight and it felt like I was slowly suffocating. Melody cleared her throat, ready to project another wave of verbal vomit at me, but this time I was quite grateful, as she might just drown my mum out.

"I think someone should stand up to Jake Bishop, don't you? Didn't you used to be friends with him once? Back in elementary school? Was he always so nasty?"

I shrugged.

"Well, I think he's gotten away with being an idiot for far too long . . . Are you sure you're okay? Your face has gone gray."

"I've got a bad headache."

She frowned, and I wondered if she was thinking she might be the cause.

"I can come to your house one day if you like? We can hang out during vacation. Keep each other company."

Her bottom lip curled over her top and her brow furrowed as she waited for an answer. An old man shuffled by, and I tucked my legs under my chair to keep them out of the way.

"I don't think so. I haven't been well lately." I gave a little cough.

She smacked the heel of her hand onto her forehead, making me flinch.

"Oh of course, the mystery illness! Well, that's fine if you don't want to tell me what's wrong. We all have our secrets, don't we?"

Her eyes narrowed, and I was wondering what she meant when there was another loud *BEEP*.

"Melody Bird, Room 4, please."

"That's me! Well, see you later, Matty."

Her hand suddenly reached toward me, and she squeezed my forearm before she headed off along the corridor with her mum. My arm tingled where her hand had touched it. Not a good tingle—an infected tingle. Washing was imperative, but there was no way I was going to venture into the bathroom of a doctor's office. I searched the baseboard for the missing thumbtack as Mum arrived next to me with a sigh.

"She's nice, that Claudia. A bit, you know, New Agey, but she's all right. I told her she should get herself to the salon and we'll thread her eyebrows for her."

Rummaging in her bag, she pulled out her phone and started texting someone. Now was my chance. My legs wobbled as I stood up and my ears began to ring. This possibly wasn't the best idea I'd ever had, but I knew I wouldn't be able to go home and leave that poster like that. I bent down slowly, and just as my fingers reached the cold pin, everything went black.

———————————

I woke with a cold, wet washcloth on my forehead. The receptionist, Mum, and a nurse were all staring down at me. They fussed over me for a while, talking about whether I needed to go to the hospital, and all I wanted to say to them was: *Look, could someone just put that pin back in that poster over there?* My gloves had been removed, and I told Mum I had to go home immediately, but she said we were going to see Dr. Kerr even if she had to drag me.

His office was dark and musty. I perched on the edge of the chair and stared at my naked hands in the gloomy light as Mum told the doctor how anxious I'd become, how I liked to keep things clean all the time. She was using her posh voice, the one she used in front of teachers, people who work in banks, and Mr. Charles.

"We just don't know what to do anymore, Dr. Kerr. We're at a loss!"

Dr. Kerr's bones creaked as he wrote some notes and we both waited for him to answer. In the corner was an old computer covered in a thin layer of dust. Melody was right, he did look about ninety. And I counted at least six stains of various colors on his shirt. I was just beginning to think maybe he hadn't heard anything Mum had said when he suddenly burst into life.

"Not much we can do here, I'm afraid. I'll refer him to a

psychotherapist, arrange a face-to-face assessment. In all likelihood you're looking at six weeks of counseling, maybe more, and then he should be feeling right as rain."

He squinted at me, even though he hadn't actually spoken to me at all.

Great. Can I go now? bubbled across my tongue, dangerously close to escaping.

"How long will we have to wait for an appointment, doctor?" said Mum.

He looked back down at his notes, his pen scratching once more. "Well, these things take a while, unfortunately. I think the current wait time is at least three to four months. Maybe longer."

He kept his head down, writing, and then Mum suddenly slapped her hand on the desk. Dr. Kerr and I bounced in our chairs as if we'd both gone over a speed bump.

"Three months? *Three months?* Are you serious?" Mum's posh voice was obliterated. Dr. Kerr rolled his eyes.

"Mrs. Corbin, I'm sorry, but there is a waiting list and your son isn't an urgent case. I'll write a letter to his school and explain. They'll arrange a meeting with you and the local authority to discuss your son's absence if they haven't already done so."

He flicked through an old Rolodex and copied something onto a yellow Post-it note.

Creak, creak, creak.

"Here are a couple of private therapists who may be able to help you—if you're willing to pay."

He leaned forward with the fluttering note stuck to a finger and Mum snatched it from him. Then she stood up and stormed out, leaving me sitting there on my own. Dr. Kerr just sighed and carried on writing as if I didn't exist. I stood to go too, but stopped when I reached the door.

"I'm sorry about my mum shouting, Dr. Kerr. She's been a bit stressed lately. You know, because of everything."

The old man concentrated on his writing pad for a moment and then looked up. "You're a nice boy, Matthew. Stop all this messing around now, eh? There's a good lad."

He looked down again and waved his hand as if he were shooing away an annoying wasp. I had been dismissed.

I went to bed while it was still light outside. My limbs felt heavy, my brain exhausted. I must have fallen asleep within minutes to the sound of a blackbird singing outside. When I woke up it was dark. My clock glowed red: 2:34 a.m. Something had disturbed me, but in that just-awake state I wasn't sure what; and then I heard knocking on the other side of my wall.

Tap, tap, tap.

I sat up and listened again.

Tap, tap, tap.

"Can you hear that?" I whispered to the Wallpaper Lion. "She's doing it again."

I closed my eyes and listened.

Tap, tap, tap.

"Are you there, Goldfish Boy? Are you back in your tank?"

It was Casey. I clenched my hand into a fist, ready to thump back if she did it again. I waited for ten minutes, but there was silence.

CHAPTER SIX

THE GOLDFISH BOY

Dad came up to see me at lunchtime on Saturday, waving a letter addressed to "The Parents of Matthew Corbin."

"We'll soon have you sorted out, eh, son? Get you back on your feet. Blimey, it's hot in here."

Unlike Mum, he had no hesitation about coming into my room. He walked in and opened my window using his bare hands, a big grin on his face, as if this mysterious letter's arrival would suddenly cure me of all my "issues."

"Dad, what are you doing? I don't want my window open!"

I jumped onto my bed and pulled my knees up, hugging my legs.

"Course you do. Bit of fresh air won't poison you, will it?"

My curtains blew in the breeze, the germs squealing with delight as they skydived onto my carpet.

"Me and your mum are off to Auntie Jean's picnic in a bit. How about coming with us, now that you're on the mend? All your cousins will be there."

Auntie Jean's Mighty Picnic used to be the highlight of my summer. A red ring would mark the date on our calendar, and I'd count the weeks until school was over and the picnic was here. It had started off as a small family get-together for my cousin Darcy's sixth birthday, but it went so well that Auntie Jean had organized one every summer since.

Last year's picnic had been epic. We all arrived in convoy and parked next to each other by a patch of field at a big, countryside park. The grown-ups hugged and kissed one another first and then turned their attention to the kids.

"Oliver, that can't be you under all that hair, is it?"

"How old are you now, Darcy? Fourteen? Wow, is it eight years we've been doing this, Jean?"

"Make sure you're on my team later, Matthew. How many runs did you get last year?"

I grinned at Uncle Mike, who put his arm around my shoulder.

"I think it was twelve, Uncle Mike."

It was twelve. I just didn't want to sound like a show-off.

Before we unpacked the cars all twenty of us went for a long walk to work up an appetite. We followed the same path that we did every year, but as always there was a disagreement over the route:

"It's left here, Brian. I remember that tree."

"No, it's definitely right. And how can you remember a tree? They all look the same!"

Auntie Jean took charge and turned left and we laughed as we followed her. Toward the end of the walk we slowed down, with the youngest kids at the back whining about sore feet, but then someone shouted:

"Picnic ahoy!"

Our cars glinted in the sun at the top of the hill, and the thought of lunch helped speed us onward. There was a mad frenzy as everyone unpacked their coolers and wicker baskets, laying the picnic blankets out in one huge patchwork.

I scarfed down as many sausage rolls and ham sandwiches as I could, impatient for everyone to finish so that the real fun could begin. Finally, Uncle Mike announced:

"Okay, who's up for some baseball?"

I was the first on my feet as the adults tried to organize the teams fairly.

"You take Uncle Reg, and we can have little Martha."

"But Uncle Reg can't run! That's not fair!"

"Matthew can do the running for him. Can't you, Matthew?"

I grinned and nodded as I smacked the smooth bat in my palm, eager to get started.

The game went on for hours until some of the adults said they wanted a rest and the younger kids drifted off to try and catch some grasshoppers. I sat next to Mum and she patted me on the shoulder.

"So you didn't beat last year's record then, darling? How many did you get?"

"Only nine this year, Mum."

"Only nine, eh? Well, next year I'm sure you'll beat it."

Auntie Jean was passing around a huge bowl of chips and they landed in front of me.

"Go on, Matty. Dig in."

I looked down the hill at the old brick restroom hidden in a small copse of trees.

"Mum. I think I'm just going to go wash my hands. I won't be long."

I headed toward the bathroom, the long grass scratching at my ankles. The sound of my family's excited chatter faded as I stepped into the cold, dank building. The lights weren't working and there was only a tiny rectangle of window above the sinks, so it took a while for my eyes to adjust. I didn't feel bad, exactly; I just knew I'd feel happier if my hands were clean. I stood alone, listening to the steady *drip, drip, drip* of the toilet as I washed them in the darkness.

"Come on, son, it's the Mighty Picnic! You can't miss it, you've got to try and break that baseball record, remember? How many runs did you get again?"

I shrugged. "I don't know."

Dad walked around my room, looking at my books, my desk, my papers, almost touching things. I sensed he was daring me to ask him to leave.

"You've certainly been busy keeping things nice and tidy in here. Where are your dirty socks? Moldy cups? Empty soda cans? The things *normal* boys would have lying around?"

Did you hear how he said normal, *Lion? Did you hear that? That's not right, is it?*

I said this in my head as I looked up at the misshapen wall-paper in the corner of my room. Dad's mouth was smiling, but the rest of his face didn't mean it. You had to be careful with him sometimes.

"So, how about it, then? The barbecue? Auntie Jean's? You going to come?"

I stood up and began to look at the things on my desk as if I had something really urgent that I had to deal with.

"I can't. I've got a load of schoolwork to do. Tons of it," I said, shaking my head with the utter annoyance of it all.

Dad was still grinning. He knew I was lying to him. Hovering next to me, he reached out and picked up one of my note-books. A navy blue one that I'd filled from cover to cover to pass the time.

"But it's vacation now. And you can't have that much—you've hardly been there, have you?"

He began to flick through the book, licking a finger as he turned each page, his eyes scanning my writing. I shuddered.

"I've got a lot to catch up on. A . . . a big project, for a start."

He didn't look up.

"What's this about then? All these lists? Times and stuff?" He held the book out a bit and began to read. "*3:04 p.m., Mr. Charles is feeding the fish in his pond. 4:18 p.m., Mum has just come in from work.* Blimey, son. You need to get out more."

I snatched the book from him, instantly feeling infected.

"It's for the project I just told you about. On statistics. A math thing . . . And I need to get started on it as soon as possible."

He looked at me and then at the book, which I now held pinched between my thumb and index finger.

"It looks like a lot of mumbo jumbo to me, Matthew," he said, his grin gone.

"Yeah, well. You were never very good at math, were you, Dad?" I laughed nervously, not sure if I was getting away with it. "General knowledge is your thing, isn't it? Not numbers."

I sat back on the bed and glanced up at the Wallpaper Lion. His wonky eye looked down at me reassuringly. *You're doing okay,* he was saying.

"What do you keep looking at up there?"

Dad gazed at the bare wall.

"Nothing."

He walked around, scanning the corners of the room, looking at the ceiling and then back at the wallpaper.

"It could do with some decorating in here—get all this old stuff off the walls. A couple of coats of paint. It'll transform the place."

"No!"

Dad flinched.

"You said you needed to paint downstairs, didn't you? Remember? In the conservatory? You only got one coat on it after it was built and you talked for weeks about doing a couple more layers."

I dropped my notebook onto my bed and Dad stared at it. I thought he was going to pick it up again, but he stepped back and his eyes were drawn downward, under my bed. I sat quickly and dangled my legs over the side, trying to hide the box of disposable gloves with my feet.

"So what's in the letter, Dad? From the therapist? When's my appointment?"

He was still staring under the bed.

"It's this week . . . Tuesday . . ."

I stayed still.

"And who's taking me?"

I casually moved my legs, just a bit, hoping to distract him. Dad stood there, seemingly puzzled by whatever glimpse he'd had.

"We're both coming . . ."

He took a step forward and . . .

"Brian, we'll be late again!" Mum poked her head in the doorway. Her jaw fell as she saw that Dad was actually in my room. She quickly composed herself.

"Aren't you coming, Matthew? Oh come on, you know you'll enjoy it when you get there."

I kept quiet.

"Says he's got a load of homework," said Dad, apparently forgetting about getting a better look at what he'd seen under my bed.

"Leave that for another day, eh?" pleaded Mum. "Come with us! It'll be fun! I know Auntie Jean would love to see you."

I looked at them both. Mum was grinning, but her eyes were pleading. She hadn't stepped over the threshold into my room.

"Sorry, Mum."

Dad cleared his throat.

"Right, well, give us a call if you need us. We won't be long. Come on, Sheila. We don't want to be late."

I'm not sure he realized that I hadn't used a phone in months. Mum gave me a feeble smile and closed the door. I got up from the bed and listened to them talking quietly outside my room.

"Come on, don't get yourself all upset, Sheila. Let's just go and have a nice time, forget our worries for a bit."

"We're losing him, Brian. Did you see his face? He's terrified! Our little boy is so frightened and there's nothing we can do."

"He'll work it out. He's tough, remember? Remember how good he was after we lost Callum?"

They slowly walked downstairs and I heard the front door closing behind them. I stood there for a while, in the middle of my room, listening to the silence as I wiped away my tears.

"What's wrong with me, Lion?" I said. "Why can't I stop?"

The Wallpaper Lion stared back at me blankly.

I bent down and took out my secret box and pulled on a pair of gloves (two pairs remaining) and then closed my window. I got some antibacterial solution from the bathroom and gave my notebook a light spray and wiped it with a clean cloth. Dad had left the letter on my desk and I peeked over the folds, not wanting to touch it.

. . . for your son Matthew Corbin to attend a psychology assessment with Dr. Rhodes at 10 a.m. on Tuesday, 29 July . . .

I picked the letter up by a corner and, standing at the top of the stairs, let it flutter down to land on the mat by the front door. I then went to the bathroom and washed my hands twelve times.

From: Melody Bird

To: Matthew Corbin

Subject: You Fainted/Verrucas!

Hi Matty!

I heard you fainted at the doctor's. Well, actually I saw you.

Flat out on the carpet.

Are you OK? I told you, you didn't look good.

Melody x

PS. Oh and there is good news about my verrucas! I didn't have to have them burnt off after all, but I've got to use a cream every day, which is a real pain.

I stared at the screen for a while, not sure how to reply. I decided polite but distant was probably best and began to type. On my right hand I wore one latex glove (three left) and I kept my other hand in midair, not touching anything. I was trying to ration them and only wear one at a time.

I clicked Send and stood up. There was a lot of noise outside.
Mr. Charles was attempting to water his front yard as Casey and
Teddy ran around him, jumping through the spray and squealing
every time they got a blast of cold water. The old man was bright
red and trying to get them to calm down, but the more he shouted,
the faster they hurtled around and around. Old Nina's lamp in the
front room window of the Rectory was barely visible in the bright
sunlight. I could just make out a soft, orange glow.

There was a trumpet blast as another message pinged into
my inbox.

there's something wrong with you. Whatever that might

be . . . I'm not being nosey! I'll come over and see you later,

OK?

Mel. x

PS. Your mum gave my mum your email address at the

doctor's. I think she thinks you need a friend, and anyone

who hates Jake is fine with me!

She typed like she talked.

To: Melody Bird

From: Matthew Corbin

Subject: Busy

I'm really busy at the moment trying to catch up on

schoolwork, so there's no need to come over. And I have

plenty of friends, thank you. And I don't hate Jake. I just

don't like him very much—there is a difference.

M.

There was no way I wanted a verruca-ridden girl in my house.

Mr. Charles was yelling outside.

"Casey, stop it right now! Look at the mess you've made."

He hosed the path, washing away a patchwork of child-sized,

muddy footprints. Teddy squealed as the water sprayed his ankles;

he did a funny little jump and then ran around the side of the

house toward the back. Mr. Charles blasted the muddy remains of the footprints down the path to the front gate. While he wasn't looking, Casey stepped into a muddy puddle that had settled at the edge of the yard. The back of her pink summer dress was freckled with dirt as she walked brown footprints along where Mr. Charles had just cleaned. Seeing this, he threw the hose onto the lawn and grabbed her by the tops of her arms.

"I told you to stop it, didn't I? Why won't you do as you're told, you naughty girl?"

His hands left behind two bright red strips like raw bacon. Casey looked as if she was going to cry, but instead she scowled at him, refusing to allow any tears to escape.

"Now, be a good girl and go and play," he said, patting her three times on the head. "And keep an eye on your brother, don't let him near that pond!"

He picked the hose up again and continued washing the path. Casey folded her arms and went around to the backyard.

Saturday, July 26th. 12:15 p.m. Bedroom. Cloudy and hot.
Number of toys on next door's lawn = 17
Number of children in next door's yard = 2
Number of children glaring at me from next door's yard = 1

Teddy was sitting cross-legged on the grass studying the bottom of his muddy foot. He scraped at the skin with his fingernail and inspected the dirt, then swapped to the other foot. Casey had been dancing, holding the edge of her pink dress, tiptoeing here and there in her imaginary ballet show. As she pirouetted she suddenly stopped and glared up at me. Her mouth smacked up and down and she started to laugh.

"Look, Teddy! It's the goldfish! Look! The Goldfish Boy is in his tank!"

Teddy stood and gazed toward my window, his eyes squinting in the bright sunlight. A big smile spread across his face and he looked about ready to raise an arm to wave at me, but I quickly ducked out of sight, my heart pounding in my chest.

CHAPTER SEVEN
MELODY AND JAKE

The sky from the office window looked almost turquoise, like the sky from a manga cartoon. It was going to be another hot day.

Monday, July 28th. 9:35 a.m. Office/nursery. Hot and sunny.
Gordon and Penny left together in their blue Fiat at 09:34 a.m.
Old Nina's lamp is on as usual in the front room window of the Rectory. Jake Bishop is cycling around in a figure eight in the middle of the road. He stops now and then to look at his phone and then carries on. Leo left for work earlier in his car that sounds like a tank.

Leo was Jake's older brother and was famous in our area. On his last day of high school he organized a group of kids to lift the headmaster's car and wedge it between the school gates. A crane had to be hired to get it out. A photograph of this, along with the headmaster watching through his hands, made the front page of the local paper with the headline:

SCHOOLBOY PRANK CAUSES HEADACHE

Not long after Leo was approached by the owner of a local garage who said he liked his initiative and would he be interested in an apprenticeship? He'd worked there ever since and could regularly be seen taking his silver Mini to pieces on their oil-stained driveway.

"Jake! Your inhaler!" called Jake's mum, Sue, from the doorstep of number five. She went back inside, leaving the door ajar.

Jake did two more figure eights and then sped toward his driveway, his legs pumping furiously, braking just at the last second before hitting the step. Discarding the bike with a clatter he went in, slamming the door.

I sat back in the office chair. My reflection in the computer screen showed a blank face with hollow eyes, my skin almost translucent. I rubbed at the small dent of a scar above my right eyebrow, which seemed more noticeable than usual. I hated that scar. It was always there: my little reminder. The beetle in my guts twisted.

Callum would have been five now, probably incredibly annoying and fussing over me all the time, wanting my attention. He'd be getting to the age where he'd be embarrassed by the baby-yellow walls, maybe asking Mum and Dad for a new "big boy's bedroom" with a dinosaur theme. The elephant mobile would have been packed away in the attic as Dad painted the room a prehistoric green. When it was ready, I'd appear with my old tub of dinosaur figures, which I'd found at the bottom of my wardrobe.

Here you go, Callum. You can have these if you like.

He would have skipped around his room shaking the tub excitedly while I pretended to be irritated, telling him to calm down a bit. He'd yank his new *T. rex* duvet off his bed to create a large, swirling mountain in the middle of the room. Tipping the tub of figures upside down, he'd make each one walk up the fabric's winding pathways, finishing with a mighty battle between a triceratops and a brontosaurus at the top. I'd wander off, leaving him roaring and squealing in delight.

It might sound strange, but I miss the brother I never met. The one who died because of me.

My daydreaming was distracted by voices in the street. Melody was at the end of the alleyway beside Old Nina's house, attempting to get across the cul-de-sac and home to number three. It looked like she'd been on one of her secret trips to the graveyard again. She had some small pieces of white paper in her hand.

Jake was circling around the road, blocking her way each time she tried to cross. Her long hair was tied back and she was wearing black leggings, a black T-shirt, and the same old black cardigan. The only evidence that she was aware we were in the middle of a heat wave were the bright pink flip-flops that slapped against her feet as she walked left and right, trying to get past. He was saying something, but I couldn't hear what. Finally he pedaled off, and I thought he was leaving her alone, but then he raced back, skidding to a halt just a few inches in front of her. Melody flinched, not looking at him. Stepping to one side, she went to go forward but bluffed him, turning away and walking in the opposite direction, toward my house. Even though I was watching, I still jumped when the doorbell rang. I stayed at the window but stood to one side so I couldn't be seen. The doorbell rang again as Jake shouted at her.

"Why aren't you answering my texts? Who do you think you are, ignoring me?"

He'd stopped at the end of our path, his bike barring her exit. I could see the top of Melody's head as she waited for me to answer.

"What ya knocking at his house for? I thought dead people were your thing, not freaks."

He threw his head back and laughed, showing the bright red creases of raw eczema in his neck. My stomach was in knots.

The doorbell rang once more and then Melody turned away, giving up on me. When she reached Jake at the end of our path she said something quietly to him, but I couldn't tell what. Her head was low, her hand up to her face as she chewed on a nail. This wasn't the happy, chatty girl I'd met in the doctor's waiting room.

Jake leaned forward on his handlebars and glared at her. She tried moving from one side to the other, but he just rolled his bike back and forth, blocking her way.

"You're forgetting the magic word, Melody."

She mumbled something else.

Jake put a finger to his chin as if he was thinking about letting her pass but hadn't quite decided yet, and then he leaned toward her and grabbed her wrist. Twisting around, she looked straight up at me. She must have known I was there all along, watching her like an idiot. I held her gaze for a moment.

"Please, Jake, just let her go," I whispered. He held up his phone and started taking photos of her before she managed to wrench her arm away and shield her face.

"Come on, Melody. Smile! I'm going to keep this one forever."

I couldn't bear it any longer. I raced downstairs and opened the front door using my shirt to cover the handle.

"Hi! Melody! Sorry about that, I was in the back . . ."

Jake scoffed. "Oh I see, the weirdos like to stick together, do they? You know she's only got a thing for corpses, don't you?"

He tipped his head back as if he was going to do that horrible snorting thing he does, but then he stopped, his mouth open as he looked across the street. The door of the Rectory had opened and Old Nina stood there watching us. After a long moment she made her way carefully down the steps to her gate. Very slowly she lifted her arm, and a long, white finger unfurled as she pointed directly at Jake, his mouth still wide as he stared back at her. Melody quickly ran over and stood beside me in the hallway. Jake hurried to get his foot on the pedal of his bike and then he turned around and sped off down the road. Old Nina dropped her hand, and Melody and I watched as she went back inside and the door of the Rectory was closed once more.

Melody paced around our small hallway, her flip-flops slapping against her feet as I tried to dodge her movements.

"Did you see that? Old Nina chased him off! Do you think she saw him being mean to me?"

"I don't know, Melody."

I looked down at her flip-flops on our carpet.

"He's such a nasty piece of work. Ha! I can't believe he ran off!"

She walked up and down, up and down. I felt dizzy. I wondered if I should ask her to take the flip-flops off inside the house, but then I remembered the verrucas.

In her hand she had some small, white pieces of paper, which she must have gotten from the graveyard. They looked like business cards. Maybe it was something to do with the church. A choir, perhaps? No, they didn't have one. I knew this from Callum's funeral and our feeble attempts at singing "All Things Bright and Beautiful" over my mother's sobs. The black beetle woke up deep within my stomach. Its sharp little feet began to dig in as it scurried around again.

"He's gone now . . . You can go back home if you like . . ." I said. I was going to pull the door open a bit more, but I didn't want her to see me use my shirt to touch it.

"He was scared, Matty! He actually looked scared."

She stopped and stared at me as I huddled in the corner. Beads of sweat began to run down my face.

"You okay? You're not going to faint again, are you?"

I shook my head and tried to look calm, even though I wasn't feeling it.

"I reckon he thought she was casting some kind of spell on him, don't you? Did you see her finger? Maybe Jake knows something because he lives next door to her and he's seen something we haven't. Do you think she's a witch?"

Her flip-flops slapped again as she walked back and forth.

"A witch?"

Melody was grinning at me, thrilled from the excitement of seeing Jake beaten for once. I must admit it did feel good seeing him scared, but at that moment I was more concerned about the tiny pieces of black fluff from Melody's cardigan slowly appearing on our carpet. My heart was pounding. The girl in my hallway—the girl who hung out in graveyards—needed to leave immediately.

"And what about that lamp in her window? What's that all about? I've never *ever* seen it turned off." Melody was jumping up and down, and she clapped her hands together. "Maybe it's some kind of beacon! Like a symbol to other witches that a real witch lives there! What do you think?"

I watched her for a second as she practically bounced off the walls, but when she saw my face she stopped.

"Matthew? What? What is it?"

I risked her seeing me use my shirt as protection and opened the front door widely as she stared at me.

"I'm sorry, Melody, but I'm really busy at the moment. Can you go?"

She looked outside, then back at me.

"What?"

"I said, can you go?"

Lots of little lines crinkled across her forehead and her bottom lip protruded over her top lip as she took in what I'd said.

"But . . . but we've got things to talk about. Don't you want to discuss Old Nina?"

I shook my head.

She blinked at me a few times and took a step toward the door.

"But you let me in. You let me in when Jake was being mean!"

I could feel the germs from her cardigan nipping at my ankles, burrowing their way under my skin. The feeling brought tears to my eyes.

"I didn't mean to. I made a mistake."

She pressed her lips together and glared at me before stomping out of the house and across the street.

I quickly slammed the door and ran upstairs.

CHAPTER EIGHT

PLAYING WITH PETALS

The Wallpaper Lion woke me up.

In my dream I'd asked him a question: *How does it feel being stuck up there all day, Lion? Just watching the world go by?*

Sounding a bit nervous, like he knew he shouldn't be talking but really couldn't help himself, he said: *Surely you know how that feels . . . don't you, Matthew?*

I jumped when he spoke and woke up. My heart raced and for a moment I felt disoriented, like I always did when I fell asleep in the daytime.

I was facing my floor, my head at an angle on the edge of my pillow. A yellow rectangle of sunlight stretched across my carpet from my desk to the bookshelves. I listened, waiting to see if he was going to carry on, but all I could hear was the drone of a distant lawn mower. Rolling onto my back, I watched the small area of wallpaper that resembled a lion's face. His eye still drooped downward, his matted mane circling his head like a blazing sun, his nose flat and wide, and his mouth now, thankfully, tightly shut.

My clock said 12:45 p.m. I'd been asleep for over an hour. It was weird; the less I did, the more tired I felt. I got up and stretched.

Outside, a sagging blue wading pool, filled with a summer soup of water, grass, and dead flies, sat in the middle of Mr. Charles's backyard. Casey and Teddy were nowhere to be seen. Our yard was also deserted. Mum's empty lounge chair crisped in the baking sun, and behind it Dad's gardening wigwams were all dark and shriveled.

Taking my notebook with me, I crossed the landing into the office to see if anything was going on outside at the front.

Monday, July 28th. 12:47 p.m. Office/nursery. Very hot.

Teddy is in the front yard next door. He's wearing a pull-up diaper and a white T-shirt with a cartoon ice-cream cone on the front. He doesn't have any shoes on. There is no sign of Casey or Mr. Charles. The gate is shut, the small lever on the latch in place.

Reaching toward some bright pink roses, Teddy picked a fistful of petals and scattered them onto the path, dancing as they tickled his sunburnt feet. A trowel and a green kneeling pad lay next to him. Mr. Charles must be in the middle of some gardening. When he reappeared he wasn't going to be happy with what Teddy was doing, not after all the hours he spent fiddling with those flowers.

In his left hand Teddy clutched the little square, blue blanket he'd been holding when he first arrived in the big, posh car with Casey. He let the blanket fall to the ground, then grabbed more petals and watched as they rained down on top of it. When the last petal had dropped he stretched toward a large rose but caught his forearm on a thorn.

"Owwww!" he said and he did a little jig as his face crumpled into a scowl.

For a moment I thought he was going to go and get Mr. Charles, but instead he just squatted down and inspected the cut on his arm, dabbing at it with the blanket.

I heard a door bang open, and Mr. Jenkins appeared from next door wearing his running gear and studying his iPod as he looped some white headphones around his neck. His teeth shined bright against his tanned skin as he smiled to himself. Fortunately there was no sign of Hannah or her swollen belly. Mr. Jenkins turned left out of his driveway and then broke into a jog, oblivious to the toddler crouching down in the garden next to him.

Teddy stood up. There was a tiny trickle of blood running down his arm, but it didn't seem to bother him; he reached for more petals and then stopped. Something out of the corner of his eye had distracted him.

Me.

He turned and pointed a chubby arm toward my window as he gasped:

"Fishy!"

I watched him bounce up and down, clearly ecstatic that he'd spotted the Goldfish Boy all on his own. He looked around for someone to tell.

"Fishy, Casey! Look! Fishy! Granda!"

But nobody came.

I turned away from the window and glanced at the time in the corner of the computer screen.

12:55 p.m.

That time was important.

I don't know why it stuck in my mind but it did, even without writing it down.

At some point after 12:55 p.m. on that bright, scorching day, Teddy Dawson went missing.

CHAPTER NINE

TEDDY IS MISSING

Mr. Charles hadn't been gardening after all. The trowel and kneeling pad I'd seen had just been left over from the previous day, forgotten in the madness of trying to look after two young kids. While Teddy was picking the petals, Mr. Charles was inside having an afternoon nap in his armchair. I was cleaning my room when, at 2:37 p.m., I heard a shout from the garden.

"Teddy! Teddy, where are you? Don't hide from Granddad now."

I looked outside and saw the top of Mr. Charles's red head as he stood on his patio, his hands on his hips.

"Something's going on," I said to the Wallpaper Lion.

"Teddy? Teddy! You come out here this instant, young man!"

He walked around the side of the house and I ran to the office. Claudia, Melody's mum, was just reversing her old car out of their driveway, and as she drove past number eleven, she put her hand up and waved at Mr. Charles, unaware of the panic he was in. The old man ignored her and trotted down his path, his head darting this way and that. I took some notes.

"Teddy! Teddy! Stop hiding and get back here—now!"

A few pastel pink petals fluttered along the path toward the front gate, which was now wide open. Mr. Charles walked quickly around the semicircle of the cul-de-sac, looking over garden fences and into car windows.

"Where are you, Teddy? Teddy!"

His voice sounded different. It was much higher than usual and it was shaking. As he walked past number five, Jake's mum, Sue, appeared in her supermarket uniform.

"Everything all right, Mr. Charles?" she called.

"He's gone. Teddy's gone. TEDDY!"

This last cry reverberated off the windows and we all listened for any reply, but the only sound was the low hum of some distant traffic and a group of sparrows, chirruping madly in the dusty road. Mr. Charles staggered forward, and Sue ran down her path and put an arm around him. She talked to him as they slowly made their way to number eleven.

". . . give the police a call . . . best to be on the safe side . . ."

". . . could he have got to? I was just in the lounge . . ."

I watched them go inside, then looked around at all the houses. Everything was still.

At 3:05 p.m. a police car rolled onto the street and Mr. Charles and Sue rushed to the front gate to meet them. Two uniformed police officers got out of the car as Mr. Charles launched into a trembling speech.

". . . grandson is missing . . . mother is in New York . . . doesn't know yet . . . is it day or nighttime there? Do you think I should call?"

A female officer put a hand on his arm and guided him back to the house while the other, older officer said something into his radio.

I went back to my room and looked out at the backyards to see if I could spot Teddy hiding in a bush or, worse, floating facedown in the pond. But there was no sign of him.

Casey was busy beside the half-deflated wading pool. Her hideous doll was propped against the blue lining, its face leaning toward the water as if it were looking for something on the bottom. She skipped back toward the house, and I stepped to one side in case she spotted me. When she reached the patio she turned and ran full speed up to the doll and, with a dirty, bare foot, kicked it in the back. The doll fell forward and made a small splash as it toppled into the pool. Casey stared at the drowning doll for a moment and then reached out and pulled it from the water, cradling it gently in her arms, stroking its hair. I shivered.

"She is one scary kid," I said to the Wallpaper Lion. I checked my clock. It had been nearly two hours since I had seen Teddy playing with the petals.

"He's probably hiding in a cupboard or under the bed or something. They're bound to find him. But then why is the gate open? He wouldn't have been able to open the latch, would he?"

I looked up at the Wallpaper Lion, who didn't seem so sure. The urge to wash my hands overtook me and I quickly rushed to the bathroom.

The thin skin between my fingers was beginning to split and the constant washing was making it worse. I splashed some cold water on my face and then I ran the hot tap until it was scalding and started washing my hands. I lost track of how long I was in there.

Back in my room I let my hands drip onto my carpet. That was fine. The water was clean, and this was a much more hygienic way to let them dry—and less painful—than using a towel. The older policeman was walking around Mr. Charles's garden looking under shrubs and behind bushes as Casey watched him. Sue appeared on the patio.

"Casey, come on inside now, there's a good girl."

She hurried the girl along while the officer studied the pond and poked at the water with the same stick that Teddy had used to prod the dead chick just last week. He opened the shed, and even I could see that all that was in there was a lawn mower, a ladder, a few plant pots, a bucket, and some garden tools. He checked around the outside, then unclipped a flashlight from his belt to peer into the dark space underneath. The female officer appeared on the lawn.

"Anything?"

The officer shook his head.

"Nothing inside either. I'm getting a ladder to check the attic. You never know."

The woman went to the shed and took the ladder out,

walking briskly back to the house as the other officer went around the side, talking into his radio.

Back at the front, things had gotten a lot busier. Another police patrol car, its blue light flashing, was just parking outside our house, and a silver Mondeo was just pulling up behind it. Two uniformed policemen emerged from the first and a man and a woman in plainclothes from the second. They all walked to number eleven and straight in through the open front door. Bumps and creaks were now coming from Mr. Charles's attic, and I imagined the policewoman was crawling around up there, searching all the dark corners.

As I looked outside, my eyes seemed to go blurry—the glass was rippling and vibrating. My chest rumbled as a police helicopter approached from behind Penny and Gordon's chimney like a giant black-and-yellow hornet. It thundered over the houses, and I rushed to my bedroom and watched it hovering over the backyards.

"This looks serious, Lion," I said to the piece of wallpaper. "This looks very serious indeed."

Our doorbell rang and I froze. Mum wasn't due back for another hour, and anyway, she'd use her key. Peering down from the top of the stairs, I could see a large, black outline of a figure standing on the other side of our frosted glass door. The doorbell rang again, and then the letterbox opened and someone peered through.

"Hello? Can you open up please, it's the police."

The flashing blue light of the patrol car swirled around the hallway like an annoying bluebottle fly. I slowly made my way downstairs and opened the door a couple of inches. The helicopter was so loud now it felt like someone was drumming on my ribs.

"Hello there. He told us you might not answer—you not well?"

A skinny policeman with a face like a tomato was standing on my doorstep holding a pad and pen. He practically had to shout to be heard over the noise of the helicopter. Behind him I could see the man who had searched Mr. Charles's backyard talking to Claudia, who was holding her dachshund, Frankie, under her arm.

"I'm Officer Campen. There's been a serious incident next door—a little lad has gone missing. Have you seen him at all? Wandering about?"

I shook my head.

"And have you seen anyone around in the area? Anyone acting suspicious?"

I shook my head again.

"Okay, well I need to have a quick check around your backyard. That all right?"

I blinked in the sunlight at the man and then looked down at his large, black shoes.

"Do you think you could go around the side?"

Officer Campen frowned.

"Look, son, let me come through, would you? This is serious."

I stood back and he pushed the door wide open and thumped his great feet onto our doormat. After giving his shoes a half-hearted wipe, he walked off toward the kitchen and into the conservatory.

"Through here?"

I nodded.

"I'll need to take a few details down in a minute," he said and he opened our back door and went outside.

I watched from the entrance of the kitchen as he looked around our shrubs and behind Dad's runner bean wigwams. The yards were small on our street, so it wouldn't take long for them all to be searched. After checking down the side of the house where we keep the trash cans and recycling, he headed for the shed. A rake, two tennis rackets, and an old swing-ball pole fell out as he opened the door. Shaking his head, he climbed in over the mess, pulling things out of the way so that he could have a good look.

I took the chance to wash my hands at the kitchen sink, turning the tap on using my elbow. Germs were more widespread down here what with the doors opening and closing and Nigel skulking around wherever he wanted. I could hear the policeman talking into his radio as he headed back to the kitchen, so I quickly shook my hands dry.

"Wow, that's better. Lovely and cool in here. Your parents at work?"

I nodded.

The policeman scraped out one of our pine chairs and sat himself down while I stayed in the doorway. He frowned at me, clearly noticing I wasn't coming into the room.

"This is number nine, isn't it? What's your name?"

He waited as I watched him wrap each ankle around a chair leg, his dirty soles now thankfully off the floor.

"Matthew Corbin."

"And how old are you, Matthew?"

"Twelve."

He looked up from his pad.

"Did you know that your neighbor, Mr. Charles, has his grandchildren staying with him?"

"Yes."

"Well, the little boy, Teddy, has possibly wandered off somewhere. And you definitely haven't seen him or heard him at all?"

I told him about the petals on the path and the gate being locked. I said that I'd thought Mr. Charles was gardening at the front and had just gone around to the back for something. I didn't tell him he'd called me a fish and pointed at the window—it didn't seem important. The policeman scribbled on his pad, his tongue sticking out at one corner as if he had to concentrate on looping the letters together. He rocked back until he was balancing on the back legs of the chair. Dad hated that.

"And did you tell anyone about this? That you'd seen a toddler on his own? Near the street?"

I blinked at him.

"I . . . I, well, no. I thought his granddad was around. I didn't think there was anything wrong. And he wasn't near the road. The gate was shut."

The policeman scribbled something, then looked up at me.

"And why would you notice a thing like that."

I felt a bit sick. "What?"

"The gate being shut."

I accidentally leaned onto the doorframe, then stood bolt upright.

"I don't know . . . I just look at things and see stuff. That's all."

Officer Campen wasn't taking notes anymore.

"And why were you looking out the window in the first place? It's summer vacation, why aren't you off playing football or frying your brain with all that gaming you kids do?"

He tapped his pencil against his lips. I looked around the room, trying to think what to say.

"I was in the office at the front of the house, checking my email."

The chair banged back down onto four legs and scraped along our tiled floor as Officer Campen stood up.

"Can I see?"

I took a step back so that I was in the hallway again.

"See what?"

"The window where you saw the boy when you were

checking your email. Get an idea of how much you could see from there, okay?"

He didn't wait for an answer and walked straight upstairs, shoes and all. His sweaty hand squeaked along our banister. I needed him to leave.

"In here?" he called and turned right, into the office. I quickly followed and stood guarding my room across the landing. I could hear the Wallpaper Lion growling quietly behind the door.

"You've got a good view of the whole road from here, haven't you?" He placed both disease-ridden hands onto the sterile white windowsill and looked around.

"So you haven't noticed anyone different hanging around? Any cars you didn't recognize? Anything that was a bit strange?"

I thought of Casey pushing him in the pond but kept quiet.

"No. Nothing."

He turned away from the window, looking around the room.

"Mum expecting again, is she?" he said, nodding toward the elephant mobile.

I shook my head, but he ignored me and headed back downstairs.

"Our neighbor went out running," I said as I followed him.

"Which one was that then?" said Officer Campen as he picked up his hat and notebook.

"Mr. Jenkins, next door at number seven. He left at . . ." I took my own notebook out of my back pocket. "12:51 p.m."

The policeman narrowed his eyes.

"You wrote it down?"

I nodded and quickly stuffed the book back into my pocket. What did I do that for? The policeman narrowed his eyes at me.

"Why would you write something like that down, eh? Something so trivial? Are you sure you didn't see anything?"

The phone began to ring, and we both stared at the black receiver lying on the kitchen work surface; the little red light blinked on the top.

"You going to answer that?"

I didn't move as the phone made three more rings. Officer Campen leaned back on the kitchen counter and folded his arms, watching me. I swallowed, my mouth bone-dry, as I walked toward the receiver. Phones harbored some of the worst germs imaginable owing to their intricate parts. I'd owned one cell phone in my life, but it hadn't lasted long. Disinfectant and cell phones aren't really made for each other.

I reached out, trying to hide my trembling hand, when the answering machine cut in and my mum's voice filled the kitchen.

"Hello, you have reached the Corbin household. We're obviously out somewhere having fun, so leave us a message and we'll call you back. Ciao!"

She never says *ciao* in real life. In fact, I've never, ever known her to say it at any other time apart from on our answering machine. Another, deeper woman's voice began to speak.

"Oh hello Mr. and Mrs. Corbin, this is Debbie from Dr. Rhodes's office. I just wanted to confirm with you that Matthew's first therapy appointment is tomorrow at ten. We look forward to seeing him then."

Officer Campen reached for his hat, avoiding my eyes.

"Right, I'd better move on and knock at your neighbor's. Mr. Jenkins, did you say his name was?" He didn't wait for an answer and strode toward the front door, opening it quickly. After hearing that message he couldn't wait to leave.

"Hopefully we'll find him soon; we usually do. But we might need to come back and talk to you again, and your parents when they're home from work, okay?"

Putting his hat on, he walked away and turned toward Hannah and Mr. Jenkins's house. I pushed the door closed with my foot and ran upstairs to grab my cleaning things and made a start on the windowsill in the office before the germs spread too much. A trumpet blast announced that I had an email.

To: Matthew Corbin

From: Melody Bird

Subject: Police

Matty! Have you heard? Teddy's gone missing!

M x

It appeared that she'd forgiven me for practically throwing her out of my house earlier. I quickly typed my answer; my fingertips felt dirty hitting the keys without any protection.

I know. The police just knocked on my door and asked me
a load of questions. Did you see anything?

Matthew

I looked out on the cul-de-sac as a small crowd formed in the
middle of the road. I took my notebook out again as I waited for
her reply.

> *Teddy Dawson has gone missing. There are police everywhere and
> it looks like they are organizing a search party. Gordon, Sue,
> and Claudia are all taking part.*

Gordon was wearing a white, wide-brimmed hat and clutch-
ing a bottle of water. He looked like he was about to go off on
safari. A policewoman was pointing toward the top of the road as
he nodded, taking in her instructions.

Hannah was talking to Officer Campen on her doorstep, and
I caught the odd sentence.

". . . he went out about one o'clock for a run and hasn't come
back yet . . . usually stops at the gym . . . works on his abs . . .
teaches PE at the school . . ." I couldn't see from the window, but I
imagined her Californian smile was there as she talked about how
great her husband was.

Old Nina was peering around her front door, head down, clearly terrified to be exposed to the outside world like this as another officer talked to her. The trumpet blasted again.

To: Matthew Corbin

From: Melody Bird

Re: Police

No, I didn't see anything. Did you?

M

To: Melody Bird

From: Matthew Corbin

Re: Police

I saw him playing in the front yard earlier. That's all.

Matthew

Mum's car crawled along the street, and she parked outside Old Nina's house because our driveway was blocked. She rushed over to the search party and her hand went up to her mouth. Melody's reply flashed up on my screen.

To: Matthew Corbin

From: Melody Bird

Re: Police

Oh wow! You're probably their best witness! And you didn't see anything strange? Nothing at all? What about that

kid Casey. Was she playing too? Wasn't Mr. Charles
with him?

Mel.

I groaned. I should have kept my mouth shut.

To: Melody Bird

From: Matthew Corbin

Re: Police

No sign of Casey or Mr. Charles. Mr. Jenkins went for a run
and that was it.

Matthew

Our front door opened and Mum yelled up the stairs.

"Matthew! Have you heard? Isn't it awful?! I'm going out with
the search party now. I'll speak to you later! Okay, darling?"

She didn't wait for an answer and the door banged shut. I
watched her hurry to join the group and link her arm in Sue's as
they headed down the road toward town.

A van pulled up, and two men went around the side of Mr.
Charles's house carrying some electrical equipment and some plastic pipes. I went back to my room.

One of the men was putting a black cylinder into the middle
of the pond while the other walked to an outdoor socket on the
patio and plugged it in. The pump began to hum, and after a few
seconds water began to gush out of a long blue pipe onto the flower

bed where it puddled in the bone-dry earth. Within minutes the pond was empty, and one of the men took his shoes and socks off and rolled up his trousers before stepping down into the dirty sludge. As he raked about in the mud I wondered if he'd find the dead chick that Teddy had thrown in there.

"Stop! Stop! What in God's name do you think you're doing?! There're fish in there! You'll kill them!"

Mr. Charles was running down his yard, waving both of his fists in the air. He'd changed clothes and was wearing a white vest over some pale blue trousers. A forest of gray hair smothered his shoulders.

"Who said you could do that? I didn't give permission for you to touch my pond!"

The man on the lawn spoke to him quietly. It was obvious without draining it that Teddy wasn't in the pond, so I can only assume they were looking for clues.

Mr. Charles ignored the man and went into his shed and came out carrying a large black bucket, which he filled from an outside tap. He then struggled with it toward the empty pond as the man in the sludge stood waiting with something scooped in his hands. I saw a sliver of orange as he dropped the fish into the bucket and Mr. Charles crouched down to inspect it.

"There are five more in there, you know. And I want every one out alive!"

Mr. Charles was really shouting now. The man on the lawn

put a hand on his shoulder as he tried to calm him down, but Mr. Charles shrugged him off. He went back to the patio and began to fiddle with a yellow hose that was on a wheel fixed to the side of his house. The man in the pond scooped out two more fish as Mr. Charles marched back down to the garden with the trigger of the hose in his hand as it unraveled behind him. He stood there, aiming the hose at the pond, and waited.

Ten minutes later the pond had been fully searched, with only one more fish making it into the bucket. The men gathered up their equipment and headed back to the front of the house, shaking their heads.

Without a word Mr. Charles pulled the trigger on the hose, and a sharp blast of water hit the plastic pond liner. He stood there, motionless, until the pond was full once more.

———————————————

At 6 p.m. I watched as two sniffer dogs ran excitedly around the neighborhood, their tails circling madly. They looked like they were onto something, only to turn around and head off in a different direction. They stopped and sniffed at a lamppost outside Penny and Gordon's house as Frankie yapped frantically from the window of number three. Melody's arms appeared briefly around the net curtain as she lifted the dog out of sight. The handlers directed them around the cul-de-sac as they searched each yard, and then they headed down the alleyway toward the graveyard.

The computer made a trumpet sound and an email appeared on the screen.

> **To: Matthew Corbin**
> **From: Jake Bishop**
> **Subject: Old Nina Took Teddy!!!**
> Old Nina's got him. She's a witch. She's probably baking him in a pie right now!!!!
> Jake

I stared at the message. Apart from the occasional yells of abuse, I hadn't really had much to do with Jake Bishop lately. In fact, this was the first contact I'd had with him without him calling me a freak or a weirdo for about two years. I wasn't really sure what to say.

> **To: Jake Bishop**
> **From: Matthew Corbin**
> **Re: Old Nina Took Teddy!!!**
> Of course she's not a witch! Did you see anything?
> Matthew

I looked back over my notes. Jake had sped off on his bike after Old Nina had pointed her finger at him when he was hassling Melody. That was the last I knew about his whereabouts.

I deleted the email without answering.

CHAPTER TEN

JAKE'S STORY

Even I found it hard to believe, but Jake and I had once been best friends. Mum got to know his mum, Sue, when they realized they were living one house apart and both expecting babies around the same time; me at the end of October and Jake at the beginning of November.

They began having coffee together, and when we would both kick at the same time, they used to joke that we were trying to talk to each other. I arrived on my due date and Jake apparently fidgeted constantly, driving his mum mad, until he was born ten days later. Sue used to tell that story every time I saw her.

"He was so keen to meet you, weren't you, Jakey? Ten days he had to wait though! Ten days before he could meet his new best friend."

Our mums carried on meeting up while we laid in our bouncy chairs, apparently babbling to each other, but then, over the weeks, Sue realized that something wasn't quite right with Jake. I thrived and outgrew my onesies, whereas he struggled to put on any weight and his skin was constantly red and sore. After months of hospital visits, the doctors discovered that he had a ton of allergies. Not long after that Jake and Leo's dad left, leaving Sue alone and on constant alert in case her son came into contact with anything deadly.

When we started school it became clear that for his entire

education he was going to be haunted by a bright yellow medical bag that followed him wherever he went. The other kids were fascinated at first.

"What's in that bag, Jake?"

"How many needles are in there?"

"Is it really true that you could die if you ate the wrong thing?"

But after a while the novelty wore off and Jake's allergies and raw skin made him a target. He turned up at birthday parties with his own specially prepared parcel of food, his mum terrified that a stray nut might have accidentally brushed against the cheese sandwiches and he'd go into anaphylactic shock. As soon as the adults were out of the way, the snide comments would start.

"You eating your baby food again, Jakey-boy?"

I'd give him a smile. Not quite sticking up for him, but at least letting him know I wasn't siding with them, and anyway, I'd already started hanging around with Tom more, so we weren't as good friends as we used to be.

Things got worse for him in fifth grade when the whole grade went on a trip to a London museum. As we filed onto the bus I saw there was an empty seat next to Jake, as usual. The understanding was that if you sat too close to him, then you could catch his scaly skin. I'm pretty sure nobody actually believed this, but no one was brave enough to say that.

"Matt! You can sit here if you want," Jake said, his eyes pleading with me as I edged down the aisle. Tom was already in the backseat, beckoning me over.

What I should have done was dive into the seat beside Jake and prove to everyone that it was fine. There really wasn't anything contagious about him.

But I didn't.

"Sorry, Jake. I said I'd sit with Tom."

I kept my face blank and carried on walking.

Everyone was chattering with excitement as we pulled onto the highway when our teacher, Mrs. Chambers, suddenly heaved herself up out of her seat, making the bus tilt to the left.

"Oh my God! Driver, turn around! I've forgotten Jake's medical bag."

A united groan rumbled around the bus as we returned to school and waited for Mrs. Chambers to heave herself down the steps, get herself to the school office, unlock a filing cabinet, clamber back onto the bus, and throw the despised yellow bag into an overhead locker.

The bus pulled away as Mrs. Chambers edged herself along the aisle, her large bosom leaning over Jake.

"There's no need to panic—we've got your medicine and EpiPen now, okay? Off we go, driver! We'll still be there in time for lunch!"

I looked along the gap in between the seats and the windows; I could see Jake, two rows ahead, slumped with his head resting against the glass.

"Why do you have to spoil everything, Jake?"

"That stupid bag! Haven't you grown out of it by now?"

That September we started middle school and Jake and I were put into different classes, so I didn't see him much anymore. I hung around with Tom, and Jake surrounded himself with some horrible kids from older years and gained some kind of admiration by becoming the school rebel. I regularly saw him slouched on the desk outside the principal's office, picking at the dried flakes of skin on his forehead and jutting out a foot every now and then to try and trip someone up. I guess in a weird way, he'd stopped being bullied by becoming the bully.

<u>Monday, July 28th. 6:14 p.m. Office/nursery.</u>
People known to be at home at the time of Teddy's
   disappearance:
Mr. Charles
Casey
Hannah
Sue Bishop
Old Nina
Gordon and Penny
Claudia
People known to be out:
Sheila and Brian Corbin (working)
Leo Bishop (working)
Mr. Jenkins (jogging)

People unaccounted for:
Jake
Melody

I stared at the names as I tapped my pencil on the desk. It didn't look like much, but it was a start. Teddy couldn't have gone far on his own—I was certain of it. If he'd wandered off, surely they would have found him by now?

I looked out on the cul-de-sac as the police bustled around, busy gathering evidence to try and piece together the mystery of what had happened to the little boy.

But they didn't know the neighborhood like I did. They didn't see the things I saw.

I looked down at the pile of pink petals that Teddy had been picking, now gathered in a small mound by the gatepost, and I knew what I was going to do.

I was going to work out who took Teddy Dawson.

CHAPTER ELEVEN
THE SEARCH PARTY

I was shaking as I stood over the bathroom sink. It had been hours since I'd last washed my hands. I'd lost track of things and not kept on top of keeping clean, and now I was in danger of becoming ill. And if I became ill, then who knew what that could lead to? I washed my hands over and over and over until my eyes streamed from the pain. I went to my room and was going to put a pair of latex gloves on, but I had to save them.

"Someone's got him, Lion," I said to the wallpaper. "Someone has taken him. I'm sure of it."

The Wallpaper Lion looked back at me sadly.

"I need to be alert. I need to keep an eye on things, see if I can spot any clues. You need someone like me, watching things. I was the last one to see him! If I hadn't seen him, they wouldn't have known he was in the front yard at all, would they?"

I began a new page in my notebook.

Teddy's Disappearance—The Facts
Mr. Charles wasn't coping very well with his grandchildren and
   now seems more worried about his fish.
Casey pushed Teddy in the pond and showed no signs of wanting
   to help him until Mr. Charles appeared.

Old Nina? Could she be involved?

Jake Bishop? Would he be capable of hurting him? Maybe hiding him for the attention?

Melody Bird. An unlikely suspect, but she does go to the graveyard A LOT. Would she know of some place to hide him over there?

The first search party returned at 7:18 p.m. They hung around in the middle of the street for a while, not quite sure what to do next. The police were still going in and out of Mr. Charles's house. Gordon turned toward home, fanning his scarlet face with his wide-brimmed hat as he went. Jake opened the door of number five, swigging from a can of Coke as Sue walked up to him and grabbed him in an awkward bear hug. He looked up at me over her shoulder and glared. Claudia went back to number three and Melody opened the door, Frankie yapping at their feet as they hugged as well. Mum turned to our house and looked up at the window. I held up my hand and gave a pathetic wave as she smiled weakly.

I stood at the top of the stairs as she came in.

"How did it go? Did you find anything?"

Mum shook her head and then rubbed at the back of her neck with her hand. She looked tired.

"I can't believe this is happening. That poor family. Is your dad still out?"

I nodded. Dad had come home from work to find the police everywhere. He'd thrown his tie and briefcase into the hallway and rushed out to join another search team along with Jake's brother, Leo, recently home from work, and Mr. Jenkins, who must have returned from his run when I wasn't watching. He didn't call up to let me know he was going like Mum had. I actually thought he'd forgotten I was there at all.

Mum leaned her head against the front door and closed her eyes.

"You know what I need right now, Matthew? I need a nice, big hug from my lovely, lovely son."

Her eyes remained closed as she took a deep breath. I stayed still at the top of the stairs as I watched her. In her mind she was probably willing me to walk down the stairs, to take her hand as I rested my head in the little dip between her shoulder and collarbone. She'd then envelope me with her kind, strong arms as we stood there breathing in and out in time with each other.

Her eyes flickered open and they glistened as she looked up at me, sitting on the top step, frozen to the spot.

"I think I'll put on the kettle," she said and she made her way to the kitchen.

When I was five we used to walk to school each day with Sue and Jake. Jake would usually have some kind of makeshift weapon on him that he'd use to attack any shrub or hedge he thought could do with a good bashing, whereas I'd walk beside my mum and hold her hand.

"Matty! Matty! Let's have a war!" he'd yell at me, thrusting a sharp stick into my chest. I turned away from him and nestled against Mum's leg. It wasn't that I didn't want to play, I just wanted to stay as close to my mum for as long as I could before I went into class.

"I don't think he wants to today, Jake," Mum said kindly. Jake huffed and ran on and began whacking at a bush with his stick.

We carried on walking, and I put my other hand over the top of hers, covering her soft knuckles.

"Jake, why don't you hold my hand like Matthew?" said Sue, grabbing his arm to try and stop him from hitting the bush.

Jake scowled and tugged his arm away, then studied his palm. His pink, angry skin seemed to hypnotize him, and he stopped to pick at the little white flakes.

"Don't do that, you'll make your eczema sore! You don't want to make it worse, do you?"

Sue dropped behind to inspect her son's hand as Mum and I walked on.

"Do you know what?" said Mum. "One day you'll be a really big boy and you won't want to hold your mummy's hand anymore."

I frowned up at her and she laughed.

"It's true! Us mummies know these things."

Swinging our arms back and forth, I giggled as we marched onward like clockwork soldiers.

"I'll always hold your hand, Mummy," I said after we'd slowed down. "I promise. Even when I'm twelve years old!"

Mum laughed so much that this time I saw her bright, white teeth.

"We'll see, Matthew," she said, smiling. "We'll see."

And then she squeezed my hand a little tighter.

———————————

At 7:30 p.m. a woman wearing a smart blue dress with a light gray jacket stood in front of number eleven and spoke into a microphone. A man with a large camera on his shoulder filmed her. I couldn't hear what she was saying, but she kept turning toward Mr. Charles's house and pointing and then she held up a large piece of paper, which must have been Teddy's photograph. It was all over in ten minutes, and as soon as she'd finished the report she took off her gray jacket and fanned at her face. A police officer in a suit approached them and I thought he was going to ask them to leave, but he seemed pleased to see them and shook their hands before checking his watch. After they'd left, Officer Campen appeared carrying a roll of yellow tape. He spoke to a few passersby who were hanging around outside Gordon and Penny's house, and they drifted off toward the end of the road.

7:43 p.m.–Still no sign of Teddy Dawson. The police are now taping off the end of Chestnut Close.

Penny Sullivan from number one was walking around the close with a tray of orange juice.

"Ice-cold orange juice?" she said to each one. "Something to cool you down, officer?"

Some of them waved her away with a nod and a smile, too busy to speak to her, and a few took a glass and drank the cold juice in one go. Penny returned to number one, probably looking through her kitchen cupboards to see what other refreshments she could rustle up.

The other search party came back at 8:17 p.m. Dad had his shirtsleeves rolled up and was carrying his suit jacket over his shoulder. Jake's older brother, Leo, was talking on his phone, and Rory Jenkins was eating some sort of nutrition bar. He looked up at me as he crossed the road toward his house and I stared back. Eating at a time like this didn't seem right. He brushed the crumbs from the front of his T-shirt, watching me all the time. Hannah came out to meet him and put her hands up to her husband's face and kissed him. He threw a heavy arm around her shoulder and they walked slowly back to the house, Hannah's huge stomach swaying from side to side. The sight of it made me feel sick, so I went to the bathroom and splashed some cold water on my face until I felt better.

Dad came in telling Mum they'd found nothing and that they'd shut the end of the road off so no one could come onto the close without permission. I heard them move into the kitchen to start on dinner. The door of number three opened and Melody jumped down the step and skipped across the road. I groaned. She was heading straight toward us.

"Hello, Melody, love," Mum said quietly when she opened the door. "Go on up, I'm sure Matthew would like some company right now."

I wouldn't. I wouldn't like any company right now.

"Hi, Matty!" Melody said as if it was just another day and nothing had happened, like a small child going missing. She came into the office and looked around, staring at the elephant mobile.

"Oh wow. Is your Mum having another baby?"

She spun the mobile with her finger and the elephants hurtled around and around.

"No. Look, can you not do that, please?"

The elephants spun faster and faster until two of them became tangled up and she stopped.

"So what's with all this stuff then?" she said as she poked about in the bags under the mobile. On one of the boxes was a photograph of a chubby, blond baby boy, a toothless smile on his face as he sat happily in a brilliant white diaper.

"It was for my brother. He died. Look, can you not touch *anything*, please?"

Melody stood up.

"Died? What do you mean he died?"

"He died, okay? What do you want, Melody?"

I stood with my arms folded. I wondered what she'd do if she knew he was dead because of me. I could tell her—just like that. *It was all my fault, Melody. Now will you go away and stop bothering me?*

She sat on the edge of the desk.

"Oh. Sorry. I didn't know." Her face looked sad. "That must be hard for you."

I nodded. In my head I was making a mental note of everything I now needed to clean after she'd gone:

Edge of the door, doorframe—whole door?

Elephant mobile—how can I clean that?!

Desk. Clear everything off and blast with antibacterial spray.

"Did you see the newspeople here earlier? My mum thinks he's just wandered off somewhere. Do you? Or do you think someone has taken him?"

I shrugged. "I would have thought if he'd wandered off he would have been found by now," I said.

She picked up my notebook, which was next to her on the desk.

"Oh wow, this is brilliant!" she said as she read. "You've got everything in here! You should show this to the police! *5:23 p.m. Mr. Charles is mowing his lawn again. It's the fifth time this week.*"

She giggled as she turned a few more pages. I stepped across the room.

"Can you give that back to me? It's private."

"*10:02 a.m. Old Nina is watering her pots.*"

Turning to the last page, she read what I'd written in silence and then glanced up at me; her face looked horrified. Looking down again, she read aloud:

"*Melody Bird. An unlikely suspect, but she does go to the graveyard A LOT. Would she know of some place to hide him over there?*"

I jiggled around in front of her, wanting to snatch the book back but not quite finding the courage to do it.

"Matthew? Do you think I took Teddy?"

She had tears in her eyes.

"I . . . I . . . No, of course not."

I quickly grabbed the book from her, forgetting I wasn't wearing any gloves. Her mouth hung open.

"It's nothing, Melody! I was just bored, writing some stuff down. It's not important."

"But . . . but I don't understand. Why would you think I did it?"

"I don't know! I just wondered why you go to the graveyard so much. That's all. I just thought there may be something over there you were hiding. It doesn't matter, I was just writing anything down."

I dropped the notebook onto the desk. Melody put her hands on her hips as she came toward me.

"I didn't take Teddy Dawson and I can't believe you'd say such a thing. I thought we were friends?"

I pressed myself against the windowsill.

"That's the first I've heard about it," I said.

Melody gasped, and then she spun around and ran down the stairs.

CHAPTER TWELVE

TV DEBUT

I made my TV debut at 9:03 p.m. Mum screamed upstairs at me.

"MATTY! Quick, get down here!"

I jumped off my bed, and for a few blissful seconds it felt like I was just running downstairs for dinner, like I used to. Dad was standing by the conservatory door, eating a bag of chips. Mum was perched on the edge of our cream leather sofa, staring at the large flat screen.

"He's just wandered off, that's all," said Dad. "They'll find him. He'll be home before it gets dark, you mark my words."

I glanced out at the yard. It was getting dark already.

Dad tipped the chips bag up and shook the crumbs into his mouth. I hated it when he did that.

"Where would he have gone though, Brian? We've looked everywhere. Penny said they're searching the building site near the old swimming pool now."

There was a large development of houses being built on the edge of town, and now I was picturing Teddy, toddling along, staring up at the giant, dinosaur-like cranes. Could he have been so hypnotized by them he missed a deep crater and fell in? It was unlikely. The whole area was pretty secure with high fencing, and besides, it was busy around there. Surely someone would have spotted a little boy wearing a diaper, all on his own?

Mum jumped out of her seat and pointed at the TV.

"Look! It's on!"

A woman was standing on our street talking into a microphone. I recognized her as the reporter wearing the gray jacket who'd been standing outside just before the police had taped off the road.

". . . the fifteen-month-old boy was last seen wearing a pull-up style diaper and a white T-shirt with a picture of an ice-cream cone on the front. The police believe he may have been holding a blue, square security blanket and wasn't wearing any shoes . . ."

She was holding a laminated photograph in one hand, and as the camera zoomed in Teddy's face filled the screen. He was wearing a white shirt with a fancy waistcoat; around his neck was a crumpled, gold necktie that he'd clearly tried to yank off. His pale blue eyes glistened with recent tears—possibly brought on from being stuffed into an outfit that made him look like a miniature magician.

It had been a long time since I'd seen the TV this close up, and it was making my eyes water. Dad scrunched up the bag in his hand and a few tiny crumbs fell onto the carpet. I needed to get back to my room. I turned to go, but then Mum leaped out of her seat again.

"Matthew, you're on the TV!"

The camera pulled back as the reporter pointed to Mr. Charles's lawn.

"... last seen playing in his grandfather's front yard here on Chestnut Close ..."

In the top left-hand corner of the screen was our house, and in an upstairs window stood a figure. It was me. I was just standing there, like an idiot, thinking nobody could possibly be looking at me.

"What do you watch up there all day, son? You looking for birds or something? Ornithology?"

Mum gave him a glare.

"I'm only asking, Sheila."

I ignored them.

"... the police are calling for anyone with information to get in touch with the incident room at ..."

The screen cut to a phone number. Mum turned to me and smiled, patting the sofa beside her.

"Why don't you stay down here with us this evening, Matthew? Watch a bit of TV to take your mind off everything? I don't expect we'll get much sleep tonight."

"No, not tonight, thanks," I said.

Mum stood up and I had the feeling she was going to try and touch me, so I quickly dodged around her and ran upstairs to wash my hands. Eleven squirts of antibacterial soap, some scalding hot water, and nine washes later and I felt a bit better.

It was still busy outside with police coming and going. Mr. Charles's front yard looked like a bizarre gift-wrapped present: The front wall and gate were draped in yellow tape. An officer I hadn't seen before stood guarding the door. Mr. Jenkins and Hannah were in their own yard, his arm draped heavily around her shoulder. I wondered if she knew what a horrible teacher her husband was. I don't suppose it was the kind of thing he mentioned at home:

Hello, darling. I made a boy cry during gym today! It was that weird kid next door. He said he had to wash his hands after throwing one javelin. Can you believe it? I told him he was on a pathway to failure and if he carried on like this he'd be a failure for the rest of his life . . .

The thought of the PE lesson made my eyes fill but I blinked the tears away, refusing to cry over it again. Hannah turned around and I saw her huge pregnant stomach, so I quickly looked away.

The computer trumpeted an email's arrival.

To: Matthew Corbin

From: Melody Bird

Subject: Urgent

If you're going to investigate Teddy's disappearance properly, then you're going to need my help.
Melody

I read the email over a few times.

To: Melody Bird
From: Matthew Corbin
Re: Urgent

What?

Matthew

I ran to my room and grabbed a new bottle of water. Next door's backyard was surrounded by four industrial lamps ready for when darkness fell. Three police officers stood on the patio discussing something. I went back to the office, drinking half of the water as I read Melody's next email.

To: Matthew Corbin
From: Melody Bird
Re: Urgent

Well, you're not doing a very good job so far by making wild accusations about me! And, I'm not being rude here but you don't go out and you can't do much from your house, can you? You're going to need someone at street level. Someone to do the *actual investigating*.

I quickly typed back.

To: Melody Bird

From: Matthew Corbin

Re: Urgent

And I suppose that someone is you?!

I found that I was smiling as I hit Send.

To: Matthew Corbin

From: Melody Bird

Re: Urgent

Yes.

Face it, Matthew, you can't do it without me! I'm willing
to forgive you for what you wrote in your notebook. I
understand that you need to write your ideas down, even if
that one was **INCREDIBLY STUPID**. [She inserted an emoji
here with its face all screwed up.]

To: Melody Bird

From: Matthew Corbin

Re: Urgent

Melody Bird, you are definitely one of a kind.

A few seconds later her reply pinged up on the screen.

<u>**To: Matthew Corbin**</u>

<u>**From: Melody Bird**</u>

<u>**Re: Urgent**</u>

I know.

When do we start?

I sat there for two minutes, thinking.

<u>**To: Melody Bird**</u>

<u>**From: Matthew Corbin**</u>

<u>**Re: Urgent**</u>

Suspects number one and two are Mr. Charles and

Casey. See if you can get into their house tomorrow.

Make an excuse, take over a cake or something? Do

some snooping around? See what mood he's in—does

he seem too happy considering his grandson has

disappeared? Is Casey acting like a girl whose brother

is missing?

<u>**To: Matthew Corbin**</u>

<u>**From: Melody Bird**</u>

<u>**Re: Urgent**</u>

Aye, aye, captain! I'll go now!

Over and out . . .

She was bonkers.

I hit Send but she didn't reply, and then fifteen minutes later
she came out of her house balancing a plate along her forearm.
As she crossed the road I could see it was some kind of long sponge
cake, and on top she'd randomly stuck loads of chocolate lady-
fingers. It looked like a strange, spiky caterpillar. I cringed, wishing
I hadn't said anything.

"Oh Melody," I whispered to myself.

The policeman on the doorstep was gone, and she struggled to
unlock Mr. Charles's gate with one hand, her tongue sticking out
of the corner of her mouth as she concentrated on keeping the cake
on the plate. As she got to the front door she glanced at my window
and gave me a thumbs-up.

I groaned as I sat back down at the desk. I couldn't bear to
watch. Ten minutes later she was sprinting across the close, an
empty plate smeared with chocolate in her hand. I waited at the
computer.

To: Matthew Corbin

From: Melody Bird

Subject: Casey

The whole cake thing worked (well done you!). He asked
me in to say hello to Casey. Boy, that kid is creepy! She just
sat in the corner playing with some horrible doll and didn't
even look up! You were right—she certainly doesn't seem
bothered about Teddy at all!

To: Melody Bird

From: Matthew Corbin

Re: Casey

And what about Mr. Charles? Did he seem upset?

To: Matthew Corbin

From: Melody Bird

Re: Casey

Kind of. His eyes were red like he'd been crying. There was
one weird thing though. He ate a GIGANTIC slice of cake!
Can you believe it? I thought stress killed an appetite?!
Anyway, let me know my next assignment!
Over and out.
Agent Mel x

I went to my room and lay on my bed, my arms beneath my
head, staring up at the ceiling.

"Where's he gone, Lion? Who's got him?"

The police had turned the lights on in Mr. Charles's yard, and they made a pattern on my wall. A yellow spotlight circled the Wallpaper Lion high up in his corner. His one puffed-up cheek grinned back at me like a tacky TV game show host.

Soooooo, the question for you, Matthew Corbin, is this: Who exactly is to blame for the mysterious disappearance of Teddy Dawson? Is it:

a) *Casey Dawson. This little darling may appear innocent, but she has an unhealthy habit of pushing small children into ponds. Could she have done something to Teddy?*

b) *Mr. Charles. Grandfatherly love does not come easy to this old man. Could he be responsible for the missing boy?*

c) *Jake Bishop. He's a bitter youth who gets kicks out of making others miserable. Could his attention seeking have taken him a step too far?*

d) *Matthew Corbin. This strange, lonely boy seemed to believe it was okay to leave a fifteen-month-old alone in a front yard in soaring temperatures. And let's not forget what he did to his baby brother, Callum . . .*

Sooooo, who could it be? The choice is yours.

CHAPTER TENPLUSTHREE
THE SLEEPOVER

Our doorbell rang and I woke with a gasp. There was something terrifying about hearing a doorbell late at night.

I looked at my clock. 11:tenplusthree glowed in fluorescent green. Not good. I closed my eyes and held my breath for three sets of seven, listening to a police siren that became louder and then faded as it passed the end of our street. When I opened my eyes, it was 11:14. I breathed out in relief.

I could hear Mr. Charles on our doorstep talking to Dad.

". . . going to the hospital for a checkup . . . probably just something I've eaten . . ."

". . . best to get it checked out . . ."

". . . Mum is on a flight right now. Can you have her here tonight?"

". . . of course, no problem . . ."

The door closed and Dad's voice went all squeaky. I recognized his "talking to small kids" voice.

"We'll make you up a nice, cozy bed in the spare room, okay? Just across the landing from Matthew. You know Matty, don't you?"

I stepped out onto the landing. Mum was heading upstairs, her eyes wide.

"Mr. Charles has got chest pains, so the police are running him to the hospital to get checked out. We've got Casey here for the night. Isn't that nice?"

"No, not really."

She ignored me and walked into the nursery and began dragging the boxes of baby stuff out onto the landing. The elephant mobile was dumped on top, its strings still tangled. Five long years of dangling in limbo and she'd gotten rid of it, just like that.

"Brian! Get Casey a little glass of milk, would you?"

I peeked over the banister and there she was, standing on our doormat wearing a long, old-fashioned-looking nightdress and hugging the bedraggled doll. As she followed Dad to the kitchen she glanced up at me, her eyes narrowing.

"Chest pains?" I said. "It's probably indigestion! What's he going to the hospital for?!"

Mum frowned at me. "When did you become the medical expert?" she said, raising an eyebrow.

I shrugged. A big slab of that cake Melody delivered was enough to give anyone chest pains.

"Can't she sleep downstairs on the sofa?"

Mum exhaled as she dumped the final box and a tiny puff of dust dispersed into the air.

"What are you talking about, Matthew? You really do say the strangest things sometimes. How can I let a small child sleep downstairs on her own, especially after her little brother has gone missing?"

She wiped her forehead.

"Where's that foam mattress gone? That will do . . ."

She wandered off to her room as I paced around on the landing. I could hear Dad squeaking away to Casey downstairs about the devil cat.

"Isn't he a silly Nigel, eh, Casey? Whoever heard of a cat who likes to sleep on a pool table! Would you like a cookie? Oh no, actually, you'd better not since you've probably brushed your teeth already. Sheila? You done yet?"

Mum reappeared dragging our dusty, old foam bed, which had seen better days. I danced around her, trying to block her way without actually touching anything as she left a trail of yellow foam behind her.

"She doesn't even know us!" I whispered. "How can Mr. Charles leave her with a family she doesn't know? Shouldn't social services be involved?"

Mum shuffled the bed into the room and positioned it in the corner near the computer desk.

"Her mum's on a flight now, so she'll be here within hours and anyway, Mr. Charles was the one who suggested she stay, and we're not going to let down one of our neighbors at a time like this, are we? Get a couple of sheets and a pillow, would you?"

I hesitated, then used my top to pull open the door to the

linen closet. Sheets, duvet covers, towels, and pillowcases were stacked up to the ceiling.

Dad delivered Casey to the top of the stairs.

"Here we are! One little girl, ready for bed. I'll leave you to it then, Sheila, okay? Looks like you've got it all under control . . ." He went back down humming to himself.

Casey had her head tucked low with her doll clutched under her chin.

"Nearly done, Casey, love. Pass me the sheets then, Matthew. Don't just stand there!"

I didn't move.

"I don't know which ones," I said.

Mum huffed and grabbed what she needed.

"Would you like a glass of water for the night, Casey?" said Mum as she got on her hands and knees to make up the bed.

"Yes, please," said Casey.

"Wow, she's a pretty thing, isn't she?" said Mum, pointing to the doll, which clearly wasn't a pretty thing at all after its dunking in the pond and wading pool.

"Has she got a name?"

Casey shrugged, then looked straight at me and smiled.

"Goldie," she whispered.

"Goldie. Ah, that must be because of her, erm, beautiful hair. Right, you wait here with Matthew while I go and get your water."

As soon as Mum left, Casey stared at me and made an O shape with her mouth and smacked her lips together.

"Is that your tank, Goldfish Boy?" she said, looking over my shoulder into my bedroom.

Smack, smack, smack.

"Doesn't it get boring swimming around in there all day? Up and down, up and down."

My eyes were stinging. "How's it any of your business?"

Smack, smack, smack.

She followed me to my door.

"Have you got one of those little treasure chests in there that open and close with all the bubbles? Hmmm, little fishy?"

She tried to look past me and into my room, but I stood in her way. Tilting her head to one side, she screwed her eyes up at me.

"How can you still breathe when you're out of your tank, Goldfish Boy? Why don't you die?"

I snatched the doll from her arms and she gasped.

"I can breathe a lot better than your brother could when you pushed him in the pond, you evil little witch."

"Give her back!"

She tried to grab the doll, but I held it high out of her reach. Germs scurried down my arm.

"What have you done to him, eh? Where's Teddy? What have you done to your brother?"

The little girl went scarlet as her feet beat on the carpet.

"I want her back! Give her to me, now!"

I could hear Mum starting up the stairs.

"Is everything all right?"

I gripped the doll's head and twisted it until it made an awful cracking noise and flopped to one side, and then I thrust it into her chest and slammed my door.

I woke, sweating, at 2:18 a.m. I needed to wash again. I could still feel the doll's matted hair in my hand, brittle like dried-up seaweed.

The house was silent and I quietly opened my door and crept onto the landing, peeking in on Casey. She had both her arms stretched high above her head. Her mouth was open and dried, and chalky saliva trailed down the side of her cheek as she snored gently. The broken doll was dangling off the side of the bed, its half-decapitated head resting on the carpet. Her eyes suddenly opened and I jumped.

"Goldfish Boy?" she whispered.

I ignored her and turned toward the bathroom, but she carried on.

"The old lady's got him, Goldfish Boy."

I stepped into the room

"What do you mean? What old lady?"

Her face was blank, her eyes closed again. She looked like she was asleep.

"Casey," I whispered. "Do you know who took Teddy?"

She frowned in her sleep, and then holding the doll to her chest, she rolled over and turned her back to me.

Through the open curtain I looked down at Old Nina's house. It looked darker than usual. Something was different. I was just about to turn away when I realized what it was. The yellow lamp—the one that glowed all day and all night in the front room window—wasn't glowing anymore.

It had been switched off.

CHAPTER FOURTEEN

DR. RHODES

"Maybe we should have canceled it, Brian. It doesn't feel right going out now. We should be helping with the searches."

We were all in the car in the driveway waiting to back out, but a white van was blocking the way.

"They've got hundreds of people helping, Sheila. That policeman said we can help when we get back." He nodded his head toward Officer Campen, who was standing by Mr. Charles's gate. Dad had spoken to him about moving the van so that we could get going.

"*. . . so sorry to bother you now, but we've got to get to an appointment for my son. We're seeing a specialist . . .*"

I felt sick and my knees were trembling. I just wanted to go back inside.

"I don't mind going another day. Perhaps it would be better to wait," I said. Mum looked over at Dad, but they both ignored me and Mum changed the subject.

"That poor Casey. Imagine being dragged out of bed this morning like that. She could have waited until she'd woken up, surely?"

Casey and Teddy's mum, Melissa Dawson, had come straight from the airport and picked her daughter up at 5 a.m. I'd slept through the whole thing.

"I don't think I've ever seen a child hugged quite like that before. I thought she was going to suffocate her!" Mum said. "At least it's good news about Mr. Charles."

Mr. Charles had gotten back from the hospital at 6:30 a.m. I had been right—it was indigestion.

Dad turned the engine on as if that would speed things up a bit.

Out my window I saw Melody, black cardigan on, arms folded, as she headed to the alleyway next to Old Nina's house. She looked up at me and nodded and I nodded back. I'd quickly emailed her first thing this morning.

To: Melody Bird

From: Matthew Corbin

Subject: Next Assignment—The Rectory

See what you can find out about Old Nina? Take a look around!

Matthew

I twisted around to take a look at the old Victorian house. The lamp was still off.

"I wonder where Casey and Teddy's dad is? You'd have thought he'd be around, wouldn't you?" said Mum. She pulled her sun visor down and checked her reflection in the mirror. "Penny was on the news this morning. Only for about four seconds; she wasn't on for as long as you were, Matthew."

I cringed.

"They asked her how the neighbors were feeling and she said, 'We're all praying for little Teddy.' That was nice, wasn't it? She was wearing that cream blouse she wore to her niece's wedding last year. *And* she'd put lipstick on. Bright pink. I don't think that was appropriate. A touch of gloss would have been better."

We were all quiet for a moment.

Dad fiddled with the air-conditioning and a cold blast of air hit my forehead. I was just going to ask if I could go back inside to wash my hands when two people appeared from around the side of Mr. Charles's house wearing white jumpsuits.

"Forensic scientists," I whispered. I recognized them from TV.

I watched as one of the forensic team peeled off a pair of latex gloves and pushed his white hood back as he walked to the van. If I had access to that kind of clothing I'd be fine. Cocooned in a protective layer—it looked perfect to me. The van moved out of the way and my stomach flipped as we slowly reversed out onto the road.

I was using my notebook again. The one I have in my head, not my pocket.

Tuesday, July 29th. 10:00 a.m. Dr. Rhodes's office.
Number of people in office = 4
Number of people happy to be in office = 1 (and that's only
    because she's being paid)

Dr. Rhodes wasn't what I was expecting. She was tiny, and her hair was fire-truck red and piled up high on top of her head (possibly to make herself appear taller), and her nose was pierced with a small diamond that glinted when she moved. She sat on a high-backed chair with a writing pad on her lap. Her feet barely reached the floor.

Dad, Mum, and I were all enveloped in a squishy, brown leather sofa the same shade as Mum's spray-tanned legs. Dad kept coughing like he was clearing his throat to make some kind of joke, which thankfully never arrived. Mum talked constantly about Teddy going missing and how we really didn't feel right being here at a time like this. Her posh voice was in fine form.

"We were going to cancel, weren't we, Brian? We didn't know what to do. I said it didn't seem right, just carrying on as normal. Not that this is normal. But, well—you know what I mean . . ."

Dad rubbed his forehead and groaned quietly, but I don't think Mum heard him.

Dr. Rhodes agreed that this was indeed a terrible situation and managed to reassure Mum that being here wasn't being disrespectful in any way. Mum breathed a sigh of relief having been given the all clear from a professional.

On my knees rested a black, highly dangerous clipboard that had a "checklist" that she said we'd complete together in a minute. The pen kept rolling down the paper, and I pressed one latex-gloved fingertip against it to keep it still. (I couldn't cope without wearing a glove on both hands for this, so now I had none left at all. Latex gloves = 0.)

My secret was out.

"Can I just ask who has been providing your son with gloves?" Dr. Rhodes asked with a smile.

Dad coughed again and glanced over at Mum. I quickly looked down at the form and pretended to be absorbed in the questions. One asked if any of my obsessions were accompanied by "magical thinking," and I wondered if that had anything to do with card tricks.

"Well, doctor. I can tell you that *I* certainly didn't know that my wife was supplying our son with gloves. And if I *had* known, I certainly wouldn't have agreed to it."

Every time he stressed a word he dipped his head forward like a bird pecking at a feeder.

"Brian, you're making it sound like I was doing something criminal! It was only to protect his poor skin."

Dr. Rhodes opened her mouth to chime in, but they were off.

"Protect him? How is that going to protect him? It's only going to make things worse."

"But you didn't see the state of his hands—they were blistering from the *bleach*!"

Mum screeched the word *bleach*, and to be honest, she sounded a little bit crazy.

"But giving him gloves is only going to make him do it more, isn't it? It's not rocket science . . ."

"They were blistered, Brian," said Mum, her face turning scarlet beneath her fake tan. "Blistered!"

She made it sound like a swearword. I sank down farther into the sofa, trying desperately to avoid the stray globules of saliva that were flying around. Dr. Rhodes put both her hands up to calm them down, and amazingly it had an effect. Maybe she knew how to use some of that "magical thinking."

"Mr. and Mrs. Corbin, I can honestly see both of your points of view. Mrs. Corbin, I completely understand why you would want to protect your son if he's beginning to unintentionally hurt himself, and yes, Mr. Corbin, we do find that a patient will make quicker progress if those around them do not aid their compulsions."

My parents did some synchronized arm folding accompanied by huffing as they sat back into the deep sofa, clearly each thinking they'd won.

"Now then . . ." The therapist paused to put on a pair of bright green framed spectacles as she consulted her notes. "I understand that you've been finding it hard to go to school lately. Can you tell me why that is, Matthew?"

I opened my mouth, not sure how to start, and Dad filled the silence.

"He's scared. Of bugs and stuff."

"It's not bugs, Brian. It's germs . . . germs! He thinks he's going to get sick. Don't you, darling?"

Dr. Rhodes interrupted, saying that this was more common than we realized. She said that in a school of three thousand students there were probably around twenty young people affected with Obsessive Compulsive Disorder. That was what she believed I had: OCD. But we needed to fill in a checklist to make sure.

Dad was off again.

"It's probably because he's grown up with you vacuuming the house every ten minutes. It's no wonder! You've always overdone the housework."

Dr. Rhodes took her glasses once more and glanced up at a clock on the wall. I looked as well and wished I hadn't. We were approaching tenplusthree past ten. This wasn't good.

"I'm just tidy, Brian. There's nothing wrong with that. And if you didn't leave all your stuff lying around all the time . . ."

Dad twisted across me, his bare skin pressing onto my shirt. Onto my arm.

"Oh it's my fault again, is it? It's always me!"

"Dad . . . you're touching my arm."

Dr. Rhodes leaned forward and squirmed in her chair. I watched the second hand on the clock pass the three.

"Mr. and Mrs. Corbin, it doesn't work like that. In fact, OCD isn't always about germs *or* cleanliness. If we could just—"

"Well, you're not exactly a tidy man, are you, Brian? I mean, look at the state of the shed! You just open the door and fling everything in there—"

"Don't you start on about my shed again—"

"—and then you go on and on about not being able to find anything—"

"No I don't! I never moan about that . . ."

His arm brushed against mine again, and I moved away as much as I could without touching Mum.

"Dad . . ."

Dr. Rhodes took her glasses off and pinched the bridge of her nose.

"If you put things back where they belong, you wouldn't make such hard work for yourself, would you?"

"Dad! Please move over a bit . . . You're touching my arm!"

His attention turned to me, his face now as red as Dr. Rhodes's hair. I'd pressed myself as far away as I could.

"Oh I'm touching your arm, am I? Am I not allowed to touch my own son?"

He twisted himself around and I leaned back as far as I could.

"What about a hug? Or a kiss on your birthday? When you get your exam results? When you pass your driving test? How about we shake hands on it, eh?"

He directed his hand toward me, his fingers tight together and his thumb pointing upward. His hand, which had felt so strong, so safe, when I'd held it as a young child, now filled me with terror. I hid my gloves under the clipboard, and Dad's hand fell onto his lap. His face crumbled and he turned away and quietly began to cry. I thought I should say something, but my throat was shut tight. And besides, I'd looked at the clock on the wall, and the bad luck minute was here. I kept as still as I could and counted to seven repeatedly in my head. Fortunately Dr. Rhodes stepped in.

"Actually, Mr. and Mrs. Corbin, maybe this is a good time for you both to have some time-out and for me to have a little chat with Matthew on my own. Then we can decide together how we're going to tackle this thing. Okay, Matthew?"

She looked directly at me and smiled, pretending that my dad wasn't crying and everything was just fine. I lost track of my counting and started again.

"There's a coffee shop next door. Go and get some fresh air and come back in about half an hour. That sound okay?"

Mum and Dad looked almost relieved to escape and they levered themselves out of the sofa, shuffling out with hunched shoulders and closing the door behind them.

"Okay. Now we can have a proper chat," said Dr. Rhodes, smiling kindly.

She scribbled something on her pad, then looked up at me. I kept an eye on the clock. Twenty seconds to go.

"So, let's start again. How are you, Matthew? How does it feel being here today?"

Silence.

One, two, three, four, five, six, seven . . .

My eyes darted to the clock again and she followed my gaze.

"Is there a problem, Matthew?"

Silence.

One, two, three, four, five, six, seven . . .

She tilted her head and waited. The second hand passed the twelve and I took a deep breath.

"No, no problem," I said.

She frowned. I got a feeling she'd been able to look straight into my head and see all the numbers floating around as I counted. Adding seven onto the bad number made twenty and neutralized its power. She knew that. She knew exactly what I'd been doing.

"What do you want to get out of these sessions, Matthew?"

I shrugged.

"I don't know really."

I suddenly felt ridiculous sitting there with my stupid plastic gloves. She waited, her pencil poised as she put her head to one side. I opened my mouth but couldn't seem to get any words out. The urge to escape from there, to get home and wash, was unbearable. My arm where Dad touched me was tingling with all of the germs that were now crawling under my sleeve.

"Can you remember when you first began to feel the urge to wash?"

I rubbed at the scar above my eyebrow. The mark that showed I was responsible for my own brother's death.

"A few years ago, I guess."

Dr. Rhodes smiled.

"And your parents said that things have gotten worse quite

recently. Do you know why that is? Do you know what has made you feel more anxious?"

I looked at my knees, and in my mind I pictured Hannah Jenkins next door. Her heavily pregnant stomach with its tiny helpless life cocooned inside. I shivered.

Looking back up at Dr. Rhodes, I shrugged.

"No. No idea."

The therapist leaned back in her chair.

"Okay, Matthew, let's leave that for now and start with the form I've given you, shall we? Let's see if we can see what area is bothering you the most."

I finished the form and was pleased that I hadn't ticked every box; in fact, I'd only ticked about a quarter of them. She was right, though; it did look like I had Obsessive Compulsive Disorder.

"Would you like me to explain what that means?" she asked, and I nodded.

"The 'obsessive' part refers to what is at the forefront of your mind for a lot of your day. For you, that's germs and illness. With OCD, an obsession can cause a huge amount of distress and really have an impact on your daily life—stopping you from going to school, for example."

She was certainly right about that bit.

"The 'compulsion' part means your urge to clean all the time and your need to do it over and over again until it feels right."

She waited, letting me take it all in.

It also turned out that I did have "magical thinking" after all, but it had nothing to do with tricks. Apparently I believed that my actions and thoughts were able to "magically" prevent some catastrophic illness from hurting me or my family, even though I knew deep, deep, deep down that all of my actions were completely ridiculous and this way of thinking didn't really have any power at all. All the cleaning was, well, just a waste of my time and energy.

So now that I know that, can I just go home and wash my hands? I wanted to say.

Dr. Rhodes asked if there was anything else I wanted to add, anything that wasn't covered in the questions. I thought perhaps I should mention Callum, but I couldn't bring myself to even say his name.

I shook my head, and she started talking about a technique that was going to help me called cognitive behavioral therapy. She said that together we were going to retrain my brain to stop thinking the way it does and that, after a while, I'd stop doing the things I kept doing. It wasn't going to be easy, especially the exposure therapy, but I'd made the first step by being there and . . .

I stopped listening because my ears were buzzing and panic was bubbling in my stomach. I wanted to get the hell out of there. She was talking about some relaxation techniques and asked me to close my eyes and imagine my stomach was a deflated balloon that I needed to blow up. I glanced at the clock, closed my eyes, and began to write my mental list:

<u>Tuesday, July 29th. 10:57 a.m. Dr. Rhodes's office.</u>

Facts about Dr. Rhodes:

She's a *big* coffee drinker (the smell of coffee has been absorbed into the walls)

Likes antiques, gardening, American thrillers (bookcase observations)

One daughter. Single mother? (child's drawing propped up on a bookcase shelf of two stick figures, one larger than the other; both are wearing triangular skirts and they are holding hands)

Daughter recently visited a doctor or hospital (on the sole of her shoe there is a round sticker of a smiling giraffe saying, "Star Patient")

". . . and now . . . slowly open your eyes and take one more deep breath . . ."

I opened my eyes and resisted looking straight at the clock. Time had to be up by now. I gave her a smile, trying to look relaxed, trying to look like a star patient who was feeling better and ready to go home now, thank you very much.

"Can I use your bathroom, please?"

I perched on the edge of the sofa and wriggled a little as if I really had to go. Dr. Rhodes gave me a look. A look that said, *I'm a highly experienced psychotherapist and I know exactly what you are doing.*

She paused for a moment, leaving me in suspense.

"Of course, it's just outside on the left, and if you could send your parents back in on your way out that would be . . ."

But I'd gone. I rushed past Mum and Dad, who were hovering by the door, and ran to the small bathroom, locking the door behind me.

The stall was modern, sleek, and had a small pot of potpourri on the back of the toilet tank. I quickly unbuttoned my shirt as I filled up the sink with hot, clean, cleansing water. After taking my shirt off, I tucked it into the waistband of my trousers to keep it safe and peeled my gloves off, pushing them into my back pocket. Without touching anything else, I dipped my right arm into the scalding water and used my left hand to scoop the water up and over the top of my arm, washing away all of the germs that Dad had passed on to me.

We drove home in silence. I had put my gloves back on but they felt wrong. They felt dirty. As we approached Chestnut Close, Dad pulled over next to the yellow tape that stretched across the end of our road. A large news truck was parked nearby and a small group of journalists looked up at us as we sat there, waiting to be let in.

Mum's window went down as a policeman approached with a clipboard. I hadn't seen this one before; he was older and his uniform looked much too tight around his stomach.

"Afternoon," he said. Mum gave him our names and address and he looked at his list.

"Number nine," he repeated back to her. "Right next door then?"

"Yes, it's not been very nice, officer," said Mum.

I leaned forward.

"Can we just go? I really need the toilet."

"So you must be the boy in the window," said the policeman, waggling his pen in my direction. "Matthew, isn't it? You saw him before he went missing, didn't you?"

"Yes, yes he did, officer," said Dad, sounding strangely proud.

The policeman scribbled something down.

"What are you doing out then? I thought you were one of those reclusive types."

"He's started therapy today actually," said Mum.

"Can we just get home? Please!" I said. Mum wound her window back up and the policeman unraveled one end of the tape, leaving just enough room for Dad to drive through.

Gordon was walking down the road toward his house and Mum wound her window back down again as we pulled up beside him.

"Any news, Gordon?"

He shook his head as he fanned his face with his hat. His wispy hair was wet with sweat. He looked exhausted.

"No. Nothing. We've looked everywhere. Everywhere."

He was so tired he could barely speak.

"And how's Penny? Tell her to pop over any time, won't you?"

Dad groaned, probably too loudly. He couldn't stand Penny. He called her an interfering old bat.

Gordon wiped the sweat from the back of his neck.

"Oh, Penny's Penny. You know what she's like, always keeping busy."

His shoulders slumped forward as he plodded on back toward home.

We pulled into the driveway and Dad turned the engine off as we all looked at number eleven in silence. Standing on Mr. Charles's path with her back to us was Melissa Dawson, Teddy and Casey's mum.

An officer in a suit was talking to her, gesturing at the roses as if he was just giving gardening advice and not talking about her missing son. She stood with her arms folded tightly, her head twitching briefly as if the shock was still pulsing through her. The policeman carried on; his hand waved toward the gate, which had been locked and then unlocked, then toward the house where Casey and Mr. Charles had been, and then he pointed up at our window, the office window where I had watched Teddy picking the petals.

Melissa Dawson turned to see, her face agonized, her eyes watering, and then, like a broken elevator, she plummeted to the ground, settling into a heap onto the concrete. Mum gasped and put her hand to her mouth. The man in the suit shouted to one of his colleagues and bent down beside her as she began to wail. The noise was unlike anything I had ever heard before: animal-like and agonized. I put my hands over my ears, feeling the germs from my used gloves spread all over my face. The man patted her rhythmically on one shoulder, and then a policewoman appeared and they pulled her up and into the house.

"Oh Brian, that poor woman," Mum sobbed. Dad seemed unable to speak.

When we got inside I kicked my shoes off and ran upstairs. In my room I stripped down to my boxer shorts, feeling the Wallpaper Lion laughing at me. I threw the dirty clothes outside my door and peeled off my very last pair of gloves, now ruined with sickness and disease. Back in my room I grabbed my cleaning supplies and began to spray myself with the antibacterial spray. My skin tingled as the cool mist left tiny, miniscule droplets on my arms and legs, and then I grabbed my notebook from my bedside and angrily scratched at the paper.

Tuesday, July 29th. 11:34 a.m. Bedroom.

Number of Wallpaper Lions = 1

Number of filled notebooks = 8

Number of unused notebooks = 4

Number of half-filled notebooks = 1

Number of missing neighbors = 1

Number of useless twelve-year-olds = 1

CHAPTER FIFTEEN

MELODY BIRD

To: Matthew Corbin

From: Melody Bird

Subject: OLD NINA!

She's got a cellar!!!!!!!!!!!

Agent M. x

My heart was pounding as I typed back. I had tissue wrapped around my fingers and it kept slipping.

To: Melody Bird

From: Matthew Corbin

Re: OLD NINA!

What? How do you know?!

I rewrapped the tissue around my fingers.

To: Matthew Corbin

From: Melody Bird

Re: OLD NINA!

I knocked on her door. She didn't answer, of course, but under her front room window, behind that big bush, you can

see glass. It looks like skylights to a cellar!!!! Should we tell
the police?

I sat back and thought about it. You couldn't accuse someone
because they had the perfect hiding place right there in their house.
You needed evidence. I stood up and looked down at the Rectory.
An angry-looking shrub with needle-like thorns spread across the
whole front of her bay window; beneath it something was twin-
kling in the bright sunlight. I squinted. I could just make out a tiny
triangle of glass—a sliver of window barely visible behind the
thick branches. I'd never noticed it before, but Melody was right.
Old Nina had a cellar.

To: Melody Bird
From: Matthew Corbin
Re: OLD NINA!
You're right. Good work! Can you get around the back? See
what you can see from the graveyard?

To: Matthew Corbin
From: Melody Bird
Re: OLD NINA!
I've tried. It's too overgrown and I couldn't see a thing. I
think you need to watch her house, Matthew. See if you
spot anything unusual!

Jake came out of his house and began to walk slowly around the cul-de-sac. He stuffed his hands into his jeans and scuffed his feet along the ground at a stone, kicking it until it dropped into a drain. Every now and then he looked over at the policeman standing outside number eleven and then up at me, but he didn't shout anything. He looked bored.

My hands were throbbing. They had been washed and washed, but still the germs were finding their way under my nails and deep, deep into my bloodstream. The urge to wash yet again was overwhelming.

To: Melody Bird

From: Matthew Corbin

Subject: Help

Melody. I need your help.

I stopped typing, but I had no choice. She might be a bit odd, but there was no one else I could ask. I took two deep breaths. After this email I would be exposed. Vulnerable. The tissue slipped on my index finger, so I tightened it the best I could before I continued:

I need you to get some latex gloves for me. A boxful. I can pay you when I see you next, OK? I think you should be able to get them at the pharmacy on High Street. You can't bring them here though. I'll have to meet you somewhere nearby.

Matthew

I hit Send and waited. Jake was standing outside the Rectory now, staring up at the bedroom window. I looked at where he was staring and saw a curtain move. She was watching him too.

The little clock in the corner of the screen said 12:12. I kept my eyes fixed on it until it changed to the dangerous number, and when it changed I shut my eyes and counted repeatedly to seven. *Let's just make that evil number a nice round twenty and everything will be fine and dandy.*

The trumpet noise announced that she'd answered my email, but I kept my eyes closed until I was sure that the minute had passed. When I opened them, 12:14 showed in the bottom corner of the screen. I felt my shoulders drop as I relaxed.

To: Matthew Corbin
From: Melody Bird
Re: Help
Sure.
Melody x

I exhaled, not realizing I'd been holding my breath, and then I went to the bathroom to wash.

Melody Bird wasn't someone I'd taken much notice of before. At school, she was one of those girls who always seemed to be in a rush to get somewhere, her head down low as she concentrated on the floor in front of her, somehow managing not to bump into anyone as she dashed between classes. It was only recently that I noticed her peculiar movements. My notebooks were full of her:

<u>Thursday, April 24th. Office/nursery. Cloudy.</u>
4:03 p.m.-Melody heads to the overgrown alley next to Old Nina's house. Nothing back there but the graveyard.

<u>Wednesday, May 28th. Office/nursery. Bright, light wind.</u>
4:37 p.m.-Melody goes on another graveyard visit.

<u>Thursday, May 29th. Office/nursery. Heavy rain.</u>
4:15 p.m.-Melody goes to the graveyard. And she only went yesterday? What does she do there???

<u>Sunday, June 14th. Office/nursery. Overcast.</u>
2:35 p.m.-Jake cornered Melody on her way home from school. He grabbed her bag and held it high so she couldn't reach it. He said something to her and she kept shaking her head, trying to grab her bag. Eventually he threw it into the gutter, where she grabbed it and ran home.

Melody and I were in some of the same classes at school, the worst one being drama. I hated every single millisecond of it. Miss King, our drama teacher, insisted that each one of us had an actor inside us and that it was her job to pull it out kicking and screaming for the rest of the class to enjoy. That pretty much sums up why I hated it so much.

One week we had to prance around the room pretending to be butterflies, and when she told us to stop, we had to turn and face the person nearest to us and imagine there was a sheet of glass between us as we mirrored each other's movements.

"*Okay 7A, let's see some gorgeous butterflies!*" she said, shaking her hands outward, her bracelets jangling madly. "*Are we ready to flap those little wings? Okay! On a count of three . . . two . . . one . . . FLY!*"

Miss King stood in the middle of the room and clapped her hands as we shuffled awkwardly around her. After a while, some of the girls began to get into it, and they stretched on their tip-toes and fluttered their hands at their sides. The boys were less enthusiastic and pulled faces behind Miss King's back every time they flapped past. I made discreet little arm movements, trying not to draw attention to myself, which a lot of the class seemed to be doing as well. After a couple of minutes Miss King yelled again:

"*That's wonderful, 7A! Now, get ready for that mime work. On a count of three . . . two . . . one . . . MIRRORS!*"

We all stopped and turned to the person nearest us in silence. I faced Melody Bird, who looked as uncomfortable as I felt. Tom was snorting in the corner as he faced Simon Duke, who was shaking and red from laughing.

"*Concentrate, Tom Allen! Simon Duke! Now, watch your partner and slowly, slowly copy their movements. See who takes the lead. Don't touch each other. Remember there is a pane of glass between you!*"

I looked at Melody and scratched at an itch on my eyebrow. Melody quickly scratched her eyebrow, and I laughed.

"*I haven't started yet!*" I whispered.

"No talking, Matthew," said Miss King as she passed by. *"You must all mime in silence!"*

Melody held up her hand, her palm facing outward, and I put mine a couple of inches away from hers. She moved her hand up and I copied, then she stretched it out to the side and I followed. I could feel the heat from her skin, but back then I didn't mind as much. I was washing and managing to keep it a secret, since the anxiety I had about germs hadn't gotten too bad yet. Her other hand came up and now we swayed from side to side. She stuck her tongue out, and I stuck my tongue back out at her.

"That's good, Melody! Remember you can use your faces as well, 7A. Use your whole body!"

Melody crinkled up her nose and I did the same and then she pulled her bottom teeth up over her top lip and rolled her eyes back. I spluttered with laughter and then Miss King called out again.

"And now everyone back to those butterflies . . . Three . . . two . . . one . . . GO!"

Melody smiled and then flapped off into the group as I stretched out my hands and followed her.

I heard a door bang and I looked outside to see Melody coming out of number three. Dressed in black jeans, black T-shirt, and that long black cardigan, she walked in the direction of High Street. I felt a pang of excitement. She was on her way to buy my gloves, I just knew it. Jake was outside the Rectory and he ran across the road to catch up with her. Instantly her shoulders drooped and she curled up on herself. Jake was saying something to her, waving his arms around, and then they disappeared around the corner.

About an hour later a policewoman arrived to ask me some more questions. I say *more*, but she just asked the same ones all over again: Had I seen anything suspicious or heard anything out of the ordinary? Had I noticed anyone different on the block in the days leading up to his disappearance? I said no and went over, yet again, everything that I'd seen: Teddy playing with the petals, Mr. Jenkins going for a run, and that was it. I asked if they'd questioned Jake yet.

"Why would you ask that?" the policewoman said. I recognized her as one of the police who had turned up in a silver car not long after Teddy was reported missing. One of the "too important to wear a uniform" ones.

"Matthew is friends with Jake, aren't you, darling? I guess he just wants to know if you've spoken to everyone on the street."

Mum was with us in the kitchen, halfway through tidying the cupboards to keep herself busy. She'd stopped going to the salon so she could help with the searches, and Dad had taken time off work as well. He'd been out with a search party all morning.

"Jake's no friend of mine," I said under my breath.

The policewoman leaned forward on our kitchen table.

"We've spoken to everyone in the neighborhood, yes, but if there's anything else we should know about, then you must tell us, Matthew."

"Only that he's a nasty piece of work, that's all," I said.

"Matthew! How can you say that? You used to be such good friends." Mum turned to the policewoman, clearly thinking she should explain. "Jake had troubles with his health in elementary school. He was allergic to *everything*: nuts, fish, shampoo, wool, you name it. He was always covered in rashes and having wheezing fits. It was so frightening for Sue. At school he got picked on a bit. Kids can be so cruel, you know? Not my Matthew, of course . . . But then it made him a bit bitter as he got older, I guess. You know, those sorts of kids that always seem to find trouble? His older brother, Leo, doesn't help. That's all it is really."

The policewoman stood up, clearly deciding that this was all irrelevant and that she had far more important things to do.

"How is Teddy's mum, officer? Is she coping? Can I pop over and see if there's anything I can do to help?"

The policewoman scraped her chair as she tucked it back against the table.

"She's obviously extremely distressed. She's moved to a nearby hotel with her daughter, and our liaison officer is keeping her apprised of any developments." She turned back to me. "We'll probably need to come back and talk to you again, Matthew. Okay?"

I shrugged. I couldn't think of anything else I could add that I hadn't already said.

Back in the office I was hoping to see an email from Melody about my gloves, but no such luck. Instead:

> **To: Matthew Corbin**
> **From: Jake Bishop**
> **Subject: WARNING!**
> All right? I just wanted to warn you to stay away from that
> nutty girl living opposite you. She has an UNNATURAL
> interest in the dead. Know what I'm saying? And what's this
> about you two "investigating"? How you going to find
> anything out with a loon like her?!?!
> Jake

I got some tissue from the bathroom and quickly wrapped each finger before I typed.

> **To: Jake Bishop**
> **From: Matthew Corbin**
> **Re: WARNING!**
> She's just different, that's all. Surely you know what that's
> like?
> Matthew

I hit Send and stood up to see what was going on outside. The policewoman was getting back into her car and Mum was heading over to number one, probably to fill Penny in about how Melissa

Dawson had moved into a hotel. She rang the bell and Penny came out, closing the door behind her as they stood on her driveway with their arms folded, chatting, Mum turning around every now and then to take a look at number eleven.

Officer Campen, the policeman who had knocked on our door and asked me questions the day Teddy disappeared, was standing at Mr. Charles's front door.

To: Matthew Corbin
From: Jake Bishop
Re: WARNING!
Well, I'm warning you now. Melody Bird is EVIL. Have you
seen how many times she goes to the graveyard? Do
you actually know what she does there? No, of course you
don't, cuz you don't go out, do you?

I stopped reading. Something was going on outside.

"Officer! Officer!"

Melody's mum, Claudia, was running across the street, her long skirt flowing as she dragged her dachshund behind her.

"Excuse me! I've found something! My little dog has found something in my yard! Haven't you, Frankie? There's a good boy."

Claudia waited by the gate as Officer Campen walked toward her. She held something up in her hand. It was filthy and ripped almost in two, but I recognized it straight away.

Dangling from her hand was Teddy's blue blanket.

CHAPTER SIXTEEN

THE GRAVEYARD

To: Matthew Corbin
From: Melody Bird
Subject: Gloves
I've got them.
I'll be in the churchyard from 1 p.m.
Melody

The clock on the computer read 1:06. I needed to be quick. I'd just get the gloves and come straight home—easy. I paced around the office, shaking my hands by my sides. My heart was racing and I felt like I did before I fainted at the doctor's office. I forced myself to stand still and take a few deep breaths. I shut my eyes, but it felt like the floor was moving so I opened them again. If I didn't go now, then Melody would probably come here to see what was keeping me, and Mum would answer and see the box. After the episode in Dr. Rhodes's office and Dad crying, she'd never forgive me. No, it was now or never. I took a final, deep breath and then ran downstairs.

As I sat on the bottom step and pulled on my white, barely worn sneakers Mum appeared from the kitchen with Penny. They both had mugs of tea in their hands.

"Oh hello, Matthew," said Penny. "How nice to see you face-to-face for a change and not through a window."

Mum laughed awkwardly but Penny just stared at me, her nose in the air.

"What are you doing, Matty?" said Mum. "Are you going somewhere?"

I stood up and used my elbow to open the front door.

"Yep," I said, as casually as I could.

Mum and Penny looked at each other, stunned.

"Out? But he doesn't go out, Sheila. Does he?" It was as if I wasn't there.

"Well, I am now," I said and I took a final deep breath and stepped out into the hot, humid air.

In the graveyard there was a large horse chestnut tree with a hexagonal bench surrounding its trunk. The bench was old, but the tree was ancient. I wondered if it had been mortified to find a bench being built around its base after all those years of being perfectly happy without one.

A girl in a blue dress was sitting on the bench in the shade of the tree. I hadn't seen her in color before.

"Hi, Melody," I said and I perched beside her on the very edge of the seat.

She didn't say anything, but I noticed her slip a small white card into a pocket in the skirt of her dress. Next to her there was a white plastic bag, which I tried not to stare at.

"Some of these are amazing," I said, looking at a gray stone cross with a weeping woman draped over it. Strangely I didn't feel as threatened here as I had at the doctor's or the therapist's. You'd have thought being surrounded by graves would make me more anxious, but this part of the cemetery was so ancient . . . I imagined that any germs around here were long gone.

We sat in silence for a while and I watched a few crispy leaves scuttle along the path in front of us. The breeze blew in my face like a hot hair dryer.

"Thanks for getting the gloves."

She nodded. The bag sat between us untouched, and I resisted the urge to grab it and put a pair on.

"I really do appreciate it. I know it was an odd thing to ask." I laughed nervously and she raised her eyebrows. I was expecting her to start asking questions, but she didn't.

"Come on, I'll show you my favorite gravestone," she said. "Now there's an offer you can't refuse!"

She jumped up off the bench and went to grab my hand, but I instinctively folded my arms against my chest. She looked hurt.

"I've—I've got this problem. A fear of germs. That's why I needed the gloves. I'm sorry. It's not you . . . There you go, you know my little secret now."

Melody looked away for a moment and some of her hair fell in front of her face. She tucked it behind her ear before looking back at me. She smiled but still didn't say anything. I think she was shocked that I was saying so much, and now that I'd started I couldn't stop.

"And numbers. Well, one number actually. I get anxious if I hear or see the unlucky one. That fear isn't as bad as the germs, but it's still there and it's been getting worse. If I see or hear the bad number I just need to count to seven in my head, which takes it to twenty so then it's all fine again."

I stopped as I realized I was rambling. Melody just stood there, wide-eyed. Then she spoke.

"It must have been hard for you to tell me all of this," she said.

"Well, yeah. Kind of," I said.

A big smile stretched across her face.

"No one *ever* tells me stuff like this. You know, private things about themselves."

I shrugged.

"I thought you had a thing about fingernails," she said.

"What?"

She nodded to the bag.

"I thought that's why you wore gloves all the time. Because your fingernails creeped you out or something. I thought you couldn't bear to look at them."

We both looked down at my hands.

It was then I started to laugh. It began as a giggle, an almost silent chuckle to myself, and then it swept over me and I couldn't control it. I clutched my stomach and I laughed until tears sprang in my eyes. At first she looked at me like I was mad, but then her shoulders began to shake and she laughed along with me. Every time we calmed down a bit I looked at her and we started again.

"Fingernails?" I said, trying to catch my breath.

"I didn't know, did I?" she replied and we both collapsed into hysterics again. It felt good to laugh. Really, really, really good. We eventually quieted down and she wiped her eyes.

"So, how does it feel to be outside? Properly outside," she said, smiling at me.

I caught my breath from the laughing and looked around. Over by the church I could just make out the tip of the bright white wing that belonged to Callum's angel. As soon as I saw it, I realized that being here was a very, very bad idea indeed.

"Every single cell in my body is telling me to go home right this second and wash all these germs away."

I held my hands up in front of me and turned them back and forth, seeing disease crawling all over them.

"There's nothing on them, Matthew. It's fine," said Melody.

I shook my head.

"You're wrong. They're everywhere. I can't stay here—it's too dangerous. I'm sorry, I've got to go."

I picked up the shopping bag using the cuff of my shirt and began to walk away, back toward the alley next to Old Nina's house. Melody skipped around me and walked backward, in my way.

"You can go back and wash, of course you can! But first, just come and see something with me. Please? You can do all the washing you want when you get home, just delay it for a couple of minutes—it's worth it, I promise."

She stood in my way and held her arms wide, and I hesitated for a moment. That got her smiling.

"A couple of minutes, three at the most. That's all it's going to take, Matty, honestly. And if the germs really are going to get you, then three minutes isn't going to make much difference, is it?" She laughed, but I didn't join in this time.

"Come on, follow me!"

Her hair flowed behind her as she ran off toward the corner of the churchyard where the oldest gravestones were.

I stood in the bright sun and weighed my options. I could head home and feel the relief of washing, or I could delay going home for a few more minutes and see what this crazy girl wanted to show me. I thought of something Dr. Rhodes had said at our meeting. She said that I needed to confront my fears and trust in myself and that if I took a step off my continuous wheel of worrying and cleaning, I'd be all right. I reached into the bag and ripped the top off the box, and my anxiety eased a little when I put a pair of gloves on. I looked to the left where Melody had headed, took a deep breath, and followed.

_____

This part of the graveyard was overgrown and the ground was uneven where the coffins had rotted away, leaving spongy soil ready to swallow someone up. Most of the stones were illegible, their surfaces mottled with lime-green lichen. I spotted Melody behind a cross that was leaning at an awkward angle.

"Oh good, you're here!" she said and she glanced at my hands but didn't say anything.

"I've just come to say thanks again for getting the gloves, but I'm going back now. I'm not feeling great and I think I've tried to do too much. I feel dizzy. I need some water, I think."

As she stood with her hands on her hips the dappled sunlight danced around her, picking out flecks of auburn in her hair.

"But you've come this far! Honestly, it's really worth it. Just come over, have a quick look, and then go. Okay?"

She crouched down next to a grave and pulled at some weeds. I just needed to walk five more paces, see what it was, then run home, sprint home. I could go straight upstairs and into the shower. It'd be fine. I could then clean my room, wait for the hot water to warm up again, then have another shower if I felt like it. I edged my way toward her and she turned to me, her face beaming. My feet twisted as the mounds of earth pressed against the thin soles of my shoes. I stood at the other side of the grave from her, my gloved hands tucked under my arms.

"Look," she whispered. "Have you ever seen anything so beautiful?"

At one end of the grave stood a typical oblong headstone with some faded words, but in front of it and lying on a large, gray slab of stone lay an exquisitely carved mermaid. It was about half the size of Melody, and the detail was extraordinary.

"Isn't it amazing?" said Melody and she brushed some soil and leaves off the mermaid's tail. I knelt down for a closer look.

"Wow. Did someone carve this?"

"Yep, they certainly did . . ."

She gestured at the headstone.

". . . in 1884."

The mermaid was facedown, her shoulders slightly hunched with her forehead resting in the crook of her right arm. Her hair cascaded around her in stone waves that covered her naked back. The tail curved upward, the contours of its muscles supporting the large, uncurled fan at the end, slightly chipped on one side. As the sunlight flickered along her scales, the mermaid shimmered. It was as if she was still wet from the sea and was just here resting for a moment. I bent down to take a closer look and could almost imagine I saw her back rise and fall as she breathed. I tried to see the expression on her face, but it was hidden, never to be seen.

"Is she asleep?"

Melody pulled at a few more weeds.

"I don't think so; I think she's crying. She's a mermaid in mourning."

I studied her hair and for a fraction of a millisecond was tempted to touch a curl, but I didn't.

"Why a mermaid? Who's buried here?"

I didn't want to get any closer, so I squinted at the headstone as Melody recited it by heart.

"Elizabeth Hannah Reeves. She died on the twenty-ninth of October in 1884, aged twenty-eight, but it doesn't say anything else about her. I've tried looking in the church records to see if I can find out more, but I didn't get anywhere. Maybe she went to sea once and thought she saw a mermaid but nobody believed her. Or maybe she just loved the idea of them. Who knows? But whoever she was, she's left behind this beautiful grave."

I watched her tugging at some ivy and thought maybe I'd been wrong about her all along. The constant talking I'd seen at the doctor's was probably just nerves; this calmer, relaxed Melody was actually quite nice to be around. And she'd bought me gloves without asking questions. *And* she still seemed to like me even though she knew everything. Nearly everything. Maybe knowing what I'd done to Callum would change her mind though.

"I started coming over here after school before Dad moved out to avoid all the arguing. That's when I found her."

Standing up, she folded her arms.

"When I was having a bad day I thought about the mermaid, secretly sleeping here day in and day out. It took my mind off things."

Reaching down, she brushed some more soil from the mermaid's tail.

"It's a sad grave though. On nearly all of the headstones here there's more than one name—husbands, children, parents, they all seem to share a plot, especially the older ones. But Elizabeth Reeves is here all on her own. She only has the mermaid for company."

I know how she feels. I thought about the Wallpaper Lion, and the thought of my clean, safe room sparked my anxiety again. The distraction of the mermaid faded as my chest tightened and my breathing got faster.

"Melody, I really need to go home now. The grave is great, thanks for showing me."

I turned and carefully stepped through the tall grass back onto the footpath.

"I know you watch me from the window," said Melody, catching up with me. "I know you were wondering what I get up to here. Do you think I'm weird?"

I shook my head.

"Good."

We walked along a little way in silence, and then I saw her reach into her pocket and bring out the little white card. I stopped as she held it up for me to see. In one corner there was a pale, cream-colored lily with a dark green stem. It took a moment for my eyes to adjust from the dazzling sunlight, but the pale blue printed text eventually came into focus:

IN LOVING MEMORY.

Underneath in black ink was a handwritten note:

Forever in my heart. C.

It was a memorial card.

"Where did you get it?"

She put the card back in her pocket.

"Over by the church. It was on the grave of a man who lived to ninety-eight. How great is that? To live to such an old age."

She was smiling but I wasn't smiling back.

"I don't understand. Why have you got it? Why have you got someone's memorial card in your pocket?"

"I collect them."

I stopped and faced her and her smile disappeared.

"You do what?"

She folded her arms. "I go around the graveyard and pick them up and put them in albums. I take them so that—"

"You collect them? What, like stickers? Like a kid's sticker book?"

"No, it's not like that at all. If I didn't take them, then—"

"How many of these have you got? I mean, can you just take them? Off of people's graves? These are people's private thoughts—you shouldn't be taking them, it's theft!"

She looked horrified. "No, you don't understand—"

"Don't understand what? That you're taking personal things that don't belong to you?"

Melody wiped her face with her hand. The whites of her eyes glistened with tears.

"It's not like you're saying. I'm not stealing! They'd be thrown away if I didn't take them. Why are you so angry?"

I was thinking about the card I'd written a few months ago on the anniversary of Callum's death. It wasn't a card exactly, just a scrap of paper. I'd scribbled a message to him telling him I was sorry. Saying I didn't mean for him to die. I had gone to his grave before school, tucking the paper underneath the angel's toe.

Melody stood hugging herself as a tear trickled down her cheek. I couldn't tell her.

"I'm going home," I said and I ran toward the alleyway, leaving her crying behind me. I needed to get away, from her *and* the graveyard. This whole thing had been just one big mistake. The gloves she'd bought didn't feel right—they weren't as thick as the ones Mum had gotten, so the germs were probably seeping through already.

When I passed the Rectory's backyard Old Nina was standing on a stepladder trying to reach something that was stuck in her apple tree. Something made of white fabric was twisted in the branches; she was jabbing at it using a broom. Frowning as she bit her bottom lip, she was concentrating so hard she didn't notice as I ran past, toward home.

CHAPTER SEVENTEEN

THE RECTORY

Jake was waiting for me at the end of the alleyway on his bike.

"What you two up to?" he said, his arms folded across his chest. I put the plastic bag behind my back. "You know something, don't you?"

"No."

"Do you two think you're going to find Teddy? You saw something, didn't you? From the window?"

He leaned forward on the handlebars and edged his way toward me.

"You saw something and you're not telling anyone."

"No I didn't! Now get out of my way, Jake."

He was blocking the alleyway and there was no room for me to get around.

"That Melody ain't going to be any use. If you need a partner, I can do some stuff, see what I can find out."

He shrugged as if he didn't care one way or the other, but I couldn't believe he was asking to get involved. What was he up to?

"You?" I said, stepping against the wall of his house so I could get by. "Thanks but no thanks."

He sniffed and jutted his chin toward me, and when I tried to squeeze past him he rolled his bike forward and squashed my leg against the wall.

"Jake! What do you think you're doing?"

I tried to wriggle free, but he pushed the bike harder.

"You think you're so great, don't you? Well, you know what, Weirdo Corbin?"

He leaned so close I could see the painful cracks of sore skin in the creases of his eyes.

"You're nothing."

He twisted the bike against my leg once more, then pushed away and pedaled off down the road.

When I got home Penny had left and Mum was whispering with Dad in the living room.

"It's a start, isn't it, Brian? He went out on his own accord. How long has it been since he's done that?"

I sat on the bottom of the stairs and kicked my shoes off. My leg was throbbing and every inch of me was swarming with germs. If I didn't get in the shower immediately I'd get ill. And if I got ill then Mum would get ill and then Dad and then . . . and then whatever happened next would be all my fault. All because I hadn't washed in time. Mum came out to see me.

"Give him some space, Sheila! You don't want to frighten him back into his room now, do you?" called Dad, as if I couldn't hear.

"I am giving him space! I'm just pleased to see him, aren't I?

How was your little outing, Matthew? Did you go anywhere nice? What've you got in that bag?"

I couldn't speak.

If I spoke then the germs would be able to crawl into my mouth. Dad appeared, taking his turn.

"How about that game of pool, eh, Matthew? I got all the cat hair off while you were out, so it's as good as new."

As if this was his cue to join in, Nigel appeared from the kitchen, meowing loudly as he brushed himself against Mum's legs.

"Oh look, Matty! Nigel is pleased to see you as well. Aren't you, Nigel-wigel?"

She picked him up and cradled him like a baby as the cat shut its eyes and purred loudly, tipping its head back as Mum scratched him under the chin. I had my very own welcome party.

I suddenly remembered I was still wearing the gloves, so I quickly ran upstairs as Dad yelled after me.

"Matthew? You wearing those bloody gloves again?"

I turned the shower on and twisted the dial to the hottest setting, waiting for it to heat up.

Mum knocked gently on the door.

"Are you okay, Matthew? Is everything all right?"

"Yep, fine, Mum," I called, trying to sound as cheery as possible.

There was silence but I knew she was still there, listening to the blast of water.

"I'm always here for you, darling. We both are." Her voice broke a little but she carried on. "You can tell us anything. Don't ever think we won't understand, because we will, okay? You're our very special boy."

I looked at my reflection in the mirrored cabinet. Tears were streaming down my cheeks, my nose running.

It was all because of me, Mum. The baby you wanted so badly died because of me.

I quietly cleared my throat.

"I know, Mum. I'll speak to you in a bit. Okay?"

There was more silence and then I heard her pad back downstairs. We both knew I wouldn't be speaking to her in a bit. I got in the shower and rubbed at my skin with soap. The water was scalding, but I carried on. Killing the germs was vital, and if it wasn't hot, then they wouldn't die. After the shower the tightness in my chest loosened a little, and I brushed my teeth five times to make sure nothing had reached my mouth. When I got to the office I knew there would be an email waiting for me. I used my shirt to cover my finger as I clicked the email open.

To: Matthew Corbin
From: Melody Bird
Subject: My Mistake
I thought out of everybody you'd understand.
There's not much difference between us, Matthew Corbin.

We're loners, you and I. We don't fit in. At least I don't
pretend that I do.
Melody Bird

I sat back in the office chair, stunned. A loner? She was calling me a loner? I wasn't lonely and I certainly fit in! I read the
message two more times, then put on a fresh pair of latex gloves.

A second email was waiting for me. He must have sent it
before he blocked my way in the alley.

To: Matthew Corbin
From: Jake Bishop
Subject: Old Nina Witch

What are you two up to? I saw you both heading to the
graveyard. What's going on? Is it something to do with Old
Nina? She's a witch, you know. She's probably got a whole
load of dead bodies in that house! Remember Halloween?!

Underneath the email he'd inserted a photograph of an old
lady, her face distorted and her eyes dangling in two different
directions on red-veined stalks.

I knew the Halloween he was talking about. It was the last
time I'd been trick-or-treating, three years ago . . .

It was the first time that we'd been allowed to go on our own,
but we were under strict instructions to only knock on the houses

in the cul-de-sac, including our own, and not to bother Old Nina at the Rectory. Our mums would be watching us from their living rooms, so all in all it wasn't looking like a particularly exciting Halloween.

It seemed a bit pointless knocking on our own houses, as our mums had already seen our outfits, but it was worth it for the candy. We started at Jake's and Sue opened her door and let out an ear-piercing scream when we yelled: "Trick or treat!"

"Oh my goodness, look at you two! Well hello, Mr. Scary Alien and hello, Mr. Scary Werewolf! I think you both need a treat, don't you?"

"All right, Mum, don't overdo it," said Jake as we rummaged around in the candy bowl, each taking a handful for our booty bags before we moved on.

Hannah and Mr. Jenkins's house was dark, but Jake still insisted on ringing their doorbell over and over until I told him to quit it.

My house was next and Dad answered. He'd only just got home from work and he pretended he didn't know who we were.

"Good outfit there, boy!" he said to Jake, who was wearing an all-in-one green jumpsuit with a padded tail and a white, rubber alien mask with two black slits for eyes.

"And who is this monster? It looks like you need a decent haircut!" he said to me. I was wearing normal clothes but hairy gloves with claws and a werewolf mask that went over my head. My face was sweating and I tried not to laugh.

Mr. Charles was next. He answered the door and stumbled backward when he saw us.

"Trick or treat!"

"Blimey, you nearly gave me a heart attack!" he said, resting his hand on the wall for support. "Is it that day already? Gawd. Hang on a minute . . . And I don't want any of your tricks on my garden . . ."

Jake and I giggled as he went off to try and find something to give us. He didn't need to worry about us doing a trick. We didn't have anything with us; no one ever chose "trick" instead of "treat." He came back with two apples.

"Is that it?" said Jake and I elbowed him.

"You're lucky you're not getting a clip to the ear to go with it, lad!" said Mr. Charles, and he slammed the door as we ran down the path laughing.

It was Penny and Gordon's house next. The best-decorated house in the street. Garlands of black-and-white paper spiders were strung across the window, with webs in each corner that lit up and twinkled. Three beautifully carved pumpkins glowed orange on the step. Mum had bought a pumpkin carving kit from Penny's *Harrington's Household Solutions* catalog, but ours didn't look anything like these. I glanced back at our house and saw her outline in the window keeping an eye on us.

"Trick or treat!" we yelled as we rang the doorbell of number one.

The door swung open and a faceless figure in a long, black cloak appeared. We both gasped.

"Wooooooohhhh," it said as it waved its arms at us, stepping outside as we took a step back.

"Gordon? Gordon!" yelled Penny, from the kitchen. "Come and help me with these!"

Gordon ignored her and lifted up the shroud, his face rosy as he laughed.

"Ah, who do we have here then? A scary werewolf *and* an alien!"

He bent forward to take a proper look, but Penny appeared, all elbows, and barged him out of the way. She was wearing a black-and-white polka dot dress with a tiny silver witch's hat placed at an angle on her bouffant hairstyle. She was carrying a large tray in the shape of a bat that was filled with pumpkin cookies, candy apples, and muffins decorated with miniature gravestones. The smell was amazing.

"Wow, did you make these, Penny?" I said, giving our identities away.

"Of course, Matthew. Now, you can only take one each. I've got to make sure I've got enough to go around."

I grabbed a cookie and put it in my bag as Jake surveyed the tray.

"Have you got any candy?"

Penny stood upright.

"No, I don't, young man. And if you want any of that processed rubbish I suggest you try another house."

We both jumped as the door banged shut.

Jake walked off, his alien tail dragging behind him. He could have perhaps said it better, but I knew he hadn't meant any harm. His allergies meant he couldn't eat just anything, and if it was in a packet, his mum could check the label. I joined him on the front step of number three just as Melody opened the door. She was wearing a black cat outfit with little black whiskers painted on her cheeks and two triangular ears poking out of her hair.

"MIAOWWWWW!" she shouted and pounced like a cat, her hands splayed out toward us.

"Yeah, yeah, Melody," said Jake as he shook his booty bag at her.

Melody huffed and then ducked behind the door, returning with an orange bucket full of brightly wrapped sweets.

"Miaow," she said as I took some. The end of her nose was painted black, and when she saw me looking she wriggled it at me.

Jake took two giant handfuls.

"MIAOW!" she said and snatched the bucket back. She then pretended to lick her paw and clean her ear as she purred.

"Melody? You are *so* weird," said Jake. She hissed at him and then shut the door.

"Well, that was a waste of time," said Jake, looking in his bag. "I've barely got anything!"

We turned and slowly walked back to his house, but Jake stopped at the next gate.

"Our mums said not to bother Old Nina. Come on," I said, continuing on, but Jake ran up the path and stood before the door of the Rectory. He lifted the heavy knocker and banged it three times.

"Jake!" I shouted. "What are you doing?"

I looked at our houses, but there was no outline of our mums anymore. They'd probably seen us making our way home. I quickly ran and joined him just as the large, black door slowly opened.

"Trick or treat," said Jake, but he said it quietly this time. The old lady's face was blank as she studied him.

"I said trick or treat!" He shook his bag vigorously.

Old Nina gave a little knowing nod and then went back inside, keeping the door ajar. Jake looked at me and gave me a thumbs-up as I stood staring, openmouthed. He started goofing around, doing a little dance on the step and wiggling his backside toward the house, and then the door suddenly opened again.

"You'd better come in," she said and then she went back inside, this time leaving the door wide open.

We both looked at each other, and then Jake stepped up into the large, dark hallway, taking his alien mask off. I followed. It took a while for my eyes to adjust in the gloom. I was expecting to see cobwebs and peeling wallpaper, but although it was old-fashioned and dark, the place was clean and tidy. Old Nina had disappeared through a doorway at the end of the hallway, and we slowly edged in the same direction. We walked past the door to the living room and I peeked in. Beside a small gas fire was a wing-backed chair and on the windowsill was the orange lamp, glowing warmly. Jake elbowed me in the ribs and I jumped.

"Look! Who do you think that is?"

Along the wall was a collection of framed photographs, all of the same boy at different ages. In one he gave a toothless grin as he gripped the pole of a carousel horse, in another he studied a butterfly resting on the back of his hand—he looked about my age in that one. There was a photo of his first day at school, holding up a football trophy, wearing a Santa Claus hat with his eyes crossed, and one of him at a field day wearing a big gold medal around his neck. I took off my werewolf mask and studied the photo closest to me. In this one he was standing on a beach, his arms folded against his bare chest as the sand stretched out for miles around him. It must have been windy, as his sandy hair was sticking up in all directions, his nose splattered with freckles and his eyes half-shut as he grinned back at the camera.

"Who do you think he is?" said Jake, studying the photos. "Is he her son? There're no pictures of him grown up. What happened to him?"

We both looked at each other, and I saw Jake's throat gulp as we heard Old Nina clattering around in the kitchen.

"Come in here, you two!"

Carrying on along the hall, we stopped in the kitchen doorway. In the corner was a black range cooker, and crouching down, smoke swirling around her, was Old Nina. Wearing some gray oven mitts, she reached down and lifted out a large tray of cakes, which she placed on a mat on the table.

"Ah, there you are!" she said. Taking off her oven mitts, she put her head to one side and stared at Jake.

"Do you know, I think you'll be just the right size. Just the right size indeed."

She walked toward us and Jake gripped my arm, his face deathly white as he stared at Old Nina and then at the open oven behind her.

"We've gotta get out of here, Matty," he said between gritted teeth. She got closer and closer and then Jake suddenly turned and ran.

Old Nina stopped in front of me.

"Where's he going?"

I was frozen to the spot. I wanted to run, but I was worried any sudden movement would mean she'd grab me. She was so close I could see two black hairs on her chin as she rubbed her lips together. Her thin, bony hand reached out, and then she moved toward the kitchen door beside me and took something off a hook. She gave it a shake and held it up.

"No, no, no. It's no good for you, I'm afraid. Your friend was the perfect size. What a shame he had to rush off."

It was a boy's coat. A smart, knee-length navy blue coat with shiny black buttons up the front. She held the coat close to her, rubbing the fabric with her thumb, and for a moment I think she forgot I was there. Then she sighed before hanging it back up on the door.

"Anyway. Would you like a cake?" she said.

As the sun faded on the cul-de-sac, I watched as each front room glowed and flickered simultaneously with the same news report. The same news that I could hear from our TV downstairs.

"*. . . missing child, Teddy Dawson . . .*"

I quietly crept downstairs, listening.

"*Today, Teddy's mother, Melissa Dawson, gave this emotional plea . . .*"

I sat on the middle step, where I could see the large screen. There was a row of people behind a long, white desk, and sitting in the center was Melissa Dawson. She looked very professional in a smart green dress with her dark hair tied back neatly. Speaking from memory, she looked in turn at each of the journalists sitting in front of her as if she were addressing a conference.

"*On Monday afternoon, my beautiful baby boy, Teddy, went missing from my father's yard. I urge anyone with any information as to where he is to please call the police. Anything, even the smallest bit of information, could help find him. So please, no matter how trivial you think it might be, please call.*"

She paused for a moment and took a sip of water. Then she looked down at some notes in front of her and began to read, her voice trembling slightly.

"*If there is somebody out there who is holding Teddy, they need to give* him back to me. Please. They can drop him off at a safe place—a hospital, a church, somewhere he'd be found . . ."

Her voice cracked and her posture slumped a little.

"He is a very happy, lovely boy. Please . . . please somebody bring him home to me . . . He's only little . . ."

And with that she put her hand to her mouth and her face crumbled. The professional woman had gone. The policeman beside her spoke up with details I'd heard a million times before.

"Teddy was wearing a pull-up style diaper and a T-shirt with an ice-cream cone picture on the front like this one here, and he was possibly carrying a blue security blanket . . ."

Mum dropped her head onto Dad's shoulder as he curled an arm around her and they sat on the sofa, holding each other.

I crept back upstairs to the bathroom and began to wash my hands. I was exhausted and my brain felt cloudy. I concentrated on lathering the soap correctly and covering every patch of skin, but it didn't feel right. I didn't feel clean. I rinsed my hands and started again. But after that wash it felt the same. So I started again, and again, and again. Unable to stop, I washed my hands twenty-seven times. I heard the TV switch off downstairs, and I hurried to bed before Mum or Dad could see me.

CHAPTER EIGHTEEN

TRACES OF BLOOD

The next day, Mum came up first thing to tell me that traces of Teddy's blood had been found in the fibers of the blue blanket that Claudia Bird had given the police.

Claudia told the police that she was just going out for a walk with Frankie when the dog became interested in something underneath her car. At first she thought it was an old rag, but when she pulled it out from the wheel arch she realized what it was. She had a vague recollection of driving over something in the road on the afternoon Teddy went missing. It must have been his blanket, which had then become caught up underneath her car. I checked back over my notebook, and her story seemed to add up.

Monday, July 28th. Office/nursery. Very hot.
2:39 p.m.–Claudia waves to Mr. Charles from her car as she drives
  off.

"It doesn't look good, Matthew. That poor mum," said Mum.

She dabbed at the corner of her eyes with a tissue, used it to blow her nose, then squeezed it in her hands like one of those squishy stress balls. I had been about to go and wash my hands, but she was now blocking my doorway.

"Have the police searched the Rectory?" I asked.

"Old Nina? She wouldn't hurt a fly, Matthew. Why would they want to search her house? She's staying in that posh hotel in town. You know the one? With the huge baths and the free dressing gowns."

"Who? Old Nina?"

She rolled her eyes. "No, not Old Nina! Melissa Dawson!" My mum does this a lot—she flits from subject to subject. I think it's from following so many conversations at once in the salon.

"It's a bit odd, isn't it? You'd think she'd want her family around her at a time like this, or at least to stay close in case he turns up. Penny said yesterday that she probably blames Mr. Charles for not looking after Teddy properly. She likely can't bear to be anywhere near him."

I wondered if it had more to do with her being so used to hotels, what with all the business traveling she must do. They probably felt like home to her.

My hand wash was becoming urgent now. A deadly disease could easily have been spreading from my wrists up toward my elbows, and from there it wasn't far to my shoulders, my neck, and then my mouth. And once they'd gotten inside your mouth . . . Well, that was pretty much it, really. There was no hope then.

I could hear Dad clattering around downstairs doing something in the conservatory. Mum showed no sign of leaving and leaned toward me. I quickly took a step back, my heart pounding. A low growl rumbled from the Wallpaper Lion in the corner of my room.

"There's no father around, apparently."

My breaths were coming in short bursts and I was practically panting.

"Are you all right, Matthew? You really need to get a bit of sun, you know. You're fading away up here."

I could hear "The Macarena" playing somewhere in the distance. Mum frowned at me as we both tried to place where the music was coming from, and then Dad bellowed up the stairs.

"Sheila! It's your phone again!"

Mum's face lit up.

"That's probably Penny. I'll be back in a minute."

Back in my room after washing my hands, I watched Dad from the window. There was a tower of old cans of paint on the grass, and he stumbled out of the shed holding an old roller and a dirty, black plastic tray. Grabbing a can from the top of the pile, he headed indoors.

I remembered then—decorating was Dad's way of keeping busy when he felt helpless. After Callum died he took two weeks off of work and painted the kitchen, lounge, hallway, and their bedroom. Mum's way of coping back then was to sort through the attic. She spent hours up there, rummaging away as I stared up from the bottom of the ladder. Once or twice she'd gone up there but didn't make any noise and kept the light turned off. I think she'd finished sorting and just wanted to sit there quietly in the darkness for a bit.

A lawn mower fired up next door. Mr. Charles had cleared all of Teddy's and Casey's toys off the grass and had piled them like rubbish in a heap beside the shed. He stood on the edge of the patio and then set off, pushing the orange machine at arm's length as a light green stripe appeared behind him. When he turned back toward the house, he raised one liver-spotted arm at me and waved. There was a smile on his face.

Wednesday, July 30th. Bedroom. Very hot. Cloudy.
9:35 a.m.–Mr. Charles is mowing his lawn. Appears almost
   happy . . . Is this normal behavior?

The mower turned on and off as Mr. Charles carefully cut around the edge of the fishpond. He dipped the blades up and down, trying to avoid damaging any of the plants. Two more strips and he was returning back to the patio for the last time, expertly turning the mower off just as he reached the end. Stretching his arms behind him, he looked back up at me, a strange grin on his face. He held up a finger as if to say, _Wait there just a second, young man_ before he dashed off to the kitchen, leaving the mower clicking and popping as it cooled down. My stomach churned a little. Something didn't seem right. He emerged back into the sunshine holding a glass of something clear and fizzy in each hand. It looked like lemonade. My heart was racing. He walked toward the fence between our gardens and stretched an arm upward, the sun glinting on the glass. Did he think I could just reach down and take it? I stared back at him and shrugged my shoulders. I didn't know what to do. He put one of the glasses down on the patio table and beckoned for me to join him. His other arm held the lemonade high, as if it were some ridiculous trophy waiting to be presented to me.

And the award for "Removing Oneself from One's Bedroom Goes to . . ."

Mr. Charles's grin began to wobble. I shook my head and stepped away from the window. Then I saw it. He dropped his gaze, and his face contorted into a sinister snarl as he said something under his breath. I'd never seen his face like that before, all twisted and nasty. I quickly pulled the curtains.

"Did you see that, Lion? Did you see his face?"

I glanced up at the Wallpaper Lion. His eye was directed toward my window, and I knew immediately what I'd done wrong—I'd pulled the curtains too fast and now death and disease were escaping from the folds of fabric and swarming everywhere. If I did nothing then before long the whole room would need to be decontaminated. I closed my eyes and tried to ignore the germs, but I could hear the scurrying of their dirty feet as they ran across the walls and ceiling. I sat up, wiped my eyes, took a deep breath, and reached down for my cleaning things.

———————

There were two emails in my inbox, both from my old best friend, Tom.

To: Party Crowd
From: Thomas Allen
Subject: Invitation

Venue: My House
Event: Barbecue!!!
When: Saturday, August 9th at 3 p.m.
Reason: Summer!
RSVP to TOM!
(BRING A FRIEND)

Along the bottom of the email there was a row of yellow emo-jis all doing random things like blowing raspberries, winking, or spinning around. I clicked on his other email.

To: Matthew Corbin
From: Thomas Allen
Re: Invitation
Hey bud! How's it going? Haven't seen you in ages! I heard about that little kid next door to you going missing. That's awful! [Here he had inserted a sad emoji with a tear running down its face.] I hope they find him soon!
I'm happy it's summer vacation. How great is that!? Hope you can make the BBQ!! I know things have been a bit weird, but get in touch if you want to go out or something!!!!!
Tom

I cringed. It appeared that he had developed an affliction for overuse of exclamation marks. Next to the word *weird* he'd inserted another smiley face that looked like it was straining to go to the toilet. It was obvious that I'd missed far too much school and my best friend had become an idiot.

> **To: Thomas Allen**
> **From: Matthew Corbin**
> **Re: Invitation**
> Hi Tom,
> Thanks for the invite—it sounds amazing!

(I allowed myself one exclamation mark to make him feel comfortable.)

> I don't think I'll be able to make it unfortunately. Things have been pretty crazy around here after Teddy went missing. There's police everywhere. The woman across the street found his blanket, and this morning they said they found some of his blood

I stopped. I suddenly had a thought. I looked down from the window and saw Officer Campen standing outside next door. He was rocking onto his toes and then back onto his heels like he was on some kind of invisible swing. I quickly ran downstairs and opened the front door. The step looked too filthy for my bare feet, so I held onto the doorframe with my fingertips and leaned forward.

"Officer Campen!"

The policeman was staring across the street vacantly as he stifled a yawn.

"Hey! Officer Campen!"

He looked around, frowning.

"I need to tell you something. It's about Teddy!"

The policeman darted over to the fence between our front gardens.

"What is it? You saw someone, didn't you? I knew it . . ."

My fingers hurt as I dangled around the doorframe at an awkward angle.

"No, no I didn't, but it's about the blood. The blood they found on the blanket? Teddy scratched himself when he was picking the petals off the roses. I remembered just now—I didn't write it down for some reason."

The policeman kept turning behind him, making sure no one was venturing near the house.

"How do you know all this?"

"Because I was watching him. He was picking petals and caught his arm on a thorn and he dabbed at the bloody scratch with his blanket. Get it? The blood they found doesn't mean he's been hurt."

Officer Campen stared at me as I waited.

"Where on his arm?"

I was dangerously close to falling out of the house.

"On his forearm. The right one. Look, I've got to go."

I pulled myself back inside and closed the door, knowing that before long the police would be knocking again and asking the same question in ten different ways. Dad was in the conservatory using a roller to paint beneath the window ledges; the pool table was covered with an old, stained beige cloth.

"What's going on, Matthew?" he called.

I walked to the edge of the conservatory, stopping at the white, shiny tiles that harbored a trillion germs. Nigel was nowhere to be seen.

"I remembered something, so I told the policeman next door. Teddy scratched his arm when he was in the front garden; that's probably why there was blood on the blanket."

"And what did the police say?"

I just shrugged, and Dad huffed. I knew he was embarrassed that I looked out the window so much. He'd have preferred me to be on an Xbox or something, doing something *normal*.

"Pass me that brush, would you, son? I need to get around the edges."

In the corner of the conservatory and lying on top of a few sheets of newspaper was a thin, black brush. It was just within my reach. Without stepping onto the tiles I stretched awkwardly around and picked up the brush between my bare thumb and index finger. There was no way I was going to walk across Nigel's vomiting playground, but Dad wasn't making any sign that he'd walk toward me, so I was now stuck with the brush in my hand.

"Come on, Matthew. Give it here, I haven't got all day."

Dad stared at me, his roller in one hand, as I stared back, the brush in mine. We stood there like two bizarre cowboys waiting to see who was going to draw first. Just when I was considering throwing the brush at Dad and making a run for it, the doorbell rang.

"I'll get it!"

The brush clattered to the floor as I made my escape. Officer Campen was on the step with the man in the suit who'd tried to comfort Melissa Dawson when she'd collapsed.

"Matthew Corbin? Can we come in for a chat?"

I stood back and let them in as Mum and Dad appeared.

"Mr. and Mrs. Corbin, your son has said he remembered something else about the day Teddy went missing. We just need to ask him a few more questions."

We all shuffled silently toward the kitchen.

"Everyone for tea?" said Mum and she got some mugs out of the cupboard and filled the kettle up even though no one had said yes. The policeman in the business suit introduced himself as Detective Bradley and gave Dad his business card. He then asked me more of the same questions I'd heard before. How could I see so much from the window? What was I doing looking out in the first place? Was I aware the boy was on his own? And then he moved on to the blood. How much blood was there? Did I actually see it drip onto the blanket? Did I see Teddy use the blanket to wipe the blood? Why did he not call out to his granddad if he'd hurt himself enough to bleed?

"I don't know. He just looked at the cut for a bit and then carried on doing what he was doing. He's quite a tough kid, actually."

The detective looked up, puzzled.

"And why would you say that?"

I was on a bit of a roll now.

"Well, he didn't seem that bothered when he got pushed into the pond . . ."

I screwed my eyes shut. The detective looked at Officer Campen, who shrugged.

"What pond? Who pushed him in the pond?"

Mum and Dad stopped fiddling with the tea things and everyone stared at me. The kettle rumbled away and then clicked off.

"The day after they came to stay, Casey pushed Teddy into Mr. Charles's pond. He went in headfirst and she just stood there watching him."

The detective rubbed his face and his hand made a scratching noise against stubble that hadn't been there yesterday.

"And you saw this out of your window as well?"

I nodded, and then Mum piped up.

"It was a different window though, detective. It would have been in his bedroom, which is at the back and looks out on the yards. Isn't that right, Matthew?"

I nodded, uneasy. A sinister, dank fog oozed out of the creases of the kitchen cupboards. I coughed a little as it caught in my throat.

"Okay. We'll need to take a look at that. And then what happened? While you stood there in your bedroom watching a small child nearly drown."

The kitchen fell silent and I bit my lip as tears filled my eyes. I opened my mouth to say something but Dad stepped in.

"Look, detective, I think you should know that my son, my Matthew, has a serious condition that renders him practically housebound. You might think he's a bit of an oddball, but did you know that in a school of three thousand students around twenty of them have this condition?"

I gave Dad a smile as Detective Bradley raised his hands.

"I just want to establish how this child was put in danger and why it appears that an adult wasn't supervising him. Again. I'm not blaming your son, Mr. Corbin."

"I didn't just stand there," I said, my voice gruff. "I ran to the front of the house and shouted for Mr. Charles. He was across the street talking to Penny and Gordon, and when he got back to the pond, Casey had pulled him out."

Detective Bradley went to say something, but I spoke over him.

"Isn't it a bit odd that Mr. Charles hasn't told you about this himself? And don't you think it's unusual that he's been out in that yard today, mowing his lawn while the rest of the world is out looking for his grandson?"

My voice had become louder until I was practically shouting at him. It felt good, and to make it even better, Dad winked at me. Detective Bradley glared at Officer Campen.

"You didn't stop him mowing the lawn?"

Officer Campen looked stunned.

"I-I didn't know he was . . . I heard a mower but thought it was a few doors down, I . . ."

The policemen began to discuss who was where and when and then Officer Campen began to bark orders into his radio. Mum switched the kettle on again as she and Dad talked in hushed voices in the corner.

"I knew she looked wicked. Did you see her eyes, Brian? And that weird doll? Urgh, it gave me the creeps."

"Now come on, Sheila, you can't assume she had anything to do with him going missing."

I ran upstairs to the bathroom and washed my hands over and over. I gave a final rinse in hot water and heard the front door bang closed as the policemen left. From the top of the landing I could see the fog from the kitchen slowly rolling in waves across the floor, creeping its way upstairs.

CHAPTER NINETEEN

PENNY SULLIVAN

Back in my room, the sunlight made flickering stripes across my carpet. My room didn't feel right; everything needed to be cleaned. Every pencil, book, chair leg, lightbulb, the walls, all of it. I'd start at the top and work my way down to the baseboards and then I'd tackle the smaller items. I put on a pair of gloves and set to work.

Standing on the bed, which would need changing afterward, I began to wipe at the wall with a cloth soaked in antibacterial spray. The Wallpaper Lion had an ear—I'd never noticed that before. But it was there, peeking out from his matted mane: a small golden triangle.

"Melody thinks I'm lonely," I said to him. "Can you believe it? And she's collecting memorial cards. How sick is that? I know she got the gloves for me, but . . . that's just beyond wrong. Isn't it?"

The Wallpaper Lion's face shone and his drooping eye sparkled. He almost appeared to be smiling at me, enjoying his little wash.

I stopped and stared at him.

"What if she knows, Lion? What if she sees my note and realizes Callum's death was all my fault?"

The Wallpaper Lion carried on smiling. I imagined him shaking his mane, the tiny droplets of moisture raining everywhere.

Voices were coming from outside, and from here I could see Penny drinking from a mug as she stood on the patio talking to Mr. Charles. I got off the bed and put my cleaning stuff down, picking up my notebook.

1:25 p.m.-Penny Sullivan is next door. She's talking to Mr. Charles and every now and then she pats him on the arm.

He said something about going to see his sister for a few days and then his home phone began to ring and he lolloped back indoors. She watched him go into the house, then walked down the lawn to the mound of toys that Mr. Charles had dumped next to the shed. Shaking her head a few times, she looked over the pile and picked up a red bucket, which she tipped onto the grass. A few of Teddy's chunky, plastic cars fell out and she reached down and picked up a small, orange bulldozer, studying it closely before rolling it up and down her arm.

"What's she doing?" I said. I moved closer to the window.

Turning the bulldozer over, she spun each wheel using her thumb and then Mr. Charles reappeared.

"What is it? What's happened?" said Penny.

Mr. Charles had his head in his hands.

"It was my daughter . . . doesn't want anything to do with me . . . said it's all my fault . . ."

Penny put an arm around him as he began to cry, and they turned and slowly began walking back to the house. She was trying to hold her mug and the orange toy in one hand, and her tea slopped onto the grass.

Penny pats Mr. Charles on his back as he sobs. "He's such a dear boy," he says. "I'd never see him come to any harm. He's such a dear, dear boy." Turning her patting into a rub, Penny rests her head on his shoulder for a second. "I know, I know," she says. "He's such a funny little fellow."

I looked up from my notebook, and she was staring straight at me. I gave her a weak smile and saw her physically shudder.

Penny Sullivan hadn't liked me since Callum died.

I didn't have any grandparents—they'd died before I was born—and Mum always seemed to see Penny as a bit of a mother figure. She was around a lot when I was little, telling Mum what to cook and what to buy. She was the local agent for a catalog called *Harrington's Household Solutions*, which promised to *revolutionize your home with an assortment of items you can't live without!* Mum loved that catalog, and every month she would pore through it, oohing and aahing at some new fancy gadget that we'd never use.

Dad wasn't a fan of Penny. He thought she was too overbearing, and I don't think he liked the fact Mum took her advice so seriously. One winter Mum asked her what type of Christmas tree she should get.

"Stick with a fake one, Sheila. You'll still be hoovering up needles in

August if you get a real one. Harrington's are doing a lovely synthetic Nordic spruce in the catalog next month. That'll look picture-perfect in your window."

That particular year, Dad had wanted a real tree for a change, but Mum would never go against Penny's advice.

"She's life-experienced, Brian. That woman knows what she's talking about."

"Life-experienced? She's an interfering old bag, that's what she is. Always thinking she's right, never listening to what anyone else says. It's no wonder she's driven both of her kids away . . ."

But Mum didn't agree, and it was Penny she called in a panic when she had to rush to the hospital to have Callum. She arrived on our doorstep wearing a bright, fluffy, multicolored sweater and jeans, and she was carrying a large bag stuffed with games. I'd never seen her in casual clothes before. Gordon hovered behind her as always, a newspaper tucked under his arm. Over the afternoon and evening she taught me how to play Hangman, Dots and Boxes, and Battleship using just a pencil and paper, and we played some old board games that used to belong to her children, like Chinese Checkers. Gordon sat in Dad's armchair filling in a crossword puzzle and looked up every now and then when she told him what a good player I was.

"He's such a quick learner, Gordon! Not like our Jeremy. He could never get the hang of board games, could he, Gordon?"

Gordon just grunted and shook the paper before squinting down at it again.

Every now and then I asked if my new baby brother had arrived yet. I was so excited, and I couldn't understand why it was taking so long. Penny just answered:

"These things take time, Matthew. These things take time."

While we played our games I kept picking at a large spot that was just above my right eyebrow, which was annoying Penny.

"Pick, pick, pick, Matthew! Stop it now. If you carry on picking you'll end up with a scar, you know . . ."

She made beans on toast for dinner and we sat together at the kitchen table, waiting for news. I'd never seen anyone eat so delicately before. I remember sitting up straighter than I normally would, and I made sure I held my fork the right way.

"Penny? Do you think he'll have blond hair or brown hair like mine?"

"I don't know, Matthew. Eat your dinner now."

Pick, pick, pick.

"He might have no hair at all! Did your babies have hair, Penny? Do you have a boy or a girl?"

Pick, pick, pick.

"I have a son named Jeremy and a daughter named Anna and yes, they both had hair. Stop fiddling with that spot, now. There's a good boy."

I ate three more forkfuls of beans and put my cutlery down. Gordon got up and put his plate in the sink and then wandered off to the lounge without a word and I heard the TV turn on.

"Where are your children, Penny? Do they live near here?"

Pick, pick, pick.

"They don't, no. For some unfathomable reason they both decided to move abroad. Jeremy lives in Brazil and Anna in New Zealand."

I gawped at her.

"Wow, New Zealand is a million miles away. Do they come back to see you?"

She shook her head.

"Oh. Penny? What does un-un-fatha-umble mean?"

"It means inexplicable or incomprehensible."

She looked at my blank face.

"It means they both made a silly mistake and should have stayed here. Life would be a lot happier for both of them if they stopped being so stubborn and listened to what I said. Now eat up."

Her face was red, her lips pressed tightly together. I ate a few more forkfuls in silence, then picked at my spot again.

"Penny? Do Jeremy and Anna not like you very much?"

SLAM. Penny banged her hand down hard on the table.

"Matthew, I said stop picking that bloody spot or everyone will know what you did for the rest of your life!"

My orange juice had splashed over the edge of my cup and onto my dinner. Penny picked up her knife and fork and carried on eating as if nothing had happened.

I blinked back tears and told her that I wasn't feeling very hungry anymore, and she let me leave the table and go to my room.

It was pitch-black outside when I heard Dad's car pull up and I crept a little way down the stairs and sat quietly in the darkness.

Penny opened the door and waited as Dad lifted two suitcases out of the trunk—an overnight bag for Mum and a hospital bag for the baby, the tiny white clothes inside still unused. Mum headed straight for Penny's open arms, but just as she stepped into the hallway her legs went out from under her. It was as if she'd fallen into quicksand, and she sank slowly, deep, deep down. Penny knelt on the floor beside her and held her in her arms, stroking her hair and rocking her back and forth as my mum sobbed.

"It's okay, let it all go . . . It's okay . . . I'm here, Penny's here . . ."

I crept upstairs and went into the bathroom, locked the door, and began to wash my hands. I knew I was to blame for this, and I knew that if I washed away all the germs then they couldn't hurt anyone else. I just needed to keep on top of it from now on, like a big boy, that was all. That's all I needed to do.

And that's when it started. Secretly at first; for years I could easily sneak off to the bathroom and wash my hands over and over without anyone noticing. But then Hannah and Mr. Jenkins announced to everyone that they were expecting a baby, and *bam.* Things got a lot worse.

Fortunately I didn't think anyone had stopped to look back through time and figure out why I was doing what I was doing, but it was simple really.

I cleaned because Callum died, and Callum died because of me.

CHAPTER TWENTY

THE SIGHTING

"It'll say it on that thing that scrolls along the bottom, won't it, Brian? The tickle?"

Dad had taken time-out from decorating to watch the news.

"It's called a ticker, Sheila. A ticker. Not a tickle."

Mum had called us both into the living room saying that Penny had texted and there was some kind of update about Teddy on the news. I paced around the carpet trying to relax. My knuckles were cracked and bleeding from my constant washing; the blood had freaked me out, so I cleaned them over and over, but then they just bled even more. Around and around I spun, back on my stupid wheel.

"Stop going back and forth, Matthew. You're making me dizzy."

We all stared at the TV. Dad kept tutting, saying would it just hurry up.

"Penny's always sticking her big nose in where it's not wanted. Are you sure she's right?"

Mum fiddled with her phone to try and find the text again.

"Look—it's on!" I said. Mum dropped the phone and grabbed the remote control, turning the volume up even though it was only being reported on the ticker for now. Dad read the scrolling white words out loud.

"Breaking News. Police investigate a suspected sighting of the missing toddler, Teddy Dawson, boarding a ferry with a man and woman in Harwich yesterday. Police in Holland are working alongside the British forces."

As the ticker ended, Dad turned back to the conservatory to carry on painting.

"See?" he said. "I told you they'd find him. He'll be all over the CCTV cameras—he'll be home before long, I bet."

Mum turned the TV off and went into the kitchen. I followed, stopping when I reached the tiled floor.

"That would be good, wouldn't it? Maybe we could have a little party or something? I'll see what Penny says. She'd love to organize that."

Mum had just begun to load the dishwasher when the doorbell rang.

"Answer that for me, Matthew?"

I went to the hall and recognized the outline of the figure behind the frosted glass door. She was dressed in black with pink flip-flops. I ignored the second bell and ran upstairs.

"Matthew? Why didn't you answer it?" shouted Mum as she opened the front door.

I paced around my room, wondering if I should run to the bathroom and lock myself in, when my door was pushed open. I stood by my window with my arms folded.

"Hi, Matthew."

Her eyes looked puffy with dark rings underneath and her

hair was pulled back into a ponytail. In her arms she was carrying a large brown photograph album, and I had an awful feeling it was something for me.

"I think we need to talk. I know you think I'm some kind of lunatic after the graveyard but I'm not, okay? There's all that crazy stuff going on out there with Teddy missing, and I think we could be good friends if you just saw me for the person I am, not the person you think I am."

Her cheeks flushed pink. The little speech had clearly been rehearsed, and as she waited for me to say something her dark eyes flittered around my room, taking everything in. A deep, barely audible growl rumbled from the corner, and I glanced up at the Wallpaper Lion and glared at him.

Something caught her eye outside and she stepped toward the window.

"Is Mr. Charles watering his yard?"

I looked out and saw the old man was slowly saturating his flower bed using his hose.

"Why would you bother doing something like that when your grandson is missing?" said Melody.

We watched him move along the garden, one footstep at a time, and she rested her head against the side of the wall. I flinched.

"Melody, I think you should go now. I've got a few things I need to do. Lots of things, actually. And I really don't like people being in my room, you know? After what I told you about?"

She continued to stare at Mr. Charles.

"Did you know that if you spray a hose in a certain direction and the sun is in the right place you can see a rainbow?"

I watched as the sun glinted on the sparkling spray, but I couldn't spot any colors.

"Dad showed me once when he still lived with us. He said, 'If you look carefully enough you can see beautiful things in almost anything.' I don't think that's true though, do you?"

She turned to face me. The sores on my hands were throbbing so much I would have to ask Mum for a painkiller before long.

"Melody, I really need you to go. Please?"

But she became all businesslike and shook her head.

"No. I'm not going. This won't take long and it's really important."

She kicked her flip-flops off and sat cross-legged on my duvet. As simple as that. I felt physically sick.

"D-didn't you hear me? I asked you to go. And don't you think you should have some socks on if you've got verrucas?"

I paced to the window, to the door, to the window, and back to the door. Her head went from side to side as if she were watching a tennis match.

"I'll be quick," she said, putting the album on her lap and taking a deep breath. "I thought if I explained why I took the cards from the graveyard, then you'd understand."

Tucking a stray hair behind one ear, she watched me with

dark eyes. I forced myself to stop by my dresser and repeated a phrase in my head while she spoke.

Everything can be cleaned . . . Everything can be cleaned . . . Everything can be cleaned . . .

"The church throws away all the cards and gifts that have been left on the graves after they've been there for a certain amount of days. The relatives know about it, it's all okay with them; they don't expect to get any of it back. I just take what's lying around before it ends up in the trash."

I frowned.

"That's great. Nice to know. Right, now you can go, okay?"

She rested her chin on the album that she held to her chest and completely ignored me.

"As you know, before Dad left I used to sneak out and go to the graveyard to get away from all the shouting. One day I saw a memorial card on the ground with a muddy footprint across it. I picked it up and it said, 'My dearest Mary, I am hollow without you. Love, Jack.' I took the card home, dried it off on the radiator, and kept it. That card was so heartbreaking and it was being walked over like a piece of rubbish. It just didn't seem right. That was my first one, and I've been collecting them ever since. Now I can't bear to think that they're going to be thrown out, so I pick up what I can and keep them safe."

She took a deep breath and her cheeks flushed pink again as she held the album out to me.

"Just take a look, okay?"

The brown book dangled between us and I tucked my hands behind my back.

"Uh, can you open it for me?" I asked.

Melody waited for a second, then shrugged and put it down on my bed, turning the front cover over. I took a step closer. The folder was like a ring binder with sheets of plastic inlays—little pockets of all different sizes designed to hold cards. Postcards, antique cigarette cards, that kind of thing. But on these cards there were doves, flowers, crosses. I studied the first page.

Rest In Peace, Uncle Cyril. We will miss you always. Love, Sarah & John.

Sleep tight my darling. Christine x

Miss you forever my sweet pea. Your Frank.

Dad—my wonderful hero. Until we meet again. Your son, Tommy x

There was even some in a child's handwriting:

Granddad, you made us laugh when you snored so loud! We hope it's nice in heaven. Love, Katie, Becky, and Joshua

Melody was watching my face, trying to gauge my reaction as she slowly turned the pages. I had a lump in my throat and didn't know what to say. Then I spotted some handwriting I recognized.

"Stop there a second," I said.

In the top corner of a page there was a card with a little blue teddy bear sitting beside a white cross. Underneath, in blue ink, it read:

Our baby boy Callum. We never had the chance to see you grow, but we love you each and every day. Mummy, Daddy, and Matty xxx

Tears stung my eyes. I knew Mum visited his grave every now and then, but I didn't realize she'd left messages for him.

"Where did you get this one?" I said, pointing at the card.

"By the angel. The big, white angel near the front of the church. Why?"

"No reason."

It was me, it was all my fault he died was dancing around on my tongue, but I quickly swallowed it away. She obviously had no idea he was my brother, and there was no sign of the note I'd left saying sorry. It had probably been thrown away by the church, or lost. I relaxed a tiny bit as Melody picked up the book and hugged it again.

"So. What do you think?"

I sighed.

"Well, it's a bit weird, to be honest."

She frowned and looked down at my hands before standing up.

"Oh that reminds me. You still owe me the money for those gloves."

We glared at each other for a moment and then she smiled at me, knowing she'd made a point.

"I guess there's no harm if they were being thrown away anyway," I said. "And it must have been hard, you know . . . with your dad leaving and everything."

She nodded and bit her top lip.

"Look. Let's just forget it, okay?" I said. "I'm not saying I agree with it, but if it's not upsetting anyone, then it doesn't matter what I think."

She grinned.

"Good. We're wasting time arguing anyway. Did you hear about the sighting?"

"Yes. It doesn't mean it was definitely him though."

Melody nodded. "My thought too. We need to carry on investigating, Matty. Have you found anything out yet?"

I told her about seeing Old Nina trying to get the white fabric out of her tree after I'd left the graveyard.

"Whatever it was, she seemed very eager to get to it."

Melody frowned.

"And what's with the lamp she had in her window?" she said. "It's not on anymore! Did you see? Do you think it means something?"

I shrugged, pleased that she'd noticed it had been turned off as well.

"I don't know, I've been wondering about that myself. Is it just a coincidence that it's been off since Teddy went missing?"

"Right," she said, standing up and ready for action. "I'll go and see if I can find out what's in her tree, and you find out about the lamp. Your parents have lived here longer than my mum. Maybe they know something?"

I nodded and she smiled at me.

"You're all right, Matthew Corbin. A bit of a stress-head maybe, but I think we're going to make a great team!"

And with that she blew me a kiss and ran out the door.

CHAPTER TWENTY-ONE

OLD NINA'S LAMP

Dad poked his head around my door at 10:23 p.m. I was laying on top of my bed in my pajama shorts and T-shirt. It was too hot to get under the sheets.

"It wasn't Teddy on that ferry," Dad said sadly. "It was just a little boy who looked the same on his way to see his grandparents in Holland."

"Well, that's good, isn't it?" I said, pushing myself up onto my elbows. "If it *was* him, he could have been anywhere by now!"

Dad didn't look so sure.

"He could still be anywhere. Anyway, try not to think about it and get a good night's sleep, okay?" He turned to go.

"Dad? Can I ask you something?"

He took a couple of steps into my room.

"You know Old Nina? Why does she have that lamp on in her window all the time?"

Dad rubbed his chin.

"Ah, well, that's a sad story, actually. Really sad."

He perched himself on the edge of my desk and I laid down and looked up at the Wallpaper Lion as I concentrated on his voice:

"A long time ago, when Nina wasn't very old, she went on

holiday to Norfolk with her husband, the vicar, and their son, Michael. He was eleven years old at the time."

I looked at him.

"A son? I didn't know she had a son."

Dad nodded. That must be the boy that Jake and I had seen in the photos on Halloween.

"They'd been going to the same cottage every year since Michael had been born, spending a week by the sea. On the third day of this particular trip they settled themselves on one of the beaches and Michael headed off on the long walk to the sea. Norfolk is very flat, you know, and at low tide the sea can roll away so far that it disappears from view, so Nina and the vicar knew their son would be gone for a while.

"Midday came and Michael still hadn't returned for his lunch, but they weren't worried. Like I said, the sea was *such* a long way away, and he would have spent a good while having a swim before he made the trek back again. They kept thinking that any minute now they'd spot his figure growing bigger on the horizon as he headed toward them.

"Another hour passed, and then another, and then the sea began to rumble in. It was then that they alerted the coast guard."

Dad stopped for a moment and stared at my carpet.

"A team of boats searched into the night, but Michael was never found. They drove home in darkness, and when they got back to the Rectory, Nina switched on the lamp that was in the window. They stayed up all night waiting for news, but none came.

Morning arrived and the lamp was left on and forgotten about, but when it got dark that evening Nina looked at the warm orange glow and decided there and then to leave it on permanently. She felt the light would somehow show her son the way home."

I shivered and pulled the sheet over me.

"They never found out what happened to him?"

Dad shook his head.

"No."

"And she's still waiting? She's been leaving the lamp on, hoping her son is going to come back after all these years?"

Dad stood up.

"I doubt it after all this time. It's probably become just a comfort to her now."

He rubbed his hair and gave a yawn.

"Right, it's getting late now, young man. You'd better get some sleep."

He walked out of my room and went to close the door.

"Can you leave it open tonight, please, Dad?"

"Sure," he said and he pushed the door a little wider.

I rolled over and closed my eyes, but all I could see was the face of the boy with the freckles in the photo in Old Nina's hallway. I imagined his wet feet padding along the pavement and pictured him standing in front of the old, black door in his sodden swimming shorts, dripping sea onto the path. He'd bang the heavy knocker, a puddle circling around him as he waited on the step. Old Nina would open the door and scream in delight as she threw her arms around him. She'd usher him inside and wrap him in a towel and a warm blanket.

Sorry, Mum. That took a bit longer than I expected.

His mum would hold her hands to her face as she stood, mesmerized by the glorious boy standing in front of her.

You're back! she'd cry. *You've come back to me at last.*

And all because she'd kept the orange lamp burning brightly to guide him home.

CHAPTER TWENTY-TWO

KNOCKING AT NUMBER ELEVEN

I woke up early, the plan already formed in my mind. I put on some fresh gloves and opened the bottom drawer of my bedside cabinet and took out a pair of black binoculars that I had received four Christmases ago. No one had touched them since, which was a good thing—they'd be entirely germ-free.

I went to the office, knelt down in front of the windowsill, and rested my elbows on the ledge as I pointed the lenses outside. It took a while to adjust them properly, but slowly the red bricks of the Rectory came into focus. I looked around. The lamp was still off, and the flowers at the top of her steps, which she used to water at ten o'clock every morning, had died. One hung limply over the side, as if making a last-ditch attempt to make a run for it and find water. Why had she neglected them? And was the lamp off because she didn't need it on anymore? Had she found a replacement for her lost son, Michael? I fixed on a small triangle of space in the corner of her bedroom window and waited.

Dad got in the shower and Mum padded past without seeing me and went downstairs. I could hear her talking to Nigel, who was meowing loudly for breakfast. Twenty minutes later Dad came out of the shower and he didn't notice me either as he went downstairs.

Forty-six minutes I sat in that position. Forty-six. My arms were so numb I felt like I could just get up, walk away, and leave them there, binoculars in my hands permanently fixed on the Rectory. While I was blinking a few times to try and clear my drying eyes, I saw a flash of something brushing the curtain along the top windowsill. I tried to zoom in and fiddled with the little wheel at the bridge of my nose, but everything blurred. I twisted it the other way and the view cleared again. There was another flash as it darted one way, then back again. Whatever it was, it was quick— quicker than an old woman. My hands trembled a little and I took a deep breath and concentrated hard on a small gap in the curtain, willing it to move again. Then an old, white hand appeared and pulled the heavy curtains shut. I scanned the rest of the house, but there was nothing else to see. I sat back for a moment, my heart hammering in my chest.

"I've found him," I said aloud. "I know *exactly* who's got him!"

I ran to the bathroom, peeling off the gloves and washing my hands with lots and lots of hot water and soap, ignoring the pain. My breathing was fast, but this time it was due to excitement, not anxiety. My face felt tense, and when I looked in the mirror I saw I had a big, wide grin. I chuckled to myself and put on a fresh pair of gloves before quickly getting dressed. I ran downstairs and, not letting myself think about what I was actually doing, I marched quickly outside and over to Mr. Charles's house.

I banged on the front door with my elbow. As I stood on the path next to the rosebushes where Teddy had been picking petals so recently, my legs began to shake. Mr. Charles opened the door in his dressing gown.

"Mr. Charles! You need to get someone to go around to the Rectory. She's got Teddy in there!" I said, perhaps a little too happily.

He wasn't smiling.

"I'm sorry, Matthew. What was that?" he said and he stepped out, closing the door a little behind him. He looked left and right. Everywhere but at me.

"It's Old Nina! She's got Teddy in there!"

He folded his arms. "Now why would you think that?"

"I saw something up there in that bedroom."

I pointed up at the window now obscured by a tree. Mr. Charles looked toward the old house.

"What? What did you see?"

"I-I saw something flash across the glass. Something small and fast."

I grinned, but Mr. Charles was frowning.

"And it was Teddy? This flash you saw was my grandson?"

I shrugged.

"I think so. I-I don't know . . ."

The old man rubbed his chin.

"And her lamp's been turned off," I continued. "It's been like that since he went missing."

Mr. Charles looked at me directly now, his face blank.

"So?"

I was fidgeting and I tried to keep still.

Ring, ring. Ring, ring.

A telephone was ringing inside Mr. Charles's house. I tried not to count the rings, but I couldn't help myself.

"The lamp being turned off means she's not waiting for her lost son to come home anymore. And . . . and she's got this thing stuck in her tree that looks like a kid's T-shirt!"

The phone had rung five times now.

"A T-shirt?" said Mr. Charles, interested now.

Seven. It was up to seven rings. I shook my head. I had to stop counting.

"Yes! Maybe. I'm . . . I'm not sure."

I realized I should have at least waited until Melody had investigated that part. Mr. Charles looked around again. I was being erased from his line of vision.

"So she turned off a lamp and has got something in her tree . . ."

Nine rings. I screwed up my eyes.

"Your phone is ringing, Mr. Charles," I interrupted.

"You saw something in her window, but you don't know what it was . . ."

"Yes, but it was small and fast. *And* she's not watered her flowers."

He just stared at me. The phone sounded so loud in the silence. Eleven rings. This was getting dangerous now.

"Okay, mustn't forget the flowers. She's neglected to water her flowers. And this all makes her a kidnapper?"

"Aren't you going to answer it, Mr. Charles? I—"

I couldn't speak as I counted two more rings.

And that was it.

The phone had stopped after tenplusthree rings.

I really needed to concentrate.

"I'm sorry, Matthew. I appreciate the effort, but it all sounds pretty unlikely to me. Nina is an old friend of mine, and there is no way she's behind all of this."

The dangerous number seeped out from under Mr. Charles's front door, looking for me. Looking to take ahold of my throat and not let go. I had to be quick.

"Her lamp was always on for her dead son and it's been turned off because she's found a replacement . . . Her flowers have died because she hasn't got the time to water them anymore . . . It all makes sense!"

Mr. Charles's mouth was slightly open.

"And she's got a cellar, damn it!"

"Watch your language there!" he said sternly.

Thirteen.

13, 13, 13, 13.

THIRTEEN.

The numbers scrolled through my mind like the news ticker we had watched the other day.

. . . BREAKING NEWS . . . 13, 13, 13, 13, 13, 13, 13, 13, 13, 13, 13, 13, 13 . . .

I tried to count in my head.

"You've got to tell the police!"

One, two, three, four, five, six, seven.

It wasn't working. The counterbalancing wasn't working now and the number still had power over me. I just wasn't concentrating hard enough.

One, two, three, four, five, six, seven.

I was making twenty, but it still felt like I was stuck on tenplusthree. The number rolled toward me on a poisonous fog.

"Son, I don't want to upset you, but don't you think you've just got too much time on your hands . . . ?"

He stooped toward me, his head to one side. I coughed as the fog seeped up into my nostrils. I closed my eyes and began again.

One, two, three, four—

"Do you understand what I'm saying? I'm not trying to be rude, but . . ."

One, two, three—

". . . you're stuck in that house most days and . . ."

One, two, three, four, five—

". . . I don't know what your parents are doing to help you, but . . ."

I opened my eyes.

"Would you just shut up a minute? I'm trying to think."

One, two, three, four, five, six, seven . . .

The old man stood upright.

"Did you just tell me to shut up?"

"No—I mean yes . . . I just have to concentrate on something real quick."

The tears were close now so I began to walk backward, continuously counting to seven.

"I'm just . . . I've just got to think of something in my head . . ."

Mr. Charles unfolded his arms and stepped back into his house before he called out:

"No more interfering, eh, Matthew?"

———————

When I got back Mum was waiting for me in the hallway.

"Matthew? Where've you been?"

I didn't look at her.

"I just, I just told Mr. Charles something."

She folded her arms.

"Told him what? What's going on?"

I couldn't think what to say. Dad appeared behind her eating a slice of toast.

"I-I said I thought maybe Old Nina might know where Teddy is."

"You what?" said Dad, his eyes wide. "What on earth . . ."

"It's what you said about her son!" I said.

Mum clucked her tongue at Dad. "Brian, you didn't . . ."

"She's got him in there, I swear!"

I kicked off my shoes and ran upstairs, slamming my door.

The Wallpaper Lion looked disappointed with me. Ashamed, almost. I cleaned and cleaned while continually counting from one to seven in my head until the morning had gone. I was exhausted.

"I know why they don't believe me. They think I'm useless. That's why," I said to the Lion as I stood by the window.

"But I'm not, am I? I'm not useless. I was the last person to see him! If it wasn't for me, they wouldn't know about the blood on the blanket. And that's just for starters!"

The Wallpaper Lion's eye stared ahead. Even he was bored with me. I looked out at the pile of toys by Mr. Charles's shed. It looked like they were ready for the dump. I went to the office to write it down in my notebook, but something else outside caught my eye.

Thursday, July 31st. Bedroom. Hot and cloudy.
2:03 p.m.-The door of the Rectory just opened and Old Nina came out with a shopping bag on her arm.

That was weird. She *never* went shopping on Thursdays.

She's wearing a pale blue blouse and navy skirt. Taking a quick look around first, she makes a dash for it, heading down the street.

Maybe this was my chance to prove to Mr. Charles and Mum and Dad that something was going on. I quickly typed an email.

To: Melody Bird

From: Matthew Corbin

Re: Quick!

Old Nina has gone out. Can you follow her?!

The minutes ticked by with no reply. What if Melody was out? With every second, Old Nina got farther away. How long could I afford to wait?

I paced around the office. No one else would realize how strange this was. The only time that Old Nina ever went out was on Friday mornings, when she would leave at approximately 10:30 a.m. and return around 11:30 a.m. with one bag of shopping. I quickly flicked through my notes to check I was right. Apart from watering the flowers on her step each morning and shopping on a Friday I had never, ever seen her leave the house. She was up to something, and it was down to me to find out what it was.

CHAPTER TWENTY-THREE
FOLLOWING OLD NINA

I hadn't given myself a chance to think about it—I'd just yelled at Mum and Dad that I was going out, and then I sprinted down the road. The policeman with the yellow tape at the end of the road had gone. The neighborhood was open once more.

It wasn't long before I had to stop and walk. Aside from the fact that I was unfit, the heat was suffocating and the traffic deafening. My head vibrated with the noise.

As I got closer to town, Teddy's face began to stare out at me. On lampposts, bus shelters, on the sides of trash cans and in every shop window—"MISSING: TEDDY DAWSON" posters were everywhere. It was the same photograph the TV reporter had held up on the news—the one of him in his little suit with his still-damp eyes.

I puffed along High Street like an old man, my heart pounding, but I felt good. I'd done it! I was out and I was actually *doing* something. I was *investigating*.

I looked through every shop window that I passed to see if I could spot a pale blue blouse. I got to the crosswalk and waited for someone to press the button, my gloved hands hidden in my pockets. Suddenly she was there, on the opposite side of the road. She shuffled along, her back bent over as she put her bag down on the ground so that she could push the button. It tipped forward and two balls of blue wool dropped onto the curb. She quickly grabbed them and stuffed them back into the bag, her pink scalp showing through her thin, white hair. The lights changed and I tucked my chin low and quickly crossed, avoiding any eye contact as we passed each other in the middle of the road. A few people were waiting at a bus stop and I hovered nearby, keeping my distance from anyone as I watched her go into a newsstand.

Balls of wool. Balls of *blue* wool. Was she making an outfit for a small boy? Or maybe she was planning on knitting something to replace his blue blanket! An old man walked up behind me and placed his shopping bags down with a huff. I realized he thought I was part of the bus line so I edged back slightly, keeping an eye on the other side of the road.

My throat was dry and I needed to wash. I needed to wash very, very soon. But a tiny little voice deep inside me was telling me that I could do this. If I didn't touch anything and kept at a good distance, then I could watch Old Nina and get all the proof I needed that she had kidnapped Teddy. Then I could sprint home. Or maybe jog—yes, definitely *jog* home, then I'd tell the police and get straight into the shower and everything would be all right again.

Everyone in the line began to jostle around as a bus arrived. I turned to go but walked straight into the old man behind me, stumbling over his bags.

"Whoa, slow down! What's the rush?" he said and he put his hands up. As I fell forward my cheek brushed against his dirty, brown cardigan and I got wafts of peppermint, vinegar, and stale aftershave. There was an orange, crusty stain near the buttons that looked like dried egg. I steadied myself, revealing my gloved hands, but he didn't notice them.

"You all right, boy? You look like you've seen a ghost. I know I'm old, but I'm still alive, you know!"

As he laughed, stringy, white saliva stretched like elastic bands in the corners of his mouth.

"I-I . . . I'm sorry," I said as I stepped over his bags. "I'm so sorry."

So that was it. There was no way I could cope with that degree of exposure. I'd have to go home and wash immediately.

"Listen, son, if it's worth knocking an old man over for, it must be important. Off you go!"

And then he threw back his head and laughed again and a gold molar twinkled in the sunlight. Putting my head down, I turned toward home. It was no good; I'd failed. My face was burning where it had brushed against the old man's cardigan. I felt dizzy and my heart was pounding so badly it felt like it was about to erupt through my rib cage. My eardrums were throbbing and my throat felt gritty, but most of all I really, really needed to wash. I needed clean water—gallons and gallons of it—and lots and lots of soap. New packets of soap. Unopened and sterile.

I walked back to the traffic light and began to cross the road. Old Nina was just coming out of the newsstand, a magazine poking out of the top of her bag. She was headed in the direction of home but suddenly paused. Something had caught her eye in the window of a pharmacy. She put her shopping bag down and leaned forward, her forehead inches from the glass as she blinked at the display. I stood still, trying to look as if I was just waiting for someone. After a few seconds she picked up the bag, brushed her wispy hair from her forehead, and carried on along her way.

I jogged toward the window. Displayed symmetrically in a pyramid shape were boxes of pull-up diapers, the repeated photograph of the single toddler on its packaging faded in the sun. I looked up and watched as her pale blue blouse disappeared around a corner.

CHAPTER TWENTY-FOUR
HARRINGTON'S
HOUSEHOLD SOLUTIONS

"So you're out *again*! Who'd have thought it? The Goldfish Boy seen out *twice* in public!"

Jake grinned from ear to ear like some manic Cheshire Cat as he stood astride his bike at the top of our road. In the distance I could see Old Nina just closing her front door behind her.

"What did you call me?" I took a step toward him and he held his hands up.

"Whoa! All right, freak! No need to have a fit."

I tried to walk around him but he rolled his bike back, blocking my way like he'd done in the alleyway.

"What's with the gloves?" he said.

"None of your business," I said as I put my hands in my pockets.

Jake scratched at the back of his neck and a red mark appeared where he'd broken the skin and drawn blood. He studied his fingernails and I darted around him.

"So, you do think it's Old Nina after all then?"

I stopped and turned to him.

"What?"

He looked smug.

"I saw Melody trying to see into Old Nina's yard earlier. Is it to do with that thing in her tree?"

I didn't say anything.

He wiped his nose with the back of his hand.

"Anyway, I don't know why you're bothering. The kid's clearly dead. You and Melody are wasting your time if you ask me."

"You have no idea what's happened to Teddy Dawson, Jake."

Two plainclothes policemen were talking in front of Mr. Charles's house, and they both looked up at us for a moment and then carried on with their conversation.

"No I don't," said Jake. "But maybe *you* do, eh? Maybe you know where he went, Goldfish Boy?"

My throat tightened.

"Don't call me that."

Jake laughed.

"Ah, come on. Everyone is saying it! It was that little kid next door to you who started it. Teddy's sister. Mum told me she'd called you that when she was there phoning the police. She said, 'The Goldfish Boy probably knows where he went.'"

I swallowed.

"So, what did you see from that window of yours then, hey?"

I blinked away the tears.

"Stop it."

Jake laughed again, his head up high.

"You should be pleased—you're famous!"

He adopted a news anchor's voice.

"The Goldfish Boy was the last person to see Teddy Dawson alive. How exactly does that make him feel?"

He waved an invisible microphone at me and I took a step to the side. I felt like I was gasping for air. I swallowed and swallowed again.

"He's not dead!" I shouted and my voice echoed down the street. One of the policemen stretched his neck to watch us.

"Look, I'm sorry to burst your fluffy little bubble, but if a kid goes missing and a few days later they find blood on his blanket, then it's not exactly going to end happily ever after, is it? Life's tough. Deal with it."

He rolled his bike back and adjusted his pedal to leave. My legs were trembling.

"He scratched his arm. That's why there was blood on his blanket," I said.

Jake turned back.

"How do you know?"

"Well, you said it yourself. I was the last person to see him al—to see him. He was playing in the front garden and he scratched his arm on a thorn and blood got onto his blanket. That answer your question?"

He did a kind of shrug.

"Melody didn't even try to get the thing out of the tree, you know. She just stared at it over the fence. I can help if you want. With this investigating you're trying to do?"

I laughed.

"You? Help? When have you ever wanted to help anyone besides yourself?"

His face fell, and then he let me have it.

"Me?! You should talk! I didn't see you trying to help me when everyone said my eczema was infectious! Or when Mr. Jenkins called me a loser all those times. I didn't see you sitting next to me when no one else dared. Where were you, eh? Where were you, *friend*?" He said *friend* sarcastically, eyes shiny with tears that he quickly blinked away.

I opened my mouth to say something, but he held up his hand.

"You know what, Matthew? Forget it. I wouldn't want a friend like you anyway."

He was speaking the truth and it hurt. He pushed his pedal up with the top of his foot and cycled away.

The policemen outside number eleven had gone indoors and Gordon was just coming out of number one with a large box in his arms. He crossed the road and walked toward our house. That was all I needed. I just wanted to get home.

I followed him up our path and stood behind him as he rang our doorbell, trying to find the space to slip past. The box was covered with the *Harrington's Household Solutions* logo: Mum must have been ordering from Penny again. Tucked awkwardly under one arm was the latest catalog, which dropped onto our step.

"Could you pick that up for me, son?" he said, without saying hello. I stared down at the open pages. A man with a tanned face holding a silver cocktail shaker in one hand smiled up at me. He looked like the happiest man on earth.

"Matthew? The catalog?"

I reached down and picked it up using my finger and thumb, not caring he'd see my gloves. Dad opened the door.

"Ah, Gordon. Wonderful. Thanks for bringing it over," he said, taking the box and leaning against the doorframe. I stepped to one side to try and get around, but the entrance was completely blocked now.

"No problem, Brian. No problem at all. Sorry it's late. Penny's a bit behind with the orders, you know, what with . . ." He wiped the top of his balding head with his palm as he nodded toward Mr. Charles's house.

"Well, if she needs Sheila to help, just say."

"Thanks, Brian. And let me know if you need a hand with this." He tapped his fingers on the top of the cardboard box.

"I hate decorating, but I can't keep putting it off. Sheila won't let me anyway!"

Dad shook the box in his arms and gave a little laugh. I jiggled around on the step. I just wanted to get in and straight into the shower to wash all the disease away.

"Excuse me," I said and I made a dash for it, brushing against Gordon's arm and crashing into the box in Dad's arms. I threw the catalog onto the stairs.

"Matthew, be careful!" said Dad, stumbling. "Sorry about that, Gordon."

"No problem. Anyway, I'd better be off. You know . . . back to Penny, indoors," said Gordon, nodding toward his own house now.

"Thank you, Gordon. And remember, if Penny needs a hand, just say, okay?"

He pushed the front door closed with his foot and carried the box to the conservatory while I kicked off my shoes.

"Matthew. I need to talk to you about your room," he said, but I was already upstairs, heading for the shower.

CHAPTER TWENTY-FIVE

MR. RORY JENKINS

To: Jake Bishop

From: Matthew Corbin

Subject: Old Nina's Tree

Hi, Jake.

You're right. We do need your help. How about trying to get that thing out of Old Nina's tree?

Matthew

He replied ten minutes later.

To: Matthew Corbin

From: Jake Bishop

Re: Old Nina's Tree

I'll go into her yard tonight after dark.

Jake

It was late and I was sitting at the computer, my hair still wet from the shower. There was another message from Melody, apologizing for missing my earlier email, as she'd been out. She said she hadn't had any luck seeing what was in the tree. I hit Reply.

To: Melody Bird

From: Matthew Corbin

Re: Quick!

No problem. Jake is going to try and get the thing out of Old
Nina's tree TONIGHT. I know, I know, it's Jake Bishop—but
I think he could be useful?

And hey, guess what? I followed Old Nina today! She went out
and she *never* goes out on Thursdays. She bought balls of
wool and she was staring weirdly at some diapers in the window
of a pharmacy! She didn't buy any but isn't that a bit odd???!!!

Matthew

After I sent it I cringed. My so-called evidence looked completely ridiculous now. Melody quickly answered.

To: Matthew Corbin

From: Melody Bird

Re: Quick!

Jake Bishop? Are you mad?!!

To: Melody Bird

From: Matthew Corbin

Re: Quick!

I know, but let's give him a chance, OK? I kind of owe him.

Matthew

I turned the computer off and went to bed.

When I eventually drifted off I dreamed about Teddy . . .

I was at the window again, watching him pick the petals, but when he reached up for a flower he stumbled forward and fell straight into the roses. The branches snaked around his little body, wrapping him up tightly like a spider wraps a fly. Within seconds the bush had swallowed him whole and Teddy had disappeared.

My neighbors gathered, each of them calling out as if they were all playing a game of hide-and-seek.

"Teddy! Where are you?" called Mr. Charles.

"Come out, come out, wherever you are!" Old Nina cried.

I ran into the road and shouted at them all.

"It's the rosebush! The rosebush has got him. Listen to me! You've got to check the rosebush!"

Melody was there, and Penny and Gordon, Jake, Hannah with her swollen belly and Mr. Jenkins and Old Nina; as I ran around they started to laugh.

"Quick, get back in your tank, Matty!" said Melody, laughing so much she was nearly crying. "You're going to die out here!"

I woke with a jolt at 3:22 a.m., wet with sweat. I lay there for a bit and tried to go back to sleep, but every time I shut my eyes I saw Teddy tangled in the branches. I got out of bed and crept to the office.

Mr. Charles's front yard was empty and I could just make out a few pastel flowers bobbing in the darkness. There was no little blond boy in the roses. Teddy wasn't there.

I turned to go back to bed, but then I spotted a figure in the shadows outside the Rectory. At first I thought it might be Jake on his mission, but this figure was too tall. It began to walk toward number three and I realized it was Mr. Jenkins. What was he doing out at this time of night? Wearing pajama bottoms and a T-shirt, he clearly hadn't been out of bed for long; his hair was sticking up in all directions. In his left hand was a tiny, orange glow. I couldn't believe it: Mr. Jenkins, the fitness-crazy, know-it-all, bullying teacher, was smoking!

He walked around the close, his eyes constantly on Mr. Charles's house. When he got to Penny and Gordon's house, he threw the cigarette onto the ground and left it there, burning, as he crossed over the road. He stood by the gate of number eleven and peered around the rosebushes and hedges, having a good look around. What was he doing? I stepped out of view as he turned toward home, and a few seconds later I heard his front door shut quietly. I went back to bed and took out my notebook.

Teddy's Disappearance: New Suspects List

1. Old Nina
2. Mr. Charles
3. Casey
4. Mr. Jenkins???

Jake emailed first thing.

> **To: Melody Bird; Matthew Corbin**
> **From: Jake Bishop**
> **Subject: The Case of the Mysterious White Thing Stuck in a Tree**
> It's a tea towel!!!!!
> Well done, Sherlock and Watson.
> Jake

A few minutes later, Melody replied.

> **To: Jake Bishop; Matthew Corbin**
> **From: Melody Bird**
> **Subject: MIND YOUR OWN BUSINESS!!!**
> Look, Jake Bishop, I never asked you to get involved, so if you don't have anything useful to say, I suggest you crawl back to your pathetic excuse for a life. OK?!

> **To: Matthew Corbin**
> **From: Jake Bishop**
> **Subject: Melody**
> Geez, she can't take a joke, can she?!!
> J

I didn't want to get involved, so I switched the computer off and went to my room.

I cleaned for most of the morning and it still didn't feel right. I went over the back of my door for a fourth time and then I tackled the legs on my bed, the legs on my dresser, and the legs on my bedside cabinet. Cleaning these would mean that the germs would have less opportunity to travel upward and spread around.

Dad was outside stacking up cans of paint, brushes, and dust sheets on the lawn as Mum came out of the conservatory carrying an armful of wet laundry. Hannah and Mr. Jenkins were out as well.

"Oh hello, Hannah, love. How are you doing with all this stress going on? It can't be good for you or the baby."

Hannah rubbed her football stomach as she joined Mum at the fence. She always walked like that now. It was as if it were the only way she could gain momentum. I avoided looking at her oversized belly and watched Dad get a stepladder out of the shed, which he propped up on the grass and leaned against. Mr. Jenkins came over to talk to him. He was dressed in a fluorescent yellow running vest and black shorts and a pair of sunglasses rested on top of his head. He looked like a wasp. He said something to Dad, and Dad turned and looked up at my window and then shook his head.

"They're talking about me, Lion," I said. "What with everything going on, they still find time to talk about me."

Mr. Jenkins followed Dad's gaze and stared at me.

Mr. Jenkins was the worst teacher in our school, and for a while I'd managed to excuse myself from quite a few of his lessons (I felt sick, I'd pulled a muscle in my leg, I was getting over a chest infection, etc.). But he wasn't fooled easily, and before long he was right on my case.

"You can't be bothered, that's your problem, isn't it, Corbin?" he said when I told him I had a migraine and couldn't go swimming. "Any feeble excuse not to do any exercise. You're bone-idle! That's what you are. Now shut up, get your suit on, and get in that pool."

My anxieties weren't too bad then, so I resigned myself to just having to get on with it, but I took my towel and trunks out of my bag as slowly as possible. I certainly wasn't going to hurry.

I thought I was the only one left in the changing room, but then I could hear a boy frantically searching for something behind the forest of school uniforms hanging on rows of hooks.

"Where are you? You stupid letter! You're in here somewhere, I know it!"

It was Jake Bishop.

"You all right, Jake?"

He looked up at me, his red-rimmed eyes wet with tears.

"I've lost the stupid letter. I'm not supposed to go swimming and my mum wrote a note and now I can't find it."

He took a deep breath, then, like a scurrying animal, he scratched around again in the pockets of his backpack.

"Can't the school call your mum?"

Jake snorted.

"Yeah, right. I said that to Mr. Jenkins and he found that *very* funny. I'm Jake Bishop, remember? What do I matter?"

He turned back, pulling out his scruffy schoolbooks and ink-stained pencil case, piling them onto the bench.

Mr. Jenkins appeared from the pool and threw a pair of purple trunks at Jake, which hit him in the face.

"Get these on. You'll have to borrow a towel."

He saw me standing there.

"Why aren't you dressed yet, Corbin? Come on!" He clapped his hands together rapidly like machine-gun fire. "You're losers, the both of you! Especially you, Bishop. What are you?"

"A loser, sir," said Jake quickly. He'd clearly been in this position with Mr. Jenkins before and wasn't bothering to put up a fight.

"A pathetic excuse for mankind, that's you. Now, *hurry up!*"

I darted back to my bags. The echoing shouts of our classmates from the pool sounded sinister, like they were all being tortured. I watched Jake through the dangling coats as he wiped his eyes.

"I can help look through your bag if you want," I said.

I didn't know what I'd do if he agreed. There was no way I'd touch Jake's bag.

"What's the point? Someone's stolen it. Probably thought they'd get back at me. Well, this time they've won, but they won't be winning when I get hold of them."

He pulled his shirt over his head without undoing the buttons and tugged at the sleeves. As he turned away, I saw raw patches of eczema all over his back. I'd never had eczema before, but I knew as soon as his skin hit that chlorine-filled water it was going to hurt like crazy.

I never did find out if someone had taken Jake's letter. He was probably right, it was very likely that someone did take it, just to get revenge on him. But on that particular day, there was only one bully in the changing room, and it certainly wasn't Jake Bishop.

Mr. Jenkins rested his hands on the low fence between our yards as he babbled on to Mum and Dad. Hannah now had her arm linked through her husband's, the sunlight dazzling on her white teeth as she stared up at him. Mum shaded her eyes as she and Dad nodded, agreeing with whatever it was Mr. Jenkins was saying. They didn't have a clue how different he was from this perfect image he projected. Bullying kids, sneaking around in the middle of the night, smoking cigarettes when he was supposed to be setting a healthy example. What else could he be up to? He'd run past

Teddy on the day he went missing. Had he turned back when I wasn't looking? Had he seen him crouching down by the roses after all?

My PE teacher finished what he was saying and pulled his dark glasses down over his eyes, a mad grin on his face as Hannah began to talk. His head turned toward my window, and I had a strong suspicion he was staring right at me. When his grin twisted into a grimace, I knew I was right.

CHAPTER TWENTY-SIX

THE DEVIL'S CAT

I was back in the office making more observations. Melissa Dawson's car was parked outside Mr. Charles's house, and Officer Campen was standing on the step. He put the back of his hand over his mouth as he tried to hide a yawn. A second car was parked a bit farther up, which I'm sure belonged to Detective Bradley.

I tried to sit at the computer but I couldn't keep still, so I went to go back to my room. Nigel was sitting outside the door, blocking my way. He purred loudly and closed his eyes, his head rocking back and forth slightly.

"Get out of the way, Nigel," I said as I tried to find an angle to get into my room. The ginger cat opened his eyes and watched me dancing around in front of him. "Go away, you disgusting cat!" I reached forward and pushed my door open, intending to make a leap for it over his head, but as soon as I'd opened the door he was in. Sauntering across the carpet, he jumped up on my bed, where he padded his feet up and down, snatching at the duvet cover with his claws.

I stood in front of him.

"Nigel! Get off! Get off, you flea-ridden old bag!"

The Wallpaper Lion snarled at me but I ignored him. I looked around the room for something to use to push Nigel off with, but there wasn't anything I was prepared to get infected. The cat did three lazy turns and then curled into a furry circle, shutting his eyes. I wanted to cry. All of the cleaning I'd done that morning was ruined.

"Nigel, I hate you! I HATE YOU!" I spat at him.

The cat twitched an ear but didn't move, so I pushed at the mattress with my knee, but he just wobbled a bit. I looked out the window and wondered whether to bang for Mum or Dad to help, but Mr. Jenkins and Hannah were still out there. It was far too embarrassing to ask in front of them.

I ran into the office.

To: Melody Bird

From: Matthew Corbin

Subject: CAT!

Melody, I need your help! Can you come over? Right now?

M

I paced around, checking the street to make sure there was no sign of Melody, then I went back into my room. Nigel had stretched himself out like a long fuzzy sausage. I tensed my hands, but there was nothing I could do. I went back into the office, but there weren't any emails.

"Come on, Melody! Answer!"

I looked out at number three. There was only one thing for it. I ran downstairs, pulled on my sneakers, and headed across the close.

————————————

If you stand on Melody's doorstep (number three), you can't see the number on Penny and Gordon's house (one), so for now, I was safe from the unlucky number. I rang her doorbell, wishing I'd put on some fresh gloves.

Melody answered the door, and her eyes widened when she saw it was me. I took a breath and launched into what I had to say.

"I need your help. The cat's on my bed! Can you come over and just get him off?"

I stopped, almost panting for breath.

She leaned against the doorframe. Her hair was curled and hung down in dark waves onto her shoulders, and she was wearing the blue dress she'd worn when I'd met her in the graveyard.

"What?" she said. My gloved hands fiddled by my sides. I didn't have to hide them from her.

"Can you help me? Can you come and get the cat off of my bed?"

I knew I was fidgeting. Melody looked down at my feet, and I tried to make them stop moving. She tucked her hair behind an ear.

"Matthew? Are you scared of your cat?"

She held my gaze, and I felt the warmth spreading up my neck to my cheeks.

"No!" I said, a little too loudly. "I just, I can't touch him. You're good with animals, aren't you? What with Frankie . . ." I looked behind her, making sure the little dachshund wasn't going to suddenly appear and hurtle toward me. I couldn't bear this. I wanted to go back to my room where I could talk to the Wallpaper Lion. He'd understand. He knew how dangerous it was to have a cat on your bed.

"I can't, I'm going out with my mum now. You'll have to ask your parents."

I shook my head.

"No, they're in the garden with Mr. Jenkins and Hannah. I can't ask in front of them. Come on, Melody. Please?"

Tears stung my eyes. All I could think about were the germs on Nigel's paws now swarming, infesting every inch of my room.

"Melody, we're going now! Oh hello, Matthew." Claudia was standing behind Melody in the hall. "I hear you've been doing some investigating, is that right?"

I looked at Melody, but she was staring at the ground.

"Erm. I've just been watching from the window a bit, that's all," I said.

"I see. Come on, Melody, get your shoes on," she said and she disappeared into the kitchen. As soon as she'd gone Melody pulled the door closed a little and began to whisper.

"Matthew, Mum saw our emails! She wants me to go to the police station and tell them what I know about Old Nina: That you saw something in her house and saw her buying diapers."

"What? She wasn't buying them though."

"I know! I tried to tell her, but she said we've got to be sure."

Melody looked at her watch.

"Sorry, Matthew. I've got to go."

My heart was going so fast the beats felt like a blur and the dizziness was coming back. The glass door closed and I was faced with a brown-haired boy wearing a long-sleeved blue shirt, jeans, and white latex gloves. He looked close to tears. I couldn't bear to look at him, so I turned and walked toward the alleyway.

I passed the horse chestnut tree with the hexagonal bench and then the patch of overgrown weeds where the mermaid slept with her head resting on her arms. I carried on along the dusty path where Melody and I had walked together and found myself at the front of the graveyard near the church. I hadn't intended to come here. On my right, standing barefoot on top of a small plinth, was a brilliant white angel. Callum's angel. Its hands were pressed lightly together in a prayer, its mouth almost smiling. Beneath its creamy, carved feet I read the inscription:

Callum James Corbin
A beloved son and brother
A moment in our arms, forever in our hearts
23rd March 2010

I stood looking at the angel with its huge feathered wings and felt my face cooling in the light breeze as tears trickled onto my cheeks. The angel's eyes were almost closed, its head tilted to one side, full of concern. I stared at the angel's feet where I'd tucked the note a few months ago. There were dimples on the top of each foot showing that this angel was a child itself.

"I didn't mean for Callum to die," I whispered. "I wish he was here now. I really do. I would have been the best brother to him, Angel. Honestly."

I wiped my face on my sleeve as I watched the statue praying, and then I turned and headed home.

CHAPTER TWENTY-SEVEN

THE WALLPAPER LION'S EYE

As soon as I got home and stepped through our front door and into the hallway, I realized something was terribly wrong. A thick, damp smell hit my nostrils, and I could hear tinny pop music being played through Dad's old radio somewhere in the distance. Mum appeared from the kitchen, Nigel brushing up against her legs.

"Matthew, where have you been? Dad wanted to talk to you about your room . . ."

I didn't let her finish.

I ran up the stairs without taking my shoes off and came face-to-face with my mattress, which was propped up vertically against one wall. My bed linen was dumped in a pile, and beside that was my white bedside table, my clock and lamp still on top. Notebooks, a pot of pens, the box of gloves, and the few remaining cleaning things that had been hidden under my bed were all now on the floor next to the bathroom. The sound of the radio and Dad whistling along came from the other side of my closed bedroom door.

"Dad?" I said and I slowly opened the door. My room was unrecognizable. The frame of my bed had been moved to the middle of the room, and dust sheets covered the carpet, my desk, and the bookcase. The *Harrington's Household Solutions* cardboard box that Gordon had delivered earlier was empty and sat next to the door. The stench of wet, sodden wallpaper made me want to vomit.

"What are you doing?"

Dad was standing halfway up a stepladder, holding a wallpaper steamer in his left hand. He hadn't heard me come in, and I stood frozen in the doorway as I watched him press it against my wall. Curled vapors of smoke seeped from the edges.

"Ah, Matthew, there you are! I thought I'd freshen it up in here a bit for you as a surprise! These walls are good; I'll get this off and then give it a couple of coats of paint tomorrow and it'll be done."

He lifted the steamer off and, with his other hand, scraped the paper away in one clean sweep. The yellowing strands fell to the floor in a wet *shlump*. He moved the steamer down the wall, and it bubbled away again like a boiling kettle.

"Stop it! Stop it, Dad," I said, but I said it too quietly.

"Mum's going to make up a bed in the office for you for a couple of nights," he said loudly over the noises and the radio. "You won't want to sleep in here with all this mess, eh?"

Behind him I could see the Wallpaper Lion was still there, cowering in his little corner. A line of sweat was seeping through Dad's T-shirt, making a dark trail down his spine.

"B-but I didn't want you to decorate. Why are you doing this? IT'S MY ROOM!"

I wondered if I could just push him off the stepladder and put a stop to the whole thing. He scraped off another section, and the paper peeled away like curls of soft butter.

"Don't be silly, Matthew," he said without looking at me. "It needs doing. And it'll be nice and clean then, just how you like it!"

SCRAPE.

Another strand fell to the floor. Behind him the steamer was just inches away from the Wallpaper Lion's mane. Condensation glistened across the paper and tears streamed out of his drooping eye and down his flat, wide nose. He'd always been there for me, day and night. What would I do without him? I ran to the ladder just as Dad placed the square, plastic steamer over the Wallpaper Lion's face.

"No! Please! Take it off! TAKE IT OFF!"

He frowned down at me, his arm held still as he waited for the heat to slowly work through the layers of paint. When he turned back to the wall and released his hand, a cloud of steam escaped and, with one swift sweep of the scraper, the Wallpaper Lion was gone. A soggy curl fell down and landed on top of the mound of old paper beside me. I picked it up and desperately tried to unfurl it, but it was falling apart in my hands.

"Matthew, what are you doing? What is the matter with you?"

I began to cry.

"You don't know what you've done! You'll never, ever know! You've killed him, Dad. You've killed him!"

I ran from the room with the wet wallpaper in my hand and

locked myself in the bathroom. Laying it carefully down on the floor, I pieced it together, sobbing as I tried not to damage it any further. I couldn't make out any part of him: his mane, his flattened nose, his domed forehead. It all just looked like a slimy mess.

Dad was on the other side of the door, pounding away.

BANG, BANG, BANG!

"Matthew! What's going on? Come on out and stop being so silly."

I turned the paper this way and that, trying to work out which way was up. Another piece fell off in my hand.

BANG, BANG, BANG!

"I thought you'd be pleased! You like things clean, don't you? Make up your bloody mind!"

BANG, BANG, BANG!

And then I saw it, barely visible along the side of the paper: I spotted his eye. His weird, droopy eye, which had watched over me for so long.

"Matthew! Are you listening to me?!"

"I heard you, Dad! Can you leave me to go to the bathroom, please, or is that too much to ask?"

I braced myself for more bangs, but he just huffed and I heard my bedroom door slam shut. I gently tore around the eye and threw the rest of the paper down the toilet, flushing it with my elbow. I carefully put the piece on the windowsill in the corner and hoped it would dry.

"I'm sorry," I whispered as I washed my hands. "I'm so, so sorry."

Thirty-seven times I washed my hands. Thirty-seven times. My worst count ever. Dad came back now and then and knocked on the door, but I told him I had an upset stomach and to go away. I heard them both murmuring on the landing and then the sounds of them shifting my mattress into the office. The cupboard door opened and Mum must have got out some clean sheets.

The Wallpaper Lion's eye curled and crisped as it dried on the windowsill and eventually began to look like the old, yellowing eye I knew so well. I picked up the fragment, not much bigger than my thumbnail, and slipped it into my back pocket.

CHAPTER TWENTY-EIGHT

THE POLICE VISIT OLD NINA

When I came out of the bathroom, Mum was on her knees in the office making up a bed using my mattress. She looked like she'd been crying.

"We're just doing what we think is right for you, darling. Okay? No one is trying to upset anyone."

I didn't say anything and she turned back to tuck in the sheet. I went onto the landing to get a pair of gloves. Dad was still banging about in my room. I went back to the office and Mum stood up.

"Me and your dad have had a chat and your dad is right. We need to be tougher with you, Matthew, to help you get over this. I won't be bringing food up to you anymore. We're going to eat around the table like a proper family. Starting tonight."

She didn't look at me when she spoke.

"You're seeing Dr. Rhodes on Monday. It's a new beginning. For all of us. And *you* can make a start by getting rid of those gloves."

When she said the word *gloves,* her head jerked toward me, but she still couldn't bear to look in my direction. Then she walked out and went downstairs.

The latest *Harrington's* catalog, the one I'd picked up for Gordon, was open on the desk at a page advertising slow cookers. Still wearing my gloves, I closed the catalog. There was a headline on the front cover: *Want the Ultimate Protection from Germs? See Page 7!* I casually flicked through the catalog until I reached the cleaning section. The first two pages were dedicated to a new steam mop that promised to eliminate dirt from a variety of surfaces. Mum had already bought this mop a few months ago but I'd never seen her use it, which probably meant it had ended up in the attic along with the juicer, pasta machine, and bread maker. I carried on, but the glossy pages became more and more crumpled and creased. Someone had scrawled deep, jagged lines over the bottles of disinfectant and antibacterial wipes. They'd scribbled so hard in places the paper was torn. I slammed the catalog shut and pushed it to the back of the desk. Mum must have lost her head for a moment and taken her anger out on the catalog. Shame seeped into my veins and flooded my body.

At 5:24 p.m. Dad announced loudly to the house:

"Quick! Something's going on at the Rectory!"

I jumped up from my mattress on the floor and went to the window. The police must have taken Melody and Claudia seriously. I looked at number three, but Claudia's car wasn't back yet.

"This is it, Lion, this is it! They're going to find him!" I said to the Wallpaper Eye in my pocket.

Detective Bradley and a female officer in plainclothes were standing on Old Nina's step and appeared to be asking her some questions. She kept the large black door as closed as possible while she poked her head around the side. The female officer leaned in, her head nodding intently, and then slowly, very slowly, Old Nina opened the door and stood back as they both walked in and the door closed behind them. I could hear Mum and Dad muttering downstairs; they must have been watching as well.

I waited.

Five minutes passed. Any minute now the door would open and a grubby but happy Teddy would appear in the arms of the female officer, followed by a handcuffed Old Nina being led away by Detective Bradley. But the door remained shut. A shadow appeared behind the curtain near the orange lamp and an arm brushed against the window. Whoever it was, they seemed to be fiddling with the lamp.

Twenty minutes passed. I waited, and nothing. I heard the kettle switch on downstairs as Mum and Dad lost interest. I was just considering washing my hands again when at 6:22 p.m. the door of the Rectory opened again.

"Here we go. Come on, Teddy, where are you?"

Detective Bradley appeared first, closely followed by the other officer. They were both smiling. Any second now Teddy would appear, a little stunned but no harm done. I was surprised they weren't carrying him though. I tried to see around their legs, looking for the lost boy, but he wasn't there. Perhaps they'd called for backup. Is that what they did in cases like this?

They both stopped on her step and turned to face Old Nina, who stood at the threshold. I couldn't see any handcuffs, and she didn't seem to be following them out. She had her body turned to one side and there was something in her arms. I blinked, trying to see what it was, but Detective Bradley's head was in the way. The female officer moved slightly to one side and then reached a hand out toward the old lady as Detective Bradley took a step backward. And then I could see exactly what it was in Old Nina's arms. There was no toddler; there was no Teddy. She hadn't taken him to replace her dead son—she'd just gotten herself a little companion and had been trying to hide it so she wouldn't be evicted.

It was a kitten. A small, tabby kitten. The officer tickled it under the chin and then they walked away.

Detective Bradley glanced up at me. I swallowed. They both climbed into a black car and it slowly edged out of the close. I looked back over at the Rectory and saw the lamp in Old Nina's window was glowing once more.

CHAPTER TWENTY-NINE

MOCKINGBIRD'S BREAST

"What do you mean you're not going?"

As he spoke, Dad jabbed his forkful of roast chicken across the kitchen table at me.

"Come on, son, spit it out. Me and your mum are dying to know why you've suddenly changed your mind."

He shoveled the chicken into his mouth, dropped the fork on his plate with a clatter, and sat back, waiting for me to answer.

Up until this point things had been going quite well with my attempt at trying to eat a meal with them—my first for many months. Mum had tried to dish me up some roast chicken, salad, and potatoes, but that was just a step too far. I was quite happy with my sterile, microwave meal. The doors to the conservatory were open and Nigel was asleep on the pool table, safely out of the way. I'd started off with a bit of light chat about the cat:

"So, Nigel's still alive, I see?" I'd said, nodding toward the conservatory.

Dad smirked, a pleased look on his face at having his family all sitting around the table for a change. Plus, like me, he wasn't a big fan of Nigel.

"Flipping cat, shedding his fur over my table."

"Leave him alone, Brian. At least someone is getting some use out of it, aren't you, Nigel?"

We all looked over at the sleeping, furry mound glowing yellow in the evening sunlight.

"You still owe me that game, remember, Matty? It's not much fun playing on your own, you know."

I didn't meet his gaze but kept focused on my dinner and shrugged, noncommittal.

"Have you got any paint for my room yet?" I said. Keep it normal. Keep it neutral. Mum spooned a large dollop of mayonnaise onto her plate, tapping the spoon three times.

"You're going to love it, Matty," she said, grinning. "*Mockingbird's Breast*, it's called. Cream with a tiny touch of ocher."

Dad looked at me and we both smiled and raised our eyes.

"Those paint guys are having a laugh! Sitting around drinking tea all day while they come up with a hundred ridiculous names for something that's basically white."

He chuckled to himself.

"I figure we could do better than *Mockingbird's Breast*, don't you, Matthew?"

I smiled, took a deep breath, and went for it.

"How about: *Dirty Dishwater.*"

Dad grinned and his eyes darted to the pool table.

"Good one. I know: *Cue Ball Cream.*"

I laughed as Mum tutted and pretended to be offended.

"What about . . . Wait for it . . . *A Hint of Denture.*"

Dad put his fork down.

"Excellent! Hold on, hold on . . . How about *Tired Eyeball*?"

"I'd love that on my walls, please, Mum . . ."

We were both laughing so much we couldn't eat, and Mum had a big smile on her face.

"Come on now, you two, those paints are expensive. You know they're good quality when they've got fancy names like that."

Dad raised his eyebrows and nodded toward Mum and we both spluttered out laughing again.

"Wait a minute, wait a minute," I said, wriggling on my seat. "How about *Soiled Diaper*!"

It went quiet. Dad sort of chuckled, but I'd ruined it. The whole moment of happiness had been crushed because my imaginary paint color had reminded everyone about Teddy being missing. The kitchen fell into silence. We all picked up our forks and prodded at our food, and then I looked at the empty chair opposite me: the chair where my brother would have been sitting.

"Melissa and Casey are back staying with Mr. Charles. Did you know? I think she realized how much she needs her dad after all."

I nodded. I had noticed her car was back but was parked farther up the road so there was room for the police to come and go.

"How's your pasta, darling? Does it need another twenty seconds?"

The Bolognese steamed into my face, and I gave her my best smile as I blew on a forkful.

"It's fine, Mum. Thanks."

She smiled back at me.

After a few minutes of silence I thought it might be a good moment to divert the attention away from Teddy and explode my own little news bomb, so I told them that I wasn't going back to see Dr. Rhodes. Not ever. I just couldn't do it. There was too much bad stuff going on around me: my baby brother dying, Teddy going missing, hearing about what happened to Old Nina's son. And she'd make me talk about Callum, I just knew it. That's what they did, those therapists. They made you talk about stuff in the past that you'd rather forget. She might find out exactly what I did, and I couldn't cope with that.

I had been wrong about it being a good moment.

"Oh Matthew. Why? You've hardly even given it a chance!"

"You don't understand, Mum. It's too hard. I can't do it."

I pushed the pasta around the warped, brown plastic tray with my fork.

"Hold on a minute, hold on. So, you're telling me that you're not going back to see one of the best therapists in the area . . . because it's too hard?"

Mum put a hand on Dad's arm.

"Brian, don't shout."

He turned and faced Mum, and small pieces of chicken fell out of his mouth as he spoke.

"But he's not even started, Sheila! What does he expect? A

smiley sticker on a chart or something? Of course it's hard! If it was easy I'd cure him myself!"

He pushed his chair back and stormed out of the kitchen, through the conservatory, and into the yard. Mum stood up and scraped her food onto Dad's plate. She'd hardly eaten a thing.

"See what you've done now?" she said. "I've backed you up on so many things, Matthew, SO many things!"

It looked like dinner was over.

"Buying you those stupid gloves, bringing food to your room like some silly servant, making excuses for you when you didn't want to go anywhere. The least you can do is get some help. If not for your sake, for us."

She grabbed my dish of pasta and threw the whole thing into the bin. Keeping her back turned, she leaned on the kitchen counter as if the conversation had exhausted her.

"You're pulling this family apart, Matthew. We can't take it anymore."

She then went out into the yard and joined Dad, who was standing by his runner beans. She wrapped her arms around him, and they stood holding each other.

I had the Wallpaper Lion's eye in my pocket, but suddenly I felt very, very alone.

CHAPTER THIRTY

NUMBER ONE

The computer clicked and hummed as the little red light blinked. I began to count the flashes, then stopped when I got to ten and looked away. Not because I was worried about getting to the bad number, but because I just didn't want to count. The little black beetle was back, gnawing away at my insides. Punishing me for what happened to Callum.

The *Harrington's Household Solutions* catalog was behind the monitor where I'd pushed it after finding Mum's angry scrawls over the cleaning products. I'd move it later.

I sat and waited for the computer to get to the home screen, and then I logged into my email.

To: Matthew Corbin

From: Melody Bird

Subject: What Shall We Do Now?

So Old Nina is off the suspect list. What now?

Melody

I didn't have an answer.

A car drove into the cul-de-sac, and I stretched up to take a look. There were no police around tonight. Penny was just getting out of their blue Fiat on the driveway of number one, which was odd. Gordon usually did all the driving. I sat back. Now that I came to think of it, I hadn't seen Penny and Gordon together for a while. They were usually inseparable. How long had it been exactly? I got up and went to the landing and grabbed my notebook from my bedside table, flicking through it as I returned to the office. I sat back down and read through some of the entries.

> . . . it looks like they are organizing a search party. Gordon, Sue, and Claudia are all taking part . . .
>
> . . . Gordon got in his car at 11:27 a.m. and drove off . . .
>
> . . . Penny Sullivan is next door. She's talking to Mr. Charles and every now and then she pats him on the arm . . .
>
> . . . Gordon dropped a large box off at our house. It looks like Mum and Dad have been ordering from Penny's stupid catalog again . . .

I looked back further, to the night after Teddy went missing, and I stopped. My heart was pounding in my ears.

> . . . I can't believe Mum has agreed to let that creepy kid, Casey, stay at our house tonight. I got up at 2:18 a.m. and she was stirring in her sleep. "The old lady's got him, Goldfish Boy," she said. Could Old Nina have Teddy?

But Old Nina wasn't the only old lady in the street.

I reached for the *Harrington's* catalog and quickly found the pages covered with pen scratchings. The lines stretched from one side to the other, crazy haphazard scrawls that cut across the descriptions of the products and the photographs. But now, as I looked at it again, it didn't look so angry. Some of the lines were swirls and loops, some curled around and around, and although it was messy, it certainly wasn't menacing. And it didn't look like something my mum would have done. In fact, it didn't look like anything an adult would have done. It looked like a child's innocent scribble.

I stood up. The curtains of number one were being drawn and I saw the hall light switch on. My breaths were coming in quick pants and I took a moment to take a slow, deep breath.

To: Melody Bird

From: Matthew Corbin

Subject: Number One

Penny and Gordon have been acting peculiar . . .

I stopped and deleted the message. This time I wasn't going to say anything. Not until I was sure.

I went out onto the landing. Dad was still in my room. I could hear his paintbrush scratching against the wall.

I went downstairs. Mum was doing some ironing in the conservatory. She looked up and her eyes had dark rings circling them.

"You okay, Matthew?"

I stopped at the doorway.

"Mum. Have you spoken to Penny lately?"

"Penny? No, not today. I know all this Teddy business has been really distressing for Gordon. She said his blood pressure has rocketed up what with all the searches. He's got to be careful because of his heart, so they're going to try and go away for a bit."

Mum put the iron down.

"What's the matter, Matthew? You've gone white."

"When? When are they going?"

Mum shrugged.

"I don't know. She hasn't said. Soon, I think. She said they're hoping to be away for a few weeks at least."

She walked to the sink to fill the iron with more water. I went to the front door and took some slow, deep breaths. If I thought about it too much I wouldn't go, so I had to be quick before the anxiety took hold of me. I bent down and put my shoes on, my head pounding.

"I just need to go out for a bit. I'll be back soon," I said to Mum and I shut the door behind me before she could ask any questions.

———————————

Looking across at number one, I took the Wallpaper Lion's eye out of my pocket and tucked it into my palm for safety. For my safety. Trying not to hold my breath, I crossed the road toward Penny and Gordon's.

The television was on, blaring loudly, and I could see the screen flickering behind the curtains.

I checked their car, looking for any signs of Teddy. The seats were immaculately clean. A green air freshener in the shape of a palm tree dangled from the rearview mirror, and there was a local road map in the compartment of the passenger door. In front of the gear stick there was a tub of mints and a blue cloth that Gordon probably used to wipe the windshield. I checked the backseat. Nothing was out of place apart from a box of tissues lying on the floor. I walked around to the passenger side so that I could see the storage pocket on the driver's door. The plastic handle of something poked out of the top, probably an ice scraper, and an old newspaper. Something bright orange caught my eye underneath the passenger's seat. I couldn't quite see what it was, so I moved around to the hood and leaned across the windshield, cupping my hands around my eyes.

Beneath the passenger seat was a small, orange bulldozer. The plastic bulldozer that Penny had picked up from the pile of toys in Mr. Charles's garden.

Pushing myself upright from the car, I heard a brief double click.

"Oh no!"

The headlights began to flash on and off and the horn beeped repeatedly. I'd set off the car alarm. I froze for a moment, then ran toward the pavement just as the door of number one opened.

"Matthew? Is that you? What are you doing?"

Penny fumbled with her car keys, then pressed the fob, and the alarm stopped.

"Sorry, I-I just . . . I accidentally knocked the car and . . ."

I turned as if to go.

"But what did you want? You didn't come over here just to set off our car alarm, surely?"

I took a couple of steps toward her, taking a second to study her appearance. She pulled the front door behind her a little and folded her arms, guarding the entrance, just like I do when I don't want anyone in my room. Her hair was pinned back neatly in the usual style. Her clothes, a pale pink blouse and a sky blue skirt, were as smart as always. She looked calm, and there was no sign of stress or strain on her face—apart from the annoyance at having me standing on her driveway.

"Well, what is it? What do you want, Matthew?"

"I, erm. Mum said you're going away."

She blinked at me.

"And I wondered if you needed anything done while you're gone. Watering your plants? Drawing your curtains? Delivering your catalogs? That kind of thing."

I felt myself flushing. I wouldn't believe me either.

Half of Gordon's face appeared at the door, and the one eye that I could see widened when he saw me.

"What's going on?" he whispered.

She practically pushed him back inside, and I could hear her muffled words behind the door.

"It's fine, Gordon. Matthew was just leaving."

She reappeared, patting the front of her hair.

"Thank you, Matthew. That's very kind of you to offer, but there's no need. Everything is in order." And with that she stepped inside and closed the door.

When I got back home I went straight to the kitchen and found Detective Bradley's business card stuck to our fridge beneath a magnet in the shape of a deck chair. I could hear Mum upstairs running a bath. Dad was putting his decorating things back into the shed.

I stared at the policeman's number and then at the phone, which was lying on its side, thinking about what I could say to him.

Penny and Gordon have got him because she took a toy bulldozer?

I haven't seen them together since he went missing?

Gordon is looking a bit stressed?

They're planning a long vacation?

It was like Old Nina all over again. I had no solid proof.

And anyway, the phone's earpiece was a tiny square of mesh that looked dirty and infected. The phone looked like something that could easily kill you. So I left it where it was.

CHAPTER THIRTY-ONE

FISHY

I'd lost the Wallpaper Lion's eye.

Somehow, while I'd been investigating at Penny and Gordon's house, I'd dropped it, probably when I'd set the car alarm off. I'd looked out the window for any sign of it, but it was hard to see anything in the fading light. I'd lost him completely.

I had a fitful night's sleep on my mattress, on the floor in the office. I dreamed that someone was standing behind me, tapping me on my back. I turned around to see who it was, but they'd disappeared. When I woke up it was dark and a spring from my mattress was digging into my left shoulder. I lay there for a while, feeling the sharp point press onto the edge of my bone, and then I rolled over onto my other side. I stared at the space beneath the computer table. My clock, which I'd put next to the computer screen, read 4:55 a.m. Any minute now the birds would start singing and daylight would arrive.

Hopefully I'd be back in my room today and I could put my things exactly how I like them. Without the Wallpaper Lion, of course. I really needed to find that eye.

I heard a gate click shut outside. Someone was up early. Maybe Sue had an early shift at the supermarket. Surely not this early though?

I closed my eyes and tried to think where the eye could possibly be. I'd have to check the driveway when it was daylight and along the pavement and curb and around the front door step.

I could hear crying. A child was crying outside.

I opened my eyes and looked again at the clock. 4:56 a.m. I lifted my head off the pillow and listened.

Silence.

I must have imagined it. I lay back down, pushing the sheet off me. It was much hotter in the office than in my room, and being five inches from the carpet didn't help—the air was suffocating down there.

I closed my eyes, but there it was again. A child was crying. I sat up and listened and this time it carried on.

I scrambled out of bed, opened the curtains, and looked down on Mr. Charles's yard.

"Oh . . . my . . . God . . ."

Standing on the path by the roses and rubbing his face with his hand was Teddy. He sobbed quietly into the corner of his arm, and then he wiped his face and looked up at me and stopped.

"Fishy."

I stared back at him. Was I dreaming?

"Fishy!"

His chubby little arm pointed up at my window. He was wearing a white pull-up diaper, a T-shirt decorated with a cartoon ice-cream cone, and no shoes. Reaching his hand up, he wriggled his fingers like he was trying to encourage a small pet.

"Fishy come?"

I ran out onto the landing.

"Mum! Dad! Quick! It's Teddy!"

I ran down the stairs and out the front door and onto our driveway. The sharp concrete made me wince as I walked barefoot toward the garden fence. Teddy had crossed the lawn and was now jumping up and down ecstatically as he saw me. I stared at him, and for a second I wondered if he was a ghost. It was getting lighter now, and a solitary bird began to chirp loudly.

"Teddy?"

He looked well. Really, really well. He looked tired and his eyes were red and his hair looked like it could do with a good wash, but apart from that he looked completely unharmed. He stopped jumping and bent down to rip up a fistful of grass, which he held out as if to feed me. I walked toward him, hypnotized by his fat, little hand. The light from our hallway came on as Mum and Dad surfaced.

"Teddy," I said. "Where have you been? Who-who took you? Are you all right? Where have you been, Teddy?"

He wasn't interested in my questions and was more excited about trying to feed me with a handful of grass.

"Eat, Fishy. Eat!"

I quickly scanned my neighbors' houses. They were all in

darkness and no cars were missing. Behind Teddy I could see Mr. Charles's gate was tightly shut. I took a step back and turned to face the middle of the cul-de-sac. Inhaling a huge lungful of air, I shouted at the houses with all my might:

"TEDDY'S BACK!"

CHAPTER THIRTY-TWO

THE RETURN

If Mum had thought Melissa Dawson had hugged Casey hard when she'd returned from America, then she should have seen her hug Teddy. It was as if she were trying to inhale him, trying to absorb him into her bloodstream. After my shout she had been the first to appear, stumbling toward her son and grabbing him. She buried her head into his neck and sobbed. Teddy looked at me across his mum's shoulder and scowled; he couldn't try and feed me now. As everyone began to surface I went back inside. Mum and Dad came out our front door, virtually pushing each other out of the way to try and see what was going on.

"What's that? Teddy's back? Where? How did he get there?"

Mr. Charles appeared, followed by a bleary-eyed Casey. She took one look at Teddy and burst into tears, hiding her face in her grandfather's legs.

I went upstairs and watched everything else from the office. Melody and her mum appeared with Frankie yapping at their feet. They laughed and hugged each other when they saw the toddler in Melissa's arms. Someone must have called the police, because a patrol car appeared and two officers got out, talking urgently into their radios. The black door of the Rectory opened and Old Nina walked down her step. In her hand she held a small, blue, knitted blanket, just like the one that Teddy had been holding on the day he'd disappeared. She'd been making one all along, just as I'd suspected. Walking across to number eleven in her slippers, she held her head high and focused on Melissa. Teddy's mum took the blanket with a thank-you, then smothered her boy's head and face with a million kisses. There was only one house that was still in darkness. Penny and Gordon's.

I lay back on the mattress and stared at the ceiling, listening to the excited voices outside. There was a question being asked over and over by the crowd.

"Where have you been, Teddy?"

"Teddy, tell us!"

"Was it a lady or a man?"

"Answer us, sweetheart!"

"Teddy, who took you away from us?"

There was silence for a moment, and I pictured his hand pointing toward Penny and Gordon's house, but then he replied with just one word:

"Fishy!"

CHAPTER THIRTY-THREE

FINDING THE WALLPAPER LION'S EYE

"Look, I didn't take Teddy Dawson! He just likes me because his sister called me a goldfish once and they used to point at me when I was looking out the window, that's all!"

Detective Bradley narrowed his eyes.

"I see," he said. "It's just that every time we've asked Teddy where he's been and who took him, he just gives us the one answer." He paused for a moment as he looked down at his notepad, and then he looked back up at me.

"Fishy."

I groaned and sat back.

"You're the 'fishy' he's talking about, aren't you, Matthew? Did you tell him that was your name?"

"No! Why would I call myself that? I've never even spoken to the kid!"

Mum put a hand on my shoulder and I flinched.

"Calm down, Matthew. You're not being accused of anything."

"Well, if I'm not, then why are they asking me these questions, Mum?" I looked at the policeman sitting in my kitchen. "Why are you here? Why aren't you out there searching the other houses?"

Dad was standing by the kettle. So far he hadn't said anything. Detective Bradley looked down at his notepad.

"We only search properties where we feel there is a justified reason, and at the moment, none of your neighbors are suspects. Why did you tell Mr. Charles you thought Mrs. Nina Fennell at the Rectory had taken him?"

I needed to wash. My skin tingled from the germs crawling around on my skin.

"Matthew?" said Mum.

"We also had a visit from Ms. Claudia Bird and her daughter, Melody, down at the station. Ms. Bird also stated that you were making accusations against Nina Fennell. Is that correct?"

"Matthew!" said Mum. "I told you Old Nina didn't have anything to do with it."

"B-but how could you be sure, Mum?"

Mum could see that I was close to tears. She turned her attention to the policeman.

"How is Teddy, detective? Has he been hurt?"

He shook his head.

"He's fine. He's been taken to the hospital to be checked over, but the initial signs are that he's extremely well and appears unharmed. His clothes will be sent off for forensic tests, and that will hopefully tell us more about where he's been."

When he mentioned the forensic tests his eyes fixed on my hands, on my latex gloves. The gloves that wouldn't show any fingerprints. I slipped my hands off the table and onto my lap.

"Am I a suspect, detective? I'm in this house ninety percent of the time. How on earth could I kidnap and hide a toddler without anyone knowing? Without my parents knowing?"

Detective Bradley looked at my mum, his face searching for any clues that she was somehow in on this, and then he quickly glanced at my dad.

"You were the last person to see Teddy, Matthew, and now you're the first person to see him return. And both times you didn't see anyone else?"

"No!"

"And the time you saw him when he went missing. Did he call up at you then? When you were watching from the window?"

I opened my mouth and closed it again. Just like a goldfish. I wasn't sure what to say.

"Detective, how old is Teddy?" Dad was joining in the conversation at last. I gave him a weak smile.

Detective Bradley looked a little taken aback at the question.

"Well, he's a toddler. He's . . ." He consulted his notes again. "Fifteen months old."

"Do you have kids, detective?"

"I do, Mr. Corbin, yes. A boy aged three."

Dad smiled.

"Ah, that's lovely. So it wasn't that long ago when he was learning to talk, no?"

"I, erm, no. No, it wasn't that long ago."

Dad folded his arms.

"Well, I'm no expert, but I would have thought a child aged fifteen months wouldn't generally have much vocabulary. Would you, Sheila?"

I twisted my head around, my eyes pleading for Mum to back him up, and she burst into action.

"That's right! Well, when Matthew was that age he wasn't even talking at all! I think his first words were *bum-bum*, and that wasn't until he was *at least* eighteen months old. And he only ever said that when he'd dirtied his diaper. I was so desperate for him to say *Mummy* that I got quite upset about it, didn't I, Brian?"

On second thought, I kind of wished Mum had kept her mouth shut.

Detective Bradley looked thoroughly fed up.

"Okay, okay. Look, Mr. and Mrs. Corbin, I'm just here because I want to get an idea why young Teddy has become so attached to your son. That's all it is."

He laid his palms flat on the kitchen table.

"Now, Matthew. Just one more question before I leave, and then you can get on with your day."

I nodded.

"I want you to really think about this before you answer, okay?" He leaned in toward me.

"Matthew. Do you know who took Teddy Dawson?"

My face reddened as I considered my answer. Did I have enough evidence to accuse Penny and Gordon? No. All I had was scraps. I could see Dad chewing on a nail out of the corner of my eye.

"No," I answered. "I don't."

The top story on the news was that Teddy Dawson had been found safe and well, but that at this stage there was no indication as to where he might have been. By lunchtime it was story number four, and by 3 p.m. it wasn't reported at all. A ferry had run aground in the Mediterranean and Teddy was officially old news.

I took a quick peek into my newly decorated bedroom, and to my amazement, it looked really good. The paint was dry and Dad was going to move my furniture back in today. The walls were smooth and Mum was right, *Mockingbird's Breast* was indeed a lovely shade of white. The curtains had been washed, my window cleaned, and the whole room looked so much lighter. It was fine, better than I expected, apart from one thing. I looked at the space where the Wallpaper Lion had looked down on me, and it just looked bare. I went back onto the landing and took my binoculars out from my bedside table. Back in the office, I knelt on the carpet and steadied my elbows on the windowsill again as I focused on number one.

Melody appeared from her house and ran across the road in her pink flip-flops, heading toward the graveyard. It must be card-collecting time again.

Using the binoculars, I scanned Penny and Gordon's driveway inch by inch, then slowly moved along the pavement. The wheels of a bike filled the lenses, and I looked up to see Jake circling around the street. He got as far as number one, then bumped down the curb and crossed over to start again outside Mr. Charles's house. I carried on searching. A few stones and leaves caught my attention, but I quickly moved on when I realized they weren't the Wallpaper Eye. After a few minutes I sat back. Jake was zigzagging across the widest part of our road now, darting this way and that. He skidded outside our house and created a swirl of dust just in front of Detective Bradley's silver car, parked outside Mr. Charles's house. Something fluttered up in the breeze, and I zoomed in as much as I could. It was lying flat on the pavement, and then a light gust of wind lifted it up and it tumbled toward Penny and Gordon's house. I'd found it! I'd found the Wallpaper Lion's eye! I grinned to myself and dropped the binoculars on the windowsill with a clatter.

I had to be quick or I'd lose it again. I ran out the door, past the police car, and across the road toward number one.

"Matthew! What you doing?" said Jake, pedaling up beside me.

"Nothing, Jake," I said as I stood at the end of the driveway. He stopped his bike and watched me.

"It doesn't look like nothing," he said.

Gordon appeared from around the side of his house wheeling a black bin behind him.

"Ah, Matthew. How are you? Good news about young Teddy, isn't it?" he said, but I didn't look up.

"Yes, yes it is."

I couldn't see it anywhere.

"Is everything okay?"

Gordon walked toward me, leaving the bin in the middle of his driveway. I glanced up at him.

"I-I've lost something. I dropped it yesterday. I thought I saw it, but I can't see it now. It's blown away."

Gordon looked around on the ground.

"Oh dear, let me see if I can help. What exactly are we looking for?"

His kind face smiled, and I felt a huge sense of relief that someone was helping me. It seemed inconceivable to think that only a few hours ago I thought he might have had something to do with Teddy's disappearance.

"It's a piece of yellow paper, about this big," I said and I held up my gloved hand, making a circle with my index finger and thumb. As Gordon stared at my hand, Jake shouted.

"There it is!"

I looked to where Jake was pointing. There, by Penny and Gordon's front step, blowing in the wind so that it appeared to be dancing around in a circle, was the Wallpaper Lion's eye.

"Yes!"

Jake dropped his bike with a clatter and ran onto the driveway to join me.

The piece of wallpaper tumbled toward the front door and Jake laughed as we both tried to reach for it at the same time. I got there first, and as I picked it up I noticed something on the window. I straightened up, my eyes fixed on the glass as the veins in my body shriveled with coldness. I looked at Jake. He saw my face and I nodded my head toward what I'd seen. He frowned and took a step closer, and then he turned back to me, openmouthed.

Gordon joined us, his face beaming.

"Let's have a look at what was so important then!"

I stared at him.

"What's up, Matthew? You haven't lost it again, have you?"

I held the Wallpaper Lion's eye firmly between my thumb and finger.

"No, no. I've got it. It's nothing really. It's just a silly piece of paper. I thought I might need it."

Jake stared at him wide-eyed, his mouth still hanging open. Gordon looked at us both, puzzled by our faces. I edged myself away slowly and Jake went to pick his bike up.

"Well, it must be important if you've been running around trying to catch it," said Gordon, frowning.

I took two more steps. Detective Bradley was coming out of Mr. Charles's house and heading toward his car.

"It's nothing. Thanks. Thanks for helping me . . ."

Gordon shook his head, and then he suddenly reached out and grabbed my shoulder. I froze as he looked at me with his pale gray eyes.

"Are you sure you're okay, Matthew?"

He looked at me and then at his house, trying to figure out what it was that had made us both react like we had. I tried to shrug him off, but he gripped me hard.

"I've got to go, can you let me go, Gordon?"

He shook his head.

"What are you up to, Matthew? You're a nosey one, aren't you? Always staring out of that window over there, always looking at matters that don't concern you. Do you think it makes you look clever?"

Jake rolled up next to me.

"Didn't you hear him? He said, let him go!"

Gordon didn't even look at him; he just kept his eyes fixed on me. I heard the policeman's car start up behind us and I looked at Jake, raising my eyes. It took a split second to register, but Jake understood and ran over to the car and banged on the glass.

Thump, thump, thump!

Gordon continued to study me.

"What is it with you, Matthew? What are you trying to prove to everyone? That you're a *normal* kid with a *normal* life?"

He smiled sadly.

"I'd give up now, son, if I were you, you're better off back in your window. You know *nothing* about life out here."

He loosened his grip and I pulled my arm free.

"No, Gordon, you're wrong," I said and I stared back at him.

"I know everything."

I ran home, past Jake, who was still talking to Detective Bradley, his face bright red as he pointed urgently toward Gordon and Penny's house. I went straight up to the office without taking my shoes off and stood watching the street below. Jake was running home with his bike beside him. Detective Bradley was still sitting in his car with the engine running. Gordon had gone inside, the bin positioned at the end of the drive for tomorrow's collection.

"Please, Detective Bradley. Go and take a look. *Please*," I said quietly.

The detective pulled his seat belt across his lap, and then he stopped. The engine turned off and he slowly got out of the car, shaking his head. He looked around the street, then up at me, and he gave an exasperated sigh before casually strolling toward Penny and Gordon's house. Standing on the driveway for a moment, he surveyed the front and around the car, and then he walked toward the window, his hand shading his eyes from the sun.

"Come on, come on . . . You've got to see it! Please!" I said.

He looked at the main pane of glass first, and then he walked closer to the front door and bent down to study a corner. Standing motionless for a moment, he then suddenly snatched the radio from his belt and began to shout into it urgently.

I sat down and let out a long breath and smiled to myself as I looked at the Wallpaper Lion's eye in my palm. The relief I felt was immense.

He'd seen it.

I'd seen it, Jake had seen it, and now Detective Bradley had seen it as well.

It was there—in the corner of the side panel of glass, barely visible unless you stood at a certain angle and if the sun was in the right position.

It was a child's sticky handprint.

CHAPTER THIRTY-FOUR

THE ARREST

The residents of Chestnut Close were slowly emerging from their houses to see the events unfold at number one. Two policemen stood at the end of the street, keeping the public away. Melody and her mum stood with their arms around each other on their step.

"I still can't believe it," said Mum. "Penny and Gordon? *Penny and Gordon?*"

Dad put his arm around Mum's shoulder, and for a tiny fraction of a second I wanted to reach down and squeeze her hand, but I didn't.

The turquoise-blue sky had turned a strange shade of purple as black clouds edged toward us. The neighborhood looked like it had been covered with a large, dark blanket. The heat wave was breaking at last.

Sue stood on her step, her arm linked in Jake's. He didn't look happy about it but he didn't pull away. I met his eyes and he smiled at me, and I smiled back.

The door of number seven opened and Hannah and Mr. Jenkins walked to the end of their path, Hannah rubbing her stomach as usual. They stopped at their gate and Mr. Jenkins stood behind Hannah and circled his arms around her.

"Are you okay out here, Matthew?" said Mum, turning around to me. I nodded.

Over to our left Mr. Charles stood next to his rosebushes, the remaining flowers curled and faded. Casey was holding his hand, her eyes fixed on the house opposite; Melissa Dawson stood in the doorway with Teddy on her hip. Melody ran across the road to join me.

"How could we not have known, Matty? How could Teddy have been so close?"

She tucked her hair behind her ear. She was only about ten inches away, so I took a tiny step to my left so I didn't accidentally touch her.

"Look!" she said.

The door of number one opened and Gordon appeared wearing a pale blue shirt and beige trousers . . . and handcuffs. The policeman led him to a waiting car and Gordon looked up at us all watching him. He covered his face with his hands as the policeman eased him into the back.

As the car drove off I looked next door and saw that Melissa and Teddy had gone back inside.

"He looked so casual about it," said Mum. "How could he be so unemotional after all they've done? All the pain they've caused?"

Dad didn't say anything, just rubbed her arm.

A few seconds later, Penny appeared. She looked immaculate. A policewoman led her down the path, and Penny held her cuffed hands to one side as if they were a mere accessory. She didn't look in our direction, but as she was about to get in the car, Mr. Charles called out to her.

"*Why*, Penny?" he said, choking on his words. "Why did you do this to us?"

She looked at him over the car roof, and then she slowly looked at all of our faces.

"I cared for him like a proper mother should," she announced to us all. And then her gaze fixed on the little girl holding Mr. Charles's hand.

"Didn't I, Casey?"

After the police had gone we all let out sighs of relief.

"What did she mean? Did that little girl know?" Mum said.

Dad shrugged. "She's just been arrested; she'd probably say anything."

"I still can't get over it. *Penny?*"

Dad snorted. "I've been telling you for years what a know-it-all she is, Sheila. She obviously thinks she's better than everyone else."

They went indoors discussing it and left me and Melody on our own outside. Lightning lit us up like a camera flash, and I whispered under my breath.

"One, two, three, four, five, six, seven, eight, nine, ten . . ."

A low rumble thundered in the distance.

"Ten miles away!" said Melody, who had been listening to me counting.

"It's two, actually," I said. "You have to divide the seconds by five. Dad told me that once."

Melody looked impressed.

"Storms are a lot closer than we realize then, eh?"

The thunder rumbled again and Melody squealed.

"I'll see you later, Matty!" she said and she ran back to number three. Her mum was laughing and held out her arm, scooping her into the house. A few drops of rain began to fall, leaving dark, round circles on the pavement, and I looked around the empty cul-de-sac as the rain pounded onto the steaming concrete. Old Nina's lamp was glowing brighter than ever in the gloom. And then her door opened.

She stood there, her tiny kitten snuggled up to her neck, and then she curled her finger, beckoning me over. Putting my hands in my pockets, I opened her gate using my elbow and walked slowly up to the large, black door. She had a pale dusting of pink powder on her cheeks and her eyes were a bright, vivid green. The kitten wriggled in her arms and she pecked a quick kiss on the top of its head. Her eyes darted around the street and she took a step toward me.

"I know you probably won't . . . ," she started, stopping to clear her throat before trying again. "I know you probably won't take much notice of an old lady like me, but I'm going to say it anyway."

Her face brightened as she smiled.

"I know you've been watching me, from that window up there?"

There was another flash of lightning and a rumble of thunder so deep my heart shuddered.

"I-I'm sorry," I started, but she waved a hand at me to stop.

"No, no, no, don't you worry about that. It's nice to see everyone going about their lives each day, isn't it? Why, I watch people myself sometimes when I'm feeling a little lonely. Life isn't always easy, is it, Matthew?"

She stopped and her face became a blur as my eyes filled with tears. I hadn't even realized she knew my name.

"I've had tough times myself, you know. Things certainly haven't been a bunch of roses in my life, I can tell you." She gave a little laugh but her eyes were sad. Looking toward her glowing orange lamp, she stopped for a moment and took a few breaths. I was soaked to the skin and my hair was plastered around my face and I just wanted to get home. I shifted around on my feet, and she quickly turned back to me and leaned forward, the tiny creases around her eyes wet with tears. Then, slowly reaching out, she held my wrist, squeezing it firmly in her hand. I wanted to pull back, but she fixed her eyes on me and I froze.

"Listen to me, Matthew. Listen to what I'm going to tell you and things will start to make a lot more sense."

I waited; her forehead was furrowed and her hand gripped tighter.

"Don't ever wait for a storm to pass. You've got to *go* out there and *dance* in the rain."

Her eyes searched mine.

"Do you understand?" she said.

I thought for a moment, shivering, and then I nodded at her. Smiling, she dropped my arm and took a step back into the house. The large, black door closed behind her and I turned around and walked home.

CHAPTER THIRTY-FIVE

CASEY

Friday, August 1st. 5:41 p.m. Bedroom. Cool and cloudy.
Number of children playing in Mr. Charles's garden = 2
Number of Wallpaper Lions = 0
Number of neighbors currently held in custody = 2

I was back at the dinner table with Mum and Dad. Mum had been out for hours getting the news from Officer Campen and some of the neighbors and she was bursting to tell us.

"Apparently Penny saw Teddy playing on his own in Mr. Charles's front garden, so she crossed over to check he was okay . . ."

"That woman's always poking her nose in where it's not wanted," Dad said, squirting tomato sauce on his plate. "I never knew why you were so friendly with her, Sheila."

Mum ignored him and carried on.

"She looked through the window and saw Mr. Charles asleep in the armchair and Casey on the floor playing with her doll."

"So Casey _was_ around then?" said Dad.

"Hold on, hold on, Brian!" said Mum, wriggling in her seat. "This is the thing! Penny decided to take him home to look after him, so she picked Teddy up, and before she took him home she _waved_ at her! She _waved_ at Casey!"

Dad put his fork down.

"What? Do you mean to say that that kid knew exactly where Teddy was all along?"

I ate my pasta in silence.

"I don't know, Brian. Casey denied it. And Penny's a desperate woman! Surely she'd say anything to try and get herself off the hook?"

Mum picked up her fork and then put it down again, too agitated to eat.

"Penny told the police she only intended to look after him for a while so that Mr. Charles could have a rest. She didn't mean to keep him so long."

"No, no, no," said Dad. "I don't believe that for a minute. That woman drove her own kids away trying to interfere with their lives, trying to prove she was some kind of superior mother. No, what happened was she saw Teddy and thought: 'I can do a better job looking after him than that.' She didn't care about anyone else, so she just took him. End of story."

Dad took a big mouthful of mashed potato.

Mum carried on.

"Before they knew it the police helicopter was thudding overhead and rather than own up, Penny persuaded Gordon to keep him just a bit longer. She told the police Mr. Charles was useless."

Mum turned to me. "You know when Teddy got pushed into the pond? Penny said Mr. Charles was too busy jabbering at her to realize his own grandson was in danger. She said if it wasn't for you banging on the glass, Teddy would have drowned."

We were all quiet for a moment as we ate.

"He's always been a pushover, that Gordon," said Dad, after thinking about it for a bit. "He's never stood up to her."

Mum got up to get a glass of water.

"Well, he stood up to her in the end. It was only when she started making plans to take him abroad that Gordon cracked. He got up while she was still asleep and put Teddy back in the front yard. And that's where you came in, darling."

Mum sat back down and gave me a big smile.

"Sue Bishop is having a barbecue next week as a little celebration. The whole block is invited. That'll be nice, won't it? You'll come, won't you, Matty? Melody and Jake will be there."

I shrugged and shook my head, and we all carried on eating.

So Casey had denied ever seeing Penny Sullivan on that day. I wondered if Mr. Charles or her mum or the police believed her. I wondered if anyone believed her.

I certainly didn't.

CHAPTER THIRTY-SIX

THERAPY

"Do you think Dr. Rhodes is married?"

I didn't care if she was or not. At this particular moment in time my skin was crawling with death and I just wanted Mum to turn the car around and go home. My knees jiggled up and down uncontrollably.

"I think she's got a daughter," I said.

"Has she? I wonder how old she is."

I didn't expect Dr. Rhodes was someone who went to Mum's salon, and she was therefore off her gossip radar. I stared out the window as we passed a woman holding a blond toddler's hand.

"Did you hear Melissa and the kids leave for the airport this morning?"

I nodded. At 6:22 a.m. I'd woken up to tapping on my wall. Just three.

Tap, tap, tap.

Two minutes later a car engine started up and I listened as Melissa, Casey, and Teddy Dawson drove away. Melissa was taking them back to New York with her. She didn't want to let them out of her sight, so she planned to hire a nanny back in America and keep them with her while she worked.

We pulled up into a space on the far end of High Street and I felt like I was going to be sick. I looked at Mum and she pressed her fingers to her lips and then held them out toward me. That was as close as she could get to giving me a kiss.

"Be strong, Matthew," she said. "You can do this, okay?"

I sat there for a moment, trying to think of a reason why I couldn't get out of the car, why I needed her to turn around and take me straight home. Beside the car was a bin, and a missing child poster was still stuck on one side. Teddy's glassy eyes blinked out at me.

Go on, Fishy.

———————————

Dr. Rhodes welcomed me with a beaming smile, and I sat on the brown leather sofa and glanced at the clock on her wall.

"Thanks for coming, Matthew, and well done. I know it's not easy for you."

Smiling, she nodded her head at me, and I suddenly felt like I was a guest on a talk show.

"So, let's get started, shall we?" Dr. Rhodes paused to put her glasses on and then we began.

First she said she wanted me to explain how I felt when I came into contact with something that I deemed dirty. I felt silly, but after a while it was obvious that she wasn't going to laugh, so I told her that I basically felt like my heart was going to explode.

We then discussed my top five fears, and she drew a ladder and I had to score each one according to how it made me feel:

5) Touching public door knobs/hand rails without gloves—anxiety level 7

4) Touching a trash can without gloves—anxiety level 8

3) Touching Nigel without gloves—anxiety level 9

2) Touching another person without gloves—anxiety level 9

1) Kissing another person—anxiety level 10

I didn't mention my issues with tenplusthree or the fact that I had a piece of wallpaper in the shape of a lion's eye hidden in my pocket to bring me luck.

We talked for a long time about what triggered my anxieties, and then she put her pad to one side for a moment and removed her glasses.

"From what you've told me, I think your fear of germs stems from a worry that you might pass illness on to another person. What distresses you is not the thought of *you* being ill, but others. Is that right?"

She was talking about that "magical thinking" again. How did she know that stuff? Her head tipped to one side as she went in for the kill.

"Would you like to tell me about that?"

I cleared my throat. My eyes warmed as they moistened; I quickly blinked the tears away.

"If-if I don't clean . . . If I don't keep cleaning then I'll get sick and then someone around me could die. Because of me."

Dr. Rhodes nodded.

"Okay. So what is your evidence to back up this theory?"

I rubbed at my scar over my eyebrow and felt the deep indentation, which was all the evidence I needed. The spot I couldn't stop picking when I was little. I shrugged. Dr. Rhodes blinked at me—once, twice, and then again. I wanted to choke on the silence. Unlike Mum or Dad, she wasn't going to let me get away with not answering.

"Mum's baby died," I said, my voice trembling. "Because of me."

Any minute now I knew I'd start crying and I tried to swallow it away.

"Okay," said Dr. Rhodes, resting her chin on her fist as she leaned forward. "Go on."

I took a deep breath.

"When I was seven I woke up in the middle of the night feeling sick. I lay there for a bit, too scared to move because I really didn't want to throw up. You know that feeling?"

Dr. Rhodes nodded.

———————————

I'd laid in bed absolutely still for a few minutes, listening to my stomach gurgling and hoping the sick feeling would pass, but it didn't, so I called out for Mum. She was heavily pregnant so it took her a while to get to me, but eventually she appeared, filling the space in my doorway.

"What's up, Matthew?" she said lazily. Her long, white dressing gown was tied around her tummy as if it was anchoring a balloon, and her hands rested on top.

"I don't feel very well," I said, trying not to move.

She clicked my lamp on and sat on my bed, and my stomach churned as the mattress moved. Her wide hand swaddled my forehead, making me shiver.

"You're burning up, darling. I'll go down and get you something. Just let me wake up a minute."

Her eyes were half-shut, and rather than waking up, she looked like she was about to fall asleep right there, sitting up on my bed. I waited a couple of seconds, watching her head nod gently forward, her eyes getting heavier and heavier. I swallowed once, twice, but I just couldn't hold it in any longer and I turned on my side and threw up over the edge of the bed like I was being seasick on a boat. My carpet, duvet, bedside table, and Mum's right arm and leg were all splattered with vomit.

"Oh Matthew! Brian! BRIAN!"

I knew she wasn't really angry, just exhausted from the pregnancy and being woken up in the middle of the night. Dad appeared in his pants, his hair all sticking up.

"Oh Matthew! Urgh, look at it all . . . Come on then, let's clean you up."

Dad stripped my bed while I managed to get myself to the bathroom and vomited in the toilet as I shivered with fever.

The next morning I woke up feeling even worse. My skin prickled and every inch of my body ached—from my eyelids to my fingertips. I got myself to the bathroom, and when I saw myself in the mirror I let out a little yelp. My face was peppered with bright red spots—I was smothered with them. I lifted up my shirt and stared at my chest. It was as if they were erupting out of my skin before my eyes. I screamed out for Mum but this time Dad got to me first, his face full of panic, but when he saw my chest he laughed.

"You've got chicken pox! That's all it is. It's just chicken pox, Matty."

Mum appeared behind him.

"At last! I thought you'd never get it," she said as she stood there smiling. Dad frowned at her and nodded toward her pregnant stomach, but Mum waved an "it doesn't matter" hand at him.

"It's fine, Brian. I've had chicken pox before. I'll get dressed."

Considering the baby was due in a week's time, Mum was amazing. She looked after me like a proper nurse: putting cool washcloths on my forehead when my temperature was high, giving me any food I wanted when my appetite came back, and rubbing pink, chalky lotion onto my spots, which were driving me insane from the itching. But after a few days, things weren't going so well. I was lying on the sofa downstairs reading a comic when I overheard her talking on the phone in the kitchen. She was trying to keep her voice low, but she sounded panicked.

"There's blood, Brian. I'm scared . . . Yes, yes, a cab's on its way now . . . I know, I know, but I'm really worried . . . Penny and Gordon are coming to watch him . . ."

Her voice cracked and I could hear her crying quietly in the hallway. She must have composed herself, as there were no tears when she came into the living room to reassure me that everything was going to be okay.

Penny and Gordon arrived and Penny helped Mum into the back of the cab. She put two bags into the trunk, one for Mum and one for the baby, and then the car pulled away. As Penny shut the door, I bit my lip so I wouldn't start crying. In her rush, Mum had forgotten to say goodbye to me.

I wiped the tears from my face and I looked up at Dr. Rhodes.

"He died because of me. I was sick on my mum and then the baby died. If I hadn't been ill, if I had kept the germs away, Callum would be here now."

I put a hand over my face and sobbed. Dr. Rhodes passed me tissue after tissue until I calmed down.

"It wasn't your fault, Matthew. Bad things happen to people all the time, and sometimes there just isn't a reason behind it. But I can tell you this for sure: Your brother dying didn't have anything to do with you being sick or the chicken pox."

I nodded at her. I understood what she was saying, but a huge part of my brain still didn't believe it. It was as though that section had its own wiring and was just making up what it wanted to torment me.

"You've done so well telling me about this today. Have you ever told your parents about it?"

I shook my head.

"Why don't you think about telling them, Matthew? It would help them to understand how you're feeling."

I didn't say anything, but I nodded and wiped my eyes again. I was so tired I could have curled up and gone to sleep on her soft sofa right there and then.

She talked about how the only way I could overcome my fears was to confront them head-on and put myself into situations where I felt most uncomfortable. I had to do the opposite of what my mind was telling me. Then I would be retraining my brain to understand that the things I was so frightened of weren't so scary after all. Over the next few weeks she said we would come up with some exercises for me to do, and if I worked really hard and was really committed, then I'd see results pretty quickly. I told her that this sounded utterly petrifying and she smiled. I glanced at the clock and saw it said 10:27. The unlucky minute had passed and I hadn't even noticed.

"You've done so well, Matthew," she said as she smiled and closed her notebook. "What are your hopes for the future?"

I think I was supposed to say something like how I hoped to travel the world, get married, have a couple of kids, a black

Labrador, a nice Audi in the driveway. That kind of thing. But I just shrugged.

"I don't know," I said.

Putting her notebook on her desk, she said that before we finished, she wanted to tell me a quick story. Placing her glasses on the top of her red hair and leaning back, she looked like she was about to read me a bedtime book.

"Once upon a time there was a young boy named Timothy who was about your age and was like you in many ways. Each morning he would get ready for school just like all the other kids, but after he'd said goodbye to his mum he would grab a bright orange bobble hat that he left on a hook by the front door. He'd put it on, check himself in the mirror, and then head off to school.

"As you can imagine, wearing an orange bobble hat in class all day and every day meant that he got quite a lot of grief from the other kids. They never tired of pointing and laughing and hurling rude words at him in the hallways, but it didn't put Timothy off. Every time he left the house, without fail, he wore the hat.

"One morning, before the teacher arrived to give an exceptionally dull geography lesson, a nasty girl named Tabitha stood up with her hands on her hips and shouted across to Timothy, who was sitting at the back of the class with his bobble hat on as usual.

"'Oi! Timothy! Why d'ya wear that hat every day?'

"The whole class erupted with laughter and everyone stared at Timothy, sitting on his own in the corner, the bobble hat pulled down so low it rested on his eyebrows. He looked up, and he smiled at the faces around him and everyone fell silent.

"'Why? Well, to protect myself from the poisonous snakes, of course.'

"The entire class fell into more hysterical laughter, and when they eventually quieted down, Tabitha piped up again:

"'But you're so stupid! There aren't any poisonous snakes in the school, are there?!'

"Everyone hushed again, eagerly awaiting Timothy's response. The boy grinned back at them all.

"'Aha, that's right!' he said, a knowing smile on his face. 'But that's only because I wear my lucky orange hat, isn't it?'"

TELLING MUM AND DAD

That evening I stood at the top of the stairs, listening to Mum and Dad watching TV. A sitcom was on and every now and then Dad chuckled.

I looked in the office and out onto the street. Old Nina's lamp was on, her front room flickering as she watched TV too. I thought about what she'd said to me, about not waiting for a storm to pass but to go out and dance in the rain. I knew what she meant. I couldn't sit this one out; I had to tackle it head-on. Taking a big, deep breath, I made my way downstairs.

"Matthew? What's the matter?" said Mum, her eyes wide as I stood in front of the TV.

"Sorry, but I need to talk to you," I said. "There's something I have to tell you."

Dad quickly switched the TV off and they both sat there, waiting. I wrung my hands together, digging my thumb into my palm.

"I clean because . . . I clean because I worry if I don't, someone will die."

Mum gasped and gripped Dad's arm.

"What do you mean?" said Dad.

I couldn't look at him. I knew that if I caught his eye I'd just stop and run away. I carried on.

"In my head, I believe that if I don't keep clean, if I don't get rid of all of the germs, then I could get ill . . ."

I cleared my throat.

". . . and if I get ill then I could make you ill and then you might die. Like Callum did."

Mum's hand went to her mouth. I swallowed a lump in my throat, not looking directly at them.

"I was sick once. When you were pregnant, Mum, do you remember? I was sick all over you when I had chicken pox."

Mum nodded, her hand still at her mouth.

"After that, you went to the hospital and . . . and . . . you lost the baby." I started to cry. "I don't know how or why, but from then on, I felt like it was my fault. I felt like Callum died because I was ill."

I broke down into sobs. Mum rushed toward me and Dad stood up.

"Oh Matthew!"

"And that's why I clean so much. That's why I need the gloves, so that I don't get any germs on my hands. I'm sorry about the gloves, Dad. I know you hate them."

Dad couldn't speak. He just nodded.

"But I need them, you see? I need them so that I don't kill anyone else like I killed Callum."

I broke down then. My body shook with my sobs and I thought I'd never stop.

"Matty, of course it wasn't your fault," said Mum, pressing her fingers to her chin. "It was just one of those things, it had nothing to do with you being ill or throwing up or you having chicken pox. I had it when I was young, so I was probably immune anyway!"

She took a step toward me, but I backed away.

"Why have you kept this a secret all this time?" said Dad. "Why didn't you tell us?"

I calmed down a little.

"I just, I just couldn't tell you. But then Hannah got pregnant next door and . . . and it just got worse."

Mum was crying now, smiling through her tears as she nodded at everything I said.

"I wrote him a note, Mum," I said. "I left it by his angel before school one day."

"You did?" she said, dabbing at her eyes. "I didn't know you did that."

I nodded.

"I told him it was all my fault he isn't here and I said . . . and I said I was so, so sorry."

"Oh Matthew."

I broke down into proper sobs.

"I'm going to get better, Mum, Dad. Honestly I am." I took a breath and wiped my eyes. "Dr. Rhodes is going to help me. She said it's going to take a lot of hard work, but she said I can do it."

"Of course you can, son."

Dad put his arms out to give me a hug, a big smile on his face as tears rolled down his cheeks.

"I'm not cured yet, Dad. Don't push it." I laughed.

And then Mum and Dad laughed with me. We wiped our eyes and we actually laughed about something that had made my life miserable for the past five years.

"I'm proud of you, Matty. Do you know that? I'm very, very proud," said Dad, his voice wobbling. I smiled at him.

"Thanks, Dad."

"And if you need me to do anything, Matthew, you just say, okay? Anything at all! I can come in and talk to your school and explain things. There's no need for secrets anymore," said Mum.

"Okay," I said, wiping my sleeve across my cheeks.

I'd done it. I'd told them. I'd actually told them. My shoulders dropped and I felt the black beetle that was constantly there in the depths of my stomach loosen its grip. I was tired, so, so tired.

Dad had put his arm around Mum, and they both stood watching me.

"Actually, could you do something for me now, Mum?"

I reached into my back pocket and took out the tiny piece of wallpaper that I'd put there to keep safe. To keep me safe.

"Can you throw this away?"

I placed the Wallpaper Lion's eye on her open palm.

"What is it?" she asked as she studied it.

I sighed.

"It's nothing. I don't need it anymore."

I smiled at their puzzled faces and then went upstairs to my room.

———————————

I knew the answer to Dr. Rhodes's question now, the one about my hopes for the future. I turned to the back of my notebook and started a blank page.

My Hopes for the Future, by Matthew Corbin

One day I want to walk downstairs, put my arms around my mum, and give her a big hug. She'll start crying, I expect, so then I'll leave her to pull herself together and go and find Dad. I'll give him a big slap on the back and say, "How about that game of pool now, eh?"

Mum will cook us her finest roast dinner, popping her head into the conservatory every now and then to see how the game is going. We'll sit at the table to eat as Nigel purrs, brushing himself against my legs, so thrilled to see me. Afterward, stuffed with food, we'll collapse together onto the sofa and watch some old comedy film that makes us all laugh.

That's my ambition.

That's how I want my life to be.

I want to go downstairs and rejoin the living.

CHAPTER THIRTY-EIGHT

SUE'S BARBECUE

I could hear the laughter from my bedroom.

Every now and then a wisp of gray smoke wafted past my window and then dispersed into nothing. Sue's barbecue celebrating Teddy's safe return was in full swing.

An empty stroller sat in the shade of a tree in Hannah and Mr. Jenkins's backyard. Baby Maxwell had arrived three weeks early on Sunday night, weighing a healthy seven pounds and ten ounces. The couple were over the moon, Hannah's face now permanently fixed in a wide grin. I'd watched as she'd carefully wrapped her newborn son in a thin, white blanket before they headed to the party.

Mr. Charles had left about twenty minutes ago and Mum and Dad not long after that. Of course they tried to get me to go with them, but I said I'd rather skip it.

All those people.

All those germs.

I just couldn't do it.

Wednesday, August 6th. 7:02 p.m. Office. Sunny.

Melody and her mum have just come out of their house. It looks
like they are going to the party at number five. Claudia is

carrying a bottle of wine and Melody has a tray of chocolate brownies.

Melody had put her hair up, which I'd not seen her do before. She was wearing a pale yellow dress and brown sandals. She looked nice. They walked up Jake's driveway and went around the side of the house toward the back, and then there was a screech of delight from Sue. I looked around for something else to note, but I wasn't really in the mood, so I put my book down.

The door to the Rectory opened and Old Nina appeared carrying a small bunch of flowers that she must have picked from her garden. She walked down her path, looking around nervously and patting at her hair. Stopping at her gate, she looked right up at me. I stared back. There was fear in her eyes. Then she put her elbows out at right angles and did a funny little shimmy.

What's she doing?

Her face flushed pink. She was embarrassing herself, but she carried on doing her weird little jiggle. When she stopped, she looked up at me and smiled, then walked toward her neighbors and the party.

I got it.

She was dancing.

I thought everyone was going to turn around when I walked into the yard, but apart from a few raised eyebrows, no one really reacted.

"Oh Matthew, it's so lovely to see you! Thank you so much for coming. Would you like a drink?" said Sue.

I shook my head, my hands tucked neatly under my arms.

"No, no thank you," I said.

Mum was talking with Mr. Charles and she looked over and grinned at me. Dad was helping Jake's older brother, Leo, with the barbecue and he raised a hand and waved at me through the smoke. Old Nina put the flowers on a table and gave me a nod, and then she turned and headed down the side of the house, back toward the Rectory. It didn't look like she was staying.

Melody appeared in front of me, bouncing on the spot.

"Matthew! You came!"

"Hi, Melody."

"Do you want something to eat? They've got some *amazing* burgers!"

She rolled her eyes when she said *amazing* and I laughed.

"No, I'm good, thanks."

Jake came over, his face bright red as he held baby Maxwell wrapped in his white blanket.

"Hannah just plonked him on me! What am I supposed to do?!"

He bounced the baby up and down gently.

"Nothing! You're doing fine," said Melody, laughing.

"But what if he wakes up?" Jake said, looking more and more panicked. "What if he starts crying?"

Mr. Jenkins was standing by the fence. He had one eye fixed on his new son. I doubt he was very happy that Jake was holding him.

"It looks to me like you're doing a great job so far," I said.

Jake stared down at the sleeping baby.

"I dunno. His eyes keep flickering. Does that mean he's got gas? I don't like the look of it. I'm gonna take him back to Hannah."

Melody and I laughed as he carefully picked his way around the guests and outdoor furniture, bobbing the baby as he went.

"He's all right, really, isn't he?" said Melody, wiping her mouth with a napkin. "I think he just wants some friends. Don't you?"

"Yeah, I think you're right," I said. "He just needs another chance."

We watched as he carefully passed Maxwell back to Hannah, laughing as he got his arms in a twist. He looked back at us and smiled, shaking his head as he walked toward the barbecue to get more food.

I didn't want to stay long. I just wanted to say hello to Melody and Jake, and show Mum and Dad that I was trying to change.

"And how about you, Matthew? How are you doing? Are you going to be all right?"

I swallowed as I looked around at everyone eating and laughing together. These people were my world, my neighbors, my friends.

I turned and faced Melody.

"I think I'm going to be fine," I said.

ABOUT THE AUTHOR

Lisa Thompson worked as a radio broadcast assistant, first for the BBC and then for an independent production company, making plays and comedy programs. During this time she got to make tea for a lot of famous people. She lives in England with her family. She is the author of *The Goldfish Boy* and *The Light Jar*.

A STORY OF FEAR AND HOPE, LONELINESS AND FRIENDSHIP...

Nate and his mother are running away. Fleeing from an emotionally abusive situation, they hide out in an abandoned cottage in the middle of a forest. Though it's old and run-down, at least it's a place of their own. Then Nate's mother heads off for groceries and doesn't return. He is left abandoned and afraid, with the dark closing in on him. Will Nate find the bravery he needs to face down his fears, survive on his own, and ultimately illuminate his future?

scholastic.com

LIGHTJAR